D0065921

The Witch of Woodland

ALSO BY LAUREL SNYDER

My Jasper June

Orphan Island

LAUREL SNYDER

The
Witch
of
Woodland

WALDEN POND PRESS
An Imprint of HarperCollinsPublishers

Library of Congress Control Number: 2023930682
ISBN 978-0-06-283665-6

23 24 25 26 27 LBC 5 4 3 2 1

First Edition

HB 03.16.2023 1206

This book is for Rabbi Josh Lesser,
who holds open every door.

And for Jordan Brown,
Tina Dubois, and Debbie Kovacs.
Because they believed.

A Prologue Is a Thing That Comes Before the Story

When I told Bea I was going to write this book, she didn't get it.

"Why?" she asked, glancing over at my desk, where I'd set up a little writing studio for myself, with three freshly sharpened pencils and a new composition book neatly laid out. On the wall above my desk, I'd taped a quote from some grown-up writer that said, "A bird doesn't sing because it has an answer. It sings because it has a song." I wasn't sure exactly what that meant, but I'd found it on a site of inspiring quotes for writers, and it made me happy. I love birds.

"I just don't get it," said Bea, frowning at the sign. "Why a book? That sounds like a lot of work. What's the *point*?"

I didn't have a logical answer. I just knew I needed to tell my story. I could feel it inside me, waiting. "Because I want to," I said. "Anyway, it's going to be nonfiction. The *truth*. Or as close as I can get, anyway."

"The truth?" asked Bea. "Nobody will believe you, Zippy. *I* barely believe you, and I was there. Anyway, who's going to read your book? Twelve-year-old authors aren't a thing."

"I'm thirteen now," I reminded her.

"Same difference," said Bea. (Bea is still twelve, but she's mature for her age and looks it. She dyes her blond curls pink every couple of months. She also gets dress coded more than anyone else in our grade. Sometimes she draws tattoos on her arms with Sharpie.)

"Well, maybe I'll just leave you out of my book, then," I said. "If you're going to be like that."

"Fine by me!" said Bea. "I'm not sure I want to be on the record as part of this whole thing anyway. But whatever . . ."

"*Whatever* yourself," I said back. "Why don't you just go home if you aren't going to be any help?"

"Fine," she said, hopping up from my bed, where she'd been sitting crisscross applesauce with her dirty shoes on, even though she knows I hate that more than anything. "I think I will." And she did.

"FINE!" I shouted after her as the screen door slammed in the front room. (Door slamming is the kind of small physical detail good writers put into their books. We learned about it at school, in our unit on Powerful Language.)

In case you're wondering, Bea has been my best friend since kindergarten, and for a long time, I thought we were as alike as two people could be. When we were little, we pretended to be sisters, even though I had long dark hair and she had her mop of blond ringlets. We wore matching clothes, and whenever we wanted to change our favorite color or TV show or candy, we decided that together with a vote. We shared everything.

Our friendship isn't like that anymore, which is kind of sad and kind of not-sad. I still don't entirely understand how that happened. We both changed, I guess. But even if things are different and we fight, Bea is still my best friend. We talk on the phone, and sleep over on weekends, and sometimes she copies my math homework or I copy hers, which I should probably not put into this book, just in case someone actually does read it. But I am determined that this book will be the *truth*. And the truth is we sometimes cheat at math.

The *other* truth is that Bea is family to me. She just is. So if you're reading this and thinking that she sounds mean or rude, I hope you'll remember that no matter what, she's my person.

But irregardless, and to get back to this book I'm writing and which you are (maybe?) reading now . . . Bea was wrong that day in my room. It wasn't the *same difference*. Not really. Thirteen isn't twelve and today isn't yesterday. Sometimes important things happen and everything changes, so slowly you don't notice or so quickly you nearly miss it. Or *you* change, in ways you never expected. I guess that's what happened to me last year—I grew, whether I wanted to or not. And what Bea doesn't get is that I don't care so much if other people believe my story. That's not why I'm writing this all down. I'm writing it because *I'll* read this book. I know I will. Over and over, for the rest of my life. Trying to figure out what happened. Trying to understand it all better . . .

Look, I know that as time goes by, I'll forget the details. I've forgotten so much already! But I'm hoping I can hold on to the parts I still remember, the ones that haven't slipped away. Because someday I'll turn into a grown-up. Someday I'll have a job and a car and a dishwasher, and if I'm not careful, I'll wake up one morning and I'll be too old to remember what happened the year I turned thirteen.

So I'm writing this book. Starting today. I definitely *am* writing this book, no matter how it turns out. Even if it ends up being a total failure. And if you're reading it somewhere in the future, whoever you are, I hope you'll like it, and believe my story. That would be nice. But if you don't, that's okay too. I know now that people are going to believe what they want. And what happened *is* pretty wild. I almost couldn't believe it myself.

As a matter of fact, that was sort of where everything began, I guess. With me not believing . . .

★☆*1*☆★

How It Actually Started

Okay, I don't want to sound obnoxious, but wasn't that good? Didn't that sound like something from a real book? All that stuff about "that was sort of where everything began, with me not believing"? I hope so! I revised it over and over. I worked really hard.

Anyway, I guess *where* everything truly began was in the kitchen of my house. And *when* it began was one awful day last August, when I was still twelve. That day, I was sitting there after school, eating a bowl of rice pudding at the kitchen island and worrying about the Fall Fling. Because walking home from school that day along Woodland, Bea hadn't been able to talk about anything else. We'd started seventh grade a few weeks earlier, and that morning over the intercom, they'd announced the big fall dance. I'd barely registered the announcement myself, but the entire way home, as we'd walked past the overgrown yards and honeysuckle-covered fences and colorful old bungalows of Woodland Avenue, Bea had gone on and on about the red minidress she wanted to buy for the dance, and about how she was hoping her mom was going to let her wear actual makeup, as opposed to just boring lip gloss. We trudged along, sweating in the heat (August in Atlanta is pretty unbearable), and the whole conversation made me as uncomfortable as the weather.

Then Bea stopped walking for a minute in the shade of a huge weeping willow that hung out over the street and said, "The main thing, Zippy, is that you don't want to *overdo* it. Because that's the kiss of death in middle school. You know what I mean?"

I absolutely *didn't* know. "Kiss of death?" I asked, staring out through the willow branches that Bea and I had swung on only a few years earlier. "What are you talking about? Overdo what?"

"It!" Bea said as she parted the branches, stepped through them, and began walking again. "You know. Like, the dance, the dress, the whole deal . . . everything. Now that we're in seventh grade, you want to keep it cool."

"But . . . ," I said. "How would I *overdo* it? How would I keep it cool? I don't even understand what any of that means." I glanced down at my black leggings and matching T-shirt, the long wavy hair that fell to my waist, feeling bewildered and not remotely *cool*.

Bea laughed. Then she said, "Hey, I have an idea! What if we went to the dance with Lane and Tess and Minnah and Leah?"

"The . . . walking group?" I asked. "But we aren't *in* the walking group."

Bea shrugged. "Maybe we could be."

"Ummm, *okay* . . . ," I said.

Lane and Tess and Minnah and Leah were a bunch of girls who lived in our neighborhood. They hadn't been a friend group in elementary school, but suddenly in sixth grade, they'd all started walking home together, laughing and gossiping so loudly I was pretty sure they wanted everyone to listen in. They had matching friendship bracelets and they usually stopped at Morelli's for ice cream after school, to order the weird hipster flavors nobody really likes: rosemary olive oil or whatever. On weekends, they hung out in the church parking lot a few blocks from my house, where they met up with eighth-grade boys and left diet-soda cans behind. They all seemed endlessly comfortable and happy, and I low-key hated them. Of course, there were other groups of kids all over the neighborhood who walked home together, but if you mentioned *the* walking group, everyone knew who you meant.

"Yeah. That'd be fun, right?" said Bea.

Immediately, I felt my chest flutter. *NO*, I'd wanted to say.

No no no. Definitely not fun. Not fun at all.

For as long as I could remember, it had always just been Bea and me. Me and Bea. People had tried to split us up, and we'd been shuffled off to summer camps without each other and sorted into different classes several times, but none of that had made any difference. We'd been set up on playdates to *make new friends*. But even then, we stuck together. We wrote notes. We came up with code names for people we didn't like. If one of us had a stick of gum, we automatically tore it in half to share. You know what I mean? *Best* friends. Whenever she says something that hurts my feelings, I try to remind myself of that.

Here: I'll give you a perfect example. Something that happened a long time ago, at Bea's eighth birthday party. Bea's mom had invited a handful of other kids to her party, in an effort to *broaden her social group*, but since I was her best friend, I got to sit next to her when she blew out her candles and sleep in the foldout sofa with her while the other kids crawled into their sleeping bags on the rug. Only I did a stupid thing. I drank way way way too much root beer. At dinner and during the movie, and even after that. So then, when it was time to go to sleep, I had to pee like *whoa*. But of course the other girls were all falling asleep on the floor around us, and I was afraid of waking them up or stepping on them. I was sure I'd annoy everyone and then they'd all have to listen to me through the thin bathroom door as I peed a million gallons of root beer. So instead I closed my eyes and forced myself to sleep.

Which was fine. Until I woke up in the darkness . . . completely drenched.

Have you ever peed the bed? Do you know what that feels like? It's miserable, and hard to explain. It's like . . . the pee is warm coming out of you, and it actually feels kind of nice when you're half-asleep. But somehow, the minute you're awake and the pee is on your skin, it turns cold and sticky and everywhere, all down your legs. There was so much root-beer-pee that night! I tried to roll out of it, but the the whole bed was just stiff wet sheets. So, for a minute, I lay there, holding my breath and listening to the other kids breathing and rustling and whistling faintly in the darkness around me. What could I do? Beside me, Bea was silent, her face buried in her pillow, her hair a mass of wild, curly shadows.

Finally, I was too miserable and clammy and chilly to stand it anymore. My teeth were chattering, and I was never going to be able to sleep like that. Even if I made it through the night, Bea would wake up in the morning and discover my disaster. What would happen then? The pee would only stain and smell worse as it dried. So at last I inched over and tapped Bea's shoulder. "Pssst," I whispered. "Are you awake?" (Even though I knew she wasn't.)

Immediately, Bea flipped over and squinted at me. "Sure," she said. "You just woke me up. Everything okay?"

I shook my head. "No," I whispered, trying not to cry. "I

wet the bed. What should I do?" Around us, the room was silent and still.

Bea didn't reply at first. I remember being afraid she might laugh out loud and wake everyone up. I felt like I was holding my breath that whole time. Waiting to see what might happen as she lay there, thinking.

Then, suddenly, she nodded and said, "Okay, then. Me too."

"Huh?" I asked. "What do you mean? You too *what*?"

Bea sat up. "Me too," she said. "I peed the bed too." And then much more loudly she shouted out, "Hey, Mom, I peed the bed!"

On the floor all around us, people began to stir. But Bea didn't seem to care at all. She just stood up on the creaky-springed foldout sofa, hopped over me, and jumped down onto the floor. Then she turned on the light over the stairs and shouted up to the second floor, "Mom, hey, Mom. You need to change the sheets. I peed the bed! And I peed on Zippy. Poor Zippy!"

Somehow, her loud, wonderful lie made everything okay. Maybe because she was the birthday girl, nobody even laughed. Mel came downstairs looking sleepy and confused. She stripped our sheets and remade the bed while Bea and I both ran up to her room for fresh pajamas. Then we all went back to sleep until it was time for chocolate chip pancakes in the morning. Nobody else ever said a word about it, and Bea never mentioned it again.

So that is Bea. She will tease and laugh. She will poke and shout. She will put her filthy shoes on my nice clean quilt and mess up my neat room and slam the door and tell me when I'm being annoying. But she will also be there when I need her.

I figured it would be stressful enough to go to my first middle school dance with just Bea. But going to a dance with Lane and Tess and Minnah and Leah, who never even talked to me at school unless they needed to borrow a pencil, sounded much worse. I couldn't even imagine it. Why on earth would Bea want to do such a thing?

Still, I managed to spit out the words, "I . . . uh . . . maybe. Anyway, we don't have to decide today. I might not even go to the dumb dance. . . ."

Bea stopped walking then and turned around to look at me. "Really?" she asked. "You think it's *dumb*? Why?" There was a funny look on her face. Annoyed. Almost angry. But as a rule, when Bea was angry, she came right out and said what she was thinking.

"I don't know," I said, feeling flustered. "I don't think dances are really my thing."

"But," argued Bea, "you've never even been to a dance before, have you? We skipped it last year because of that camping trip with your dad."

I shook my head. "No, but you know. Lots of people. Noisy."

"Still," said Bea. "You could *try*. You could *try* to like the dance, if you wanted. And the walking group. You could decide to give them a chance. Couldn't you? What would be so bad?"

I shook my head again. "I don't think so," I said. "If we go with a group, we can't leave if we get bored. And anyway, what if they say no? What if they don't want me there? They're not very nice, I don't think. It's just . . . too much."

Bea looked exasperated. "Seriously?" she said. "Why don't you think they're nice? What have they ever done to you?"

"What difference does it make?" I said. "Just go without me!" I was trying so hard to sound cheerful and chill, but I could feel myself starting to get upset. "You go with the walking group and I'll stay home. I don't mind. It's really okay."

"Argh," said Bea, turning and starting to walk again. "No, it's *not* okay," she said. "Of course it isn't, and of course I'm not going to ditch you. I'm pretty sure you know that. In fact, I think that's the only reason you could suggest it, Zippy. Because you know I never would. Isn't that right?"

"I—" I wasn't sure what to say to that. Was that true? I wasn't sure. Maybe it was. It *felt* sort of true.

Bea stomped along ahead of me now, shouting back over her shoulder. "Never mind about the walking group," she said. "We'll go to the dance alone, or I guess we can stay home and watch a movie like every other boring weekend in the boring history of the boring world. It just sounded fun. To me, anyway."

I walked along behind her after that, staring down at my feet in their black sandals and at the weeds growing up through the old hexagonal paving stones in the sidewalk. We were silent for blocks and blocks, and I didn't know how to feel. I'd won the argument, somehow, and kept Bea for myself, but it didn't feel good or right. It felt like I'd fallen into a trap that I didn't know was there. I guess that's how all traps work.

Anyway, it might not sound like such a big deal to you, but at the time, it felt like something had suddenly changed. Like when the wind shifts a little and there aren't any raindrops, but you can tell it's going to storm. Bea was often annoyed with me, but this silence was unfamiliar, and I didn't know what it meant. What *wasn't* she saying? When we got to her house—an old gray Victorian with a wraparound porch and peeling paint—she opened the gate and headed up the walk. I called goodbye and waved at the back of her pink head and her backpack, but she never even turned around.

So yeah, that brings us back to my story, I guess, as well as my rice pudding. After that terrible walk home with Bea, I was just trying to mind my own business and console myself with a snack in the kitchen when Mom suddenly dashed in (she dashes a lot) and splattered me with a bunch of words I wasn't expecting.

"Zippy!" Mom shouted. "It's time to talk about your bat mitzvah!"

I swallowed my bite of pudding before I replied. "What?" I said. "*What* bat mitzvah?"

"The one you're going to have next spring," said Mom. "In February. A week after your birthday. Rabbi Dan called to tell me the date is set. February twenty-second. Huzzah! Isn't that exciting? They were able to squeeze you in."

I put down my spoon at that point. Even on a good day, I do *not* like surprises. But this was a *big* surprise on a not-good day. Though maybe I should take a moment to explain that Mom *loves* surprises. We're very different, Mom and I. She's loud when I'm quiet and quick when I'm slow. She's loose and laughs all the time, except when she's having a temper tantrum. Also, she makes friends everywhere. Do you know anyone like that? Mom will start chatting with a stranger in line at the grocery store and leave with their number and plans to get together for a drink. She's often in a hurry, and if you ever see someone running into the bank in their pajamas and messy brown pigtails, that's probably her. I love her, but she's a disaster.

"But *why* a bat mitzvah?" I asked, frowning. "Why haven't we talked about this before now? We barely ever go to synagogue. I won't know what to do." We'd been to my cousin's bat mitzvah a few years earlier and I'd had a great time at the party eating mini eclairs and drinking Shirley Temples, but I hadn't even known when to stand up or sit down during the ceremony. I knew a handful of Hebrew letters, of course, and I could speak a few words, like "shalom" (that means hello) and "todah" (that's thank you). Kind of the same way you maybe know a little Spanish from *Sesame Street*. But that's not the same as truly understanding.

Mom blinked. "Come on, Zip," she said. "Of course we go to synagogue. For the High Holidays every year, and other times too. We marched with the synagogue at Pride. Remember?"

"Well yeah," I shot back, "but that didn't exactly help prepare me for a bat mitzvah. Also, we marched with the Quakers too. Does that mean we're Quaker now?"

Mom stared at me and took a deep, annoyed breath. When she finally spoke, her voice was different. Colder and calmer. "Zipporah Chava McConnell," she said. "I thought this was good news. It's a *party*. What's not fun about that? I honestly don't know what's wrong with you today."

I wasn't exactly sure what was wrong with me either. I was confused. And sad. Between Bea and Mom, everything felt like too much. "Sorry, I guess," I said. "I'm having a hard day. But I still don't understand. *Why* do I need a bat mitzvah? We aren't religious and I thought you only got to have a bat mitzvah if you went to Hebrew school all the way through and knew the prayers and everything. I thought it was like a graduation. And I thought we were only like . . . part-time Jews."

Mom didn't answer me at first. She stared at me over the kitchen island. Then she said, "Look, Zippy, I'm not quite sure how to explain it to you, but there's no such thing as a part-time Jew. You're correct that, typically, the kids at our synagogue who become bat mitzvah have completed the Hebrew school program, but that just makes it even nicer that they're making an exception for you. Rabbi Dan is offering special tutoring if you need it, which is really generous of him. You like Rabbi Dan, don't you?"

"Sure . . . ," I said. Of course I liked Rabbi Dan. He was a nice enough person. But I didn't *know* him. I only saw him a few times a year, from a distance, when he was leading services up on the bimah. It wasn't like we were pals.

"Exactly," said Mom. "So religious or not, *we* are Jewish, *you* are having a bat mitzvah, and that's the end of it. We're part of a tradition. Those people are our community. Got it?"

"Our community?" I asked. "But I don't even know anyone's name there."

Mom shook her head. "You can argue all day long about this if you want, Zippy, but there are loads of folks who want to celebrate you. At the synagogue and in other parts of your life too. People who have watched you grow up. Family and friends. Teachers. You might not care about all of them, but they care about you, and it would be selfish not to share your big day with them."

"My big day?" I asked.

"Also," she continued, "I already sent a save-the-date to the grandmas and put down the deposit on Ziba's for the party.

So this is happening. Our first meeting with the rabbi is tomorrow." Then Mom made *the face*. I hate the face. She turned the corners of her mouth down and wrinkled her forehead in a suffering sort of way as she added, "Please, honey, can't you just *try* to like it? Everything will be so much easier if you do."

I stood there staring at her and thinking about how Bea had said almost exactly the same thing to me an hour before, about the dance. *Try to like it*. How was someone supposed to *try* to like things? Wasn't liking things just kind of automatic? Wasn't I allowed to be in charge of my own feelings?

Then—even though she'd watched me finish a huge bowl of pudding, Mom suddenly picked up her purse and shouted at the top of her lungs, "Hey! Time to reset! Change of subject! Total do-over! We're all cheering up and going out for ramen! That's an order!" Which had nothing to do with anything. Though it was, I suppose, an effective way to end the conversation. Everyone likes ramen.

⋆☆ 2 ☆⋆

A Me Problem

*O*h! I just realized I did things kind of out of order. I jumped into the story without telling you about myself. *Establishing character* is something Ms. Marty—that's my Language and Literature teacher, but I also have her for Advisory—says needs to happen in the first pages of a book. Also, you are supposed to *introduce the setting* and whatnot. Since this is my book, I guess I'm the main character, and the setting is wherever I happen to be.

Well, unless you're really not paying attention, you know by now that my name is Zippy. I'm aware that it's a weird name, but when your parents name you Zipporah Chava McConnell, I guess maybe to make up for being part-time Jews, you don't have a lot of not-weird choices. I don't ever remember not being Zippy.

When your name is Zippy (or Zipporah Chava McConnell, for that matter), you never really get the option of being a kid who fits in easily. Or anyway, that's been my experience. I *don't* fit in, and seriously, I sometimes wonder if I ever even had a chance. Like, at our school, all the Stellas are easygoing people with lots of friends, and that can't be just a coincidence, right? What would life be like as a Stella, I wonder?

Anyway, I'm *not* a Stella. I'm a Zippy. I have very long dark hair that is often kind of tangled and so sometimes I wear a single braid down my back but never two. I have a best friend named Bea—you know about her already—and I get pretty good grades, except in theater arts, which I hate, because of all the *sharing*. I don't do any serious after-school activities like some kids—no gymnastics or violin or anything—and I've lived in the same house since the day I was born. I don't have any pets, because my mom claims she's allergic. But when I'm an adult, I totally plan to get a black cat and name it Hecate. Also noteworthy: if you run into me on the street, I will always be wearing black, and there's a perfectly good reason for that, but I'm not going to explain that here, because it deserves its own chapter.

My *setting* is that I live in a little old house made of blue siding in Atlanta, in a neighborhood called Ormewood Park, on a street called Woodland Avenue. It's just me and my parents who live there, and the house has three bedrooms, but one of them is where my mom and dad work, so the house feels pretty tiny sometimes. The closets are squinchy, and there's no garage. Our bikes have to live in the hallway, and there always seems to be a pile of paper or a stack of books wherever you want to sit down. It's kind of a mess, and I am not someone who likes messes. My room is by far the neatest part of the house. When I complain about the house being too small and cluttered, Mom and Dad threaten to ship me off to the suburbs. Apparently, it's cheaper to have a big house if you live farther out, past the highway. "Plenty of room for you in Alpharetta!" Dad likes to say. "Good luck with your new family in Tucker!" He thinks it's funny, but it's not.

I don't mean to whine about the small house, and I don't mean to be ungrateful. I've been lectured all my life about how Americans are wealthy by global standards, and about how nobody should really live in giant houses anyway. I'm sure that's all true. But I remember one time when I was little and my mom set up a playdate for me with this girl named Rahel, because she wanted us to be friendly with another Jewish family in the neighborhood. Rahel walked in and said, "Ew. It looks like a yard sale in here!" I went to my room and hid right away, and Rahel never came back, though my parents didn't understand why.

Speaking of my parents, they run a business together, consulting about sensitivity. Don't ask me what that means. So far as I can tell, it means they wear pajama pants most days and talk on the phone a lot. Also, they make grilled cheese sandwiches and hard-boiled eggs at random hours, so that they usually aren't hungry when I want dinner. Dad isn't quite as chaotic as Mom. He's quieter and calmer and doesn't leave the house in his pajamas or without brushing his hair. But he's still not the kind of dad who always eats breakfast at breakfast time or wears a suit and goes to an office. He basically lives in old jeans and faded T-shirts with ancient band names on them. He's super tall and skinny, and his clothes always look too big. Mom is short and curvy, and her clothes are always a little too tight, so I guess they even each other out.

Is that enough *Setting* and *Characters*? Can you picture my life now? I hope so! But I guess if I missed anything, I can fill in the details as they come up. In any case, I want to get back to my story, which picks up after school, the day of my first meeting with the rabbi, which was also the day after I ate that bowl of rice pudding. . . .

No matter what my mom tells you, I did *not* forget about the meeting, and I wasn't avoiding it either. I didn't exactly want to go, but the real issue was that Mom neglected to mention it would take over an hour to get to Congregation Bet Hesed in rush-hour traffic. So when I left school that day, I didn't know I was supposed to hurry. And when Bea invited me to come over—I thought maybe because she felt a little guilty about the Fall Fling fight—I needed to say yes. I wanted a chance to make everything normal again, so I followed her inside and up to her room.

Bea's room is very different from mine. Honestly, she's a slob. There are clothes everywhere and the trash can is overflowing and cups and plates are always cluttering up her bedside table. Her mom used to make her clean her room, but this year she's trying an experiment where she hopes Bea will learn from natural consequences if the room gets gross enough. I'm pretty sure that won't happen, but nobody asked me.

So Bea was lying on her unmade bed doing something with her phone, and I was just kind of wandering around eating a Mallomar—which she keeps in her desk drawer, if you're ever over—when I noticed an old photograph on the dresser, next to a dirty sock and an empty Coke can. The picture was of us—me and Bea—and another girl, on monkey bars at the park.

"Ugh," I said, picking it up. "Liv Randolph. Why do you even have this around?"

"Huh?" asked Bea, looking up from her phone. When she saw the picture in my hand, she sat up. "Oh, uh, I . . . don't know. Mom pulled a bunch of boxes out of my closet the other day and that must have fallen out. I didn't even realize it was there. But Liv isn't so bad. I don't know why you have such a problem with her."

"Seriously?" I said, shaking my head. "I've just never liked her. You can tell she thinks she's so great, with all her shiny hair and her followers."

"Followers?" asked Bea, sitting up. "She just has friends, Zippy. She's popular. There's nothing wrong with that. Jeez. Why do you get so weird about this stuff lately?"

"What *stuff*?" I said. "What do you mean *weird*?"

"Just like . . . people," said Bea. "You've always been pretty shy, but lately it's like you hate *everyone*. You're so negative."

I didn't answer right away. I took a minute to think. *Was* I getting weird? *Was* I being negative? I didn't think so. I'd never liked Liv or the walking group, but it hadn't been an issue in the past because Bea had never been interested in any of them.

"Anyway," said Bea, "we all used to hang out when we were little. Remember Brownies?"

I shook my head. "We *used* to hang out," I said, "because our mothers were friends and they made us play together when we were too young to argue. But Liv was the worst. Remember how she used to tease us about our potions?"

"You have to admit," said Bea, laughing, "it was kind of weird to try to sell those potions in the school bathroom. Anyway, she never teased me."

"She *still* teases me," I grumbled.

"Really?" asked Bea. "When?"

"What do you mean, *when*?" I said.

"I mean *when?*" Bea was staring at me, unblinking. *"When did she last tease you? What day was it? This week? Last week? What exactly did she say?"*

"Well, I . . . I don't remember *exactly*," I said, feeling flustered by the questions. "But, like, she laughs at me from a distance. I can tell. And she makes faces in the hallway."

"Hmm," said Bea. "Real specific, Zippy. I think that sounds like a *you* problem."

"I . . . I guess maybe it is, then," I said, startled. "A *me* problem."

"Anyway," said Bea, *"I* like Liv a lot. I think she's funny and smart."

"Well," I said. "Lucky *her*. Maybe you should go to the stupid dance with *her*."

Bea stared at me a second then, long and hard and serious, before she threw her hands in the air and shouted, "God! Why can't you lighten up, Zippy? Why does everything have to be such a big hard deal? If she teases you, maybe it's because *you're* being uptight and kind of extra. Did you ever think of that?"

Suddenly, my eyes were full of tears, and I hated them. I *was* uptight and extra. It was true. I *couldn't* ever seem to lighten up. But the harder I tried, the heavier I felt. "I need to go now," I said, reaching down for my backpack and turning away before my stupid tears could fall in front of Bea. "I have to go to my bat mitzvah class."

"Oh, come back here, Zippy!" Bea called after me. "Chill out. Stop being such a baby."

"No, really," I said as I stepped out into the hallway. "I need to go. My mom will get mad. Bye. See you tomorrow."

"Gee, Zippy!" Bea shouted after me as I ran down the stairs. "I can't *imagine* why a cool eighth grader like Liv might not want to hang out with you. You're so *fun*!"

When I burst outside, I also burst out crying. Then I walked home slowly, to give the tears a chance to stop. But of course that made me even later, and because the day wasn't terrible enough, the second I walked in the front door of the house, Mom started shouting at me right away.

"GET IN THE CAR RIGHT NOW YOUNG LADY THIS IS NO WAY TO START OFF ON THE RIGHT FOOT WITH THE RABBI IT'S DISRESPECTFUL TO MAKE PEOPLE WAIT."

That was pretty rich, given that *she* was the one who usually ran late. But Mom didn't even glance at me long enough to see that my lashes were wet. She was already heading for the porch, keys in hand. So fast. Always so fast. Too fast for me even to catch my breath.

Then of course we sat in miserable silence for a full half hour of traffic and NPR news blaring about climate change, which only made everything worse. I stared away from Mom and out the window. I watched the traffic crawl past us, determined not to say anything until she apologized for yelling at me. But she didn't say she was sorry, and eventually I couldn't stand the quiet. I had to fill it. That's a problem I have.

"How long will it be?" I asked quietly. "This meeting?"

"Not sure," said Mom. "I've never done this before either, you know." And I think Mom must have been feeling a little sorry for shouting, or maybe she just noticed I sounded sad, because that was when she turned off the news and clicked over to my playlist. The music helped some. I felt a tiny bit better.

Then, when we got to the synagogue and went into his office (which I had never set foot in before), Rabbi Dan offered me a snack right away, and the snack was jelly beans. So that was nice. It cheered me up a little as I sat down on one of the bright green sofas arranged around a coffee table at the center of the room.

If you're reading this and you aren't Jewish, or you aren't the kind of *part-time Jews* we are, maybe this is hard to understand, but on top of my terrible day, I was feeling pretty confused about meeting with the rabbi. I didn't know him at all, and while I'd gone to Sunday school for a few years when I was little, that had mostly just been singing and eating graham crackers and drawing pictures of rainbows and doves. A bat mitzvah was much more serious. Like I already explained, I couldn't even read Hebrew. I could identify *some* of the letters and maybe sound them out slowly, but I wasn't like everyone else I saw at the synagogue on the rare occasions we went. Everyone mumbling and singing and chanting and reading intently as they swayed back and forth, as if they understood all the things they were saying and meant them too. Everyone hugging and chatting at the end.

While the rabbi shuffled a bunch of papers on the coffee table between us, I tried to distract myself by staring around at the Jewishy-themed art on the walls. There was one big Star of David made of recycled soda cans and also a couple of paintings that looked like stained-glass mountains covered in finger paints. After a minute Rabbi Dan let go of his papers and leaned back, stroking his beard.

Just so you can picture this scene correctly, I should probably clarify here and explain that Rabbi Dan's beard isn't long and gray like the ones on rabbis in movies you may have seen. He's not like in *Fiddler on the Roof* or whatever. Rabbi Dan's beard is short and dark and neatly trimmed. And honestly, if he didn't wear a kippah—that's the little cap a lot of Jews wear, in case you don't know; it's also called a yarmulke—you probably wouldn't even guess he was a rabbi, walking down the street. He looks more like a librarian or a history teacher to me, in his wire-rimmed glasses and his loose, untucked button-downs. That day he was wearing rainbow-striped sneakers. I remember thinking that he was pretty cool, for a rabbi.

"Hello, Zipporah," said Rabbi Dan in his calm, warm voice. "Welcome."

"Oh, hi," I answered. "Thanks. But . . . it's just Zippy. Nobody calls me Zipporah. Unless I'm in trouble." I glanced over at Mom on the couch beside me.

He grinned. "Zippy! That's right. I'll remember from now on. My apologies. You definitely aren't in trouble. I've just had a distracting afternoon."

"That's okay," I said. And you know, it *was* okay. There was something so soothing about Rabbi Dan's singsong voice, his quiet smile. I almost didn't mind if he called me Zipporah.

He nodded. "You know, Zippy," he said. "We don't always do this, allow kids to become b'nai mitzvah without completing their religious education at the synagogue. But I'm glad we're moving forward. You sound like an interesting young woman, and I'm eager to spend time together, get to know you."

"B'nai mitzvah?" I said, confused. "I thought it was called a *bat* mitzvah."

"Ahh, yes," he said. "But b'nai is the plural. Bar and bat mitzvah are singular terms."

Right away I blushed. "Oh, sorry," I said. "I . . . didn't know that. There's a lot I don't know, I guess, about being Jewish."

Rabbi Dan smiled. "Not to worry!" he said. "There's a lot *I* don't know about being Jewish. Learning is a lifelong journey, right?"

I shrugged. "I *guess* it is."

"Look," said Rabbi Dan, reaching down into his pile of papers and pulling out a red folder, which he handed to me. "There's plenty to do, of course, and I don't want to be unclear about that. You'll need to learn to read from the Torah, and you'll need to memorize all the melodies, so you can lead the prayers. But I'm here to answer any questions you might have, and I never want you to feel ashamed for not knowing something. We love questions, Zippy. Questions are an essential part of Judaism, and I'm confident you can manage this, if you're willing to do the work."

I glanced down at the thick folder. "I don't mind work," I said. "The *work* isn't the problem."

The rabbi tilted his head and squinted at me. "Well, then what's the problem?" he asked. "I wasn't aware that there was one."

I probably should have just made some excuse and opened my folder then. But for some reason, that was when Bea swam into my mind. *You're so negative*, she'd said. *Why does everything have to be such a big hard deal?* Why *did* I feel so hesitant? Why couldn't I be excited? Or even just do whatever I had to, to get through this, make everyone else happy? Why couldn't I just *try to like it?* "I'm not sure . . . exactly," I said.

"About what?" asked Rabbi Dan gently. "I'm sensing hesitation, but we're really all just here to support you, to celebrate this important time in your life."

"I don't know!" I said, louder than I meant to. Mom looked

over at me, startled. "But I guess I wonder . . . what *is* this important time in my life? I feel like I missed a critical piece of information. Did I?"

Rabbi Dan nodded. "That's fair," he said seriously. "So let's start at the very beginning, then. Maybe I got ahead of myself. A bat mitzvah is a life cycle event, Zippy, a way of marking change. It's also the moment you become a full member of this community. It's a kind of transformation."

"Transformation?"

"You're not a little kid anymore," said Rabbi Dan. "You're growing up, becoming a Jewish woman. It's exciting, and we just want to celebrate that with you."

"Umm . . . becoming a *woman*?" I asked, squirming a little in my seat. Jewish or otherwise, I'm not very womanly. I mean, I wear a bra, but I don't *need* one. I just more wear it so that nobody in PE class points out how I'm *not* wearing a bra when we dress out. One reason seventh grade is weird is because some people are suddenly twice as tall as they were last year, and you see tampon wrappers on the bathroom floor when you pee. But if you haven't started to change much yourself, that can all be a little awkward. Uncomfortable.

But I obviously didn't say any of that to Rabbi Dan. All I said was, "But what if I'm not ready to *transform*? What if I still feel like, well . . . a kid?"

"That's not a bad thing at all!" said Rabbi Dan with a grin.

"The truth is, *I* still feel like a kid myself sometimes. In fact, I think we should all carry our childhood with us, remember to see the world through endlessly curious eyes! All I mean to say is that no matter what you do, your mind and your heart are growing up, Zippy. You're capable of doing and feeling new things now. Taking on new responsibilities. You know?"

I nodded, because I could tell he wanted me to, and I was grateful he was trying so hard. Actually listening to me, way more than Bea or Mom. But I still didn't totally understand what he meant, or why I needed a bat mitzvah any more than a Fall Fling or a walking group. Why did everyone suddenly want me to be different? I liked my life the way it was.

"Also," he continued, "you're making important decisions for yourself now, Zippy, like the very choice to become bat mitzvah. That's part of adulthood too, that agency and power. It's a significant step, don't you agree?"

"Well," I said, "*kind* of, I guess. Though I didn't exactly *have* a choice, if you want to know the truth. It's nice here, but I didn't choose to come. Nobody asked me."

Mom gave a faint grunt from her spot on the couch. But Rabbi Dan looked straight at me, and said, "Oh! That sounds frustrating. I wonder, what would make this someplace you *did* want to be?"

I looked over at Mom and then back at Rabbi Dan. In that moment, I was also thinking about Bea—about how this was exactly what she wanted, this *transformation* thing. We hadn't been in seventh grade a month, but it already felt like she was an entirely different person.

"The thing is," I said, "I do like being Jewish, the way we *are* Jewish. The synagogue is nice enough, and it's not like I want to be anything *other* than Jewish. But I don't really feel like I fit in here, the way that other people seem to. I don't feel like we belong."

When I said that, Rabbi Dan's eyebrows knitted together and his forehead wrinkled. "Can you tell me more, Zippy? The people who you feel *do* belong here—what do you think makes them different from you?"

I thought about that for a minute. "I guess it just seems like everyone else knows each other already, and what to say and how to be. They all look at home. But I . . . I never feel like that. When we come here for the holidays, I feel . . . outside. Like I'm watching a play about a bunch of people in a synagogue. Only I never got the script."

"Hmm," said Rabbi Dan. "Well, to be entirely fair, I think maybe you're making some assumptions about how comfortable all those other people feel. But I also wonder if we can't make this a more welcoming place for you. Where *do* you feel at ease?"

I glanced at Mom, briefly, before I tried to answer his question. "Well, I, uh . . . mostly just . . . at home. I guess."

"With your family, sure," said Rabbi Dan, nodding.

"Anyplace else? At school or on a sports team? With a particular friend?"

I shifted in my seat. I'd been sitting on my foot, and it suddenly hurt. I wasn't going to talk to anyone about what had happened with Bea. And I couldn't bring myself to admit that I basically felt the same way everywhere I went lately. *Alone.* So I changed the subject. "Well, it's not just that," I said. "The other thing is that I don't know about the whole faith-y part of being Jewish. You know? I'm not sure if I actually *believe*."

"I love that you're thinking so deeply about this," said Rabbi Dan, nodding. "But I wonder which aspects of Judaism trouble you. Which faith-y part?"

"Well," I said, thinking a minute. "Like, for instance, the stories. Noah's Ark. Or the oil lasting eight days at Hanukkah. Those don't make sense to me. If God was doing miracles back then, wouldn't He be doing miracles nowadays? So that the world wouldn't all be so messed up with climate change and racism and stuff? Isn't it possible all those bible stories are just made up?"

"That's a fine question," said the rabbi. "A big question. And sure, those stories *could* all be an invention. But isn't it more fun to be open to wonder, to consider that miracles might be real? Don't you think they're nice ideas?"

"Well, sure," I said. "But I don't usually believe in things just because they're nice ideas. And it feels kind of wrong to get up in front of everyone on my bat mitzvah and read from the Torah and pretend I believe in what I'm saying if I don't. It feels like I'll be telling a lie."

Rabbi Dan waited a minute before he spoke. He looked like he was thinking hard. He picked a green jelly bean out of the bowl, then chewed it slowly. At last he said, "Well, I certainly don't want you to lie. But I wonder, Zippy . . . what makes you think you're *supposed* to believe in that way?"

"What do you mean?" I asked. "Isn't that the entire point of Judaism? To believe in it?"

"Hmmm . . . ," said Rabbi Dan. "Maybe for some. But for me, Judaism is most importantly a reason for bringing people together, so that we aren't alone in the darkness. So much about the world *is* unknowable, Zippy, and we all live in a constant state of doubt. It's easier to experience that in community. The world is full of questions, things we'll never be certain of—"

"Exactly!" I shouted, without meaning to. "I know. That's the *whole* problem. See? It's infuriating."

"Ah," said Rabbi Dan. "I think I can imagine how that might feel. But for me, the journey, the *search* for answers, is as satisfying as the answers themselves. Questions can be beautiful. Mysteries can bind us to each other. Don't you see?"

I thought about what he said but only for a moment. "Maybe," I said. "But still, I'd much rather know things for sure."

Rabbi Dan smiled. "Zippy, I hate to tell you this, but the questions you're asking right now are themselves *very* Jewish.

Your arguments are things the sages have been wrestling with for thousands of years."

"Okay," I said with a shrug. "If you say so."

Rabbi Dan sat back against his green sofa. He put his hands together and held them to his face a moment before he spoke. "Look," he said at last. "How about this—let's proceed with your classes and tutoring. I promise, if you want to stop at any time, we can do that. But learning is never wasted. Right? Even if you decide not to become bat mitzvah in front of the community next spring, you're still you, and that's significant no matter what. You're part of this congregation. So give us a chance?"

"O-kay," I said. Though it still didn't feel quite right. But he was being so understanding and flexible, I didn't see any way to escape his kindness. I couldn't seem to push him away, the way I'd managed to do with everyone else lately.

Rabbi Dan nodded. "I know we haven't spent much time together yet, but you matter to us a great deal, Zippy, and I'll be interested to see where this path leads you. This process often unfolds in ways nobody expects. Almost like magic. *You* like magic, isn't that right?"

That startled me. How did he know that?

Then a strange thing happened. I was sitting there, trying to think of how to reply, when suddenly the light in the room changed. It was weird. Like, out of nowhere, the sun shifted so that it was shining right in at us, blazing through the blinds in the window, making the green sofa glow all around me. "Oh!" I said. I had to shield my eyes from the shine, but somehow Mom and Rabbi Dan didn't seem to notice. They just sat there.

Until Rabbi Dan stood up, and we all shook hands. Mom laughed in a relieved way. And I signed this big special piece of paper called a brit without really understanding what it said. There were pictures and gold scribbles and Hebrew letters all over it. Mom was smiling as I set down the pen, and she took the red folder that Rabbi Dan had handed me, full of my prayers and instructions and a calendar of the classes I'd need to attend every two weeks. She put it in her big straw purse.

And after that, we were done. But here is the last thing I will say about that day, that meeting with Rabbi Dan. Because this is a book that I am writing, I will tell you that when I was leaning over to sign my name, Rabbi Dan looked at me, smiled, and repeated what he'd said only a moment before.

"Almost like magic," he said.

The Witch Thing

Okay, so . . . speaking of magic . . . I guess this is as good a time as any to tell you about *The Witch Thing*. It's definitely something you'll need to know, to understand the rest of my story. *The Witch Thing* is what Rabbi Dan was talking about when he said he knew I liked magic. It's also why I wear black all the time, which I already mentioned.

Probably, if I were a better writer, I would save this for some climactic moment. I'd "foreshadow" it, like Ms. Marty talks about in class. If I did that, you'd wonder if I *really* was a witch or if I just thought I was. And then, about halfway into the book, I'd shock and amaze you with my actual witchcraft. But I'm not exactly sure how to do that, and Ms. Marty isn't here to help.

I'm not sure how *The Witch Thing* began. Maybe I was born a witch, or maybe something happened to me when I was a baby before I even knew what was going on. But my very first witch memory is from one night when I was in kindergarten, when I climbed out of bed and wandered into the living room, where my parents were watching a movie. When I entered the room, there was this lady on the TV, swirling her hands all around in the mist. She had glitter on her face and rings on her long fingers, which I thought were beautiful. The witch said some magical words and the wind changed and the clouds turned purple and she flew up into the sky. I was entranced.

I don't just mean that I thought it was cool—even though I did. I mean it was like I was literally under a trance. I couldn't move my feet. I could barely breathe. Also there was an overwhelming feeling, like a shimmer beneath my skin, all over me. Like my whole body had fallen asleep and was now pins and needles. I stared at the TV, frozen.

My mom immediately turned the TV off and was like, "You can't watch this, Zippy. It's a grown-up show. Get to bed now, young lady!"

But the second the TV went dark, I came unfrozen and had a meltdown. Dad ended up carrying me back to bed over his shoulder, and I remember hanging upside down, kicking my legs and arching my back, totally freaking out. I was little, after all. But when I finally calmed down in bed and closed my eyes, that witch was still with me. That image of her arms writhing in the mist was emblazoned in my brain. The mere thought of her made me shimmer and prickle all over again. When I pictured her, it was like my skin woke back up and I could feel something special, a kind of power surging inside me. It was like that witch had reached out and grabbed me through the TV, put a spell on me. Lying in bed, I couldn't help wondering what it felt like to sail through the sky. What it felt like to have such power, to control the wind, the world.

I remember I spent recess the next day running around like I was flying. I twisted my hands over my head, whispering nonsense words, until a bunch of other kids did it too. They followed after me, twisting *their* arms in the air, flying and chanting whatever nonsense words I called out. I don't know if it made their skin prickle like it did mine, but after that, we played Witches every day.

That was the best, like I had my own little coven, before I even knew what that word meant. I'd never had so many friends before and I've never had so many since. Together, we stirred potions from weeds and stones we found on the recess field. We drew symbols in the dirt with sticks and cast spells.

And *that* was how Bea and I became friends. We started

out playing Witches on the playground, and then she began coming over and helping me with my witchcraft at home—but also eating snacks and watching TV and playing UNO and regular stuff like that. Of course, the rest of the kids got bored with being witches eventually and outgrew the game. But Bea stuck with me.

I still don't know who that lady on the TV was. I've never been able to figure it out, and Mom and Dad swear they don't remember her at all. But she truly changed my life. We have pictures of me in my witch clothes every year for Halloween after that. For those first few years, Bea was a Halloween witch too, until she got obsessed with Elsa—who, I suppose, is a sort of witch herself, if you think about it.

As fun as all that was, *The Witch Thing* was never just about Halloween or the recess coven. Because for me, witchcraft wasn't a game or a costume or something I needed other people for at all, not even Bea. Witchcraft was for me, all by myself. It mattered more than anything or anyone. It was mine alone, a serious business. I read all about witches. I studied everything in the library, and everything I could find at Bookish, the little bookstore down the street. Of course, I learned about the witches who lived in Salem (they weren't actually burned, if you want to know the truth). I read about witchcraft in China—they called them wu—and in Italy—those were called streghe. I have a real silver pentacle, and I wear it every day, even though that isn't cool in seventh grade. But I don't care what anyone else thinks, because my pentacle is antique silver with an actual opal in the middle, and I can tell there's magic in it when I hold it in my hand. It sits there all smooth and heavy. It feels warm to the touch, even on cold days. And then, there are the spells. . . .

See, all my life, I have been able to make things happen, control things with my mind. You know how some kids just seem to know when to kick the soccer ball so it goes in the right direction? Or when everyone wants a certain kind of fancy water bottle, there's that kid who already has one, like they knew exactly when it was going to become cool? Well, I'm like that, with magic. It's an instinct—like my hands and voice just know how to do it. Spells spring from me. And with them, I can handle the world.

Maybe you want to know what I mean? Well, here's an example. Last year I discovered that if I scrape the roof of my mouth with a fingernail, and then dab the spit on a pimple, and hold the finger there, pressing hard, while saying the words, "Begone begone begone begone," and then hissing until I can't hold my breath anymore . . . the pimple will disappear overnight. Or like, if I'm in Individuals and Societies, and Mr. Norbert is doing that thing where he looks around the room for someone to run an errand, all I have to do is sit on my left hand and whisper, "Em ton em ton em ton," and he will definitely *not* call on me. Or if I'm walking home from school by myself on a day when Bea is home sick, and the walking group passes me, laughing and shouting, on their way to get a snack at Hodgepodge, all I have to do is hold both thumbs in my fists behind my back, and the light will turn red just as they're crossing the street, so that it doesn't look weird when I end up standing on the corner alone, instead of walking with them.

In all kinds of ways, magic makes life easier.

Anyway, my witchcraft is probably the thing that most people would tell you about me if you asked them to describe Zippy McConnell. I know I stand out, in my black clothes and superlong hair, walking through the halls at school. Some days, even now, I can feel people staring at me behind my back. That doesn't bother me as much as it used to, but it is still a true fact that in elementary school, people like Liv Randolph used to call me Zippy the Witch, and not in a nice way. Like, she'd shout it at Morning Meeting when she saw me coming or when she ran past me on the track in gym. For a while she even had people passing around the "witch curse" like cooties at lunch. I don't know how Bea ever forgot that.

Sometimes, I've wondered what it might be like to know another witch, but I've never met one. Though, one time, my aunt Jane took me to a real occult store called Grandma's Candle Shop when I visited her in Baltimore. She bought me a black candle that smelled angry when I burned it and a ring with a stone that changed colors. I remember looking around that place, at all the incense and crystals, and thinking that if there was a store for witches, then there *had* to be other witches in the world. That maybe I wouldn't be alone with my magic forever.

⋆ 4 ⋆

The Torah Thing

*O*kay, so now we've come to the part in the story where I need to tell you a little more about the Torah, just in case you're reading this and you aren't sure what that means. Don't worry, it will only take me a second. But you need to know this if you want to understand my story.

So, here we go: Introducing . . . the Torah!

The Torah is basically the Jewish name for the bible. It's full of stories about a bunch of characters you've probably heard of—Adam and Eve and Moses and everyone—but it doesn't have Jesus in it. No Jesus. Jews don't do Jesus. What the Torah *does* have in it is a bunch of very old laws about how Jews are supposed to live. I think the idea is that as long as we keep the Torah around, we won't forget how to be Jewish. The weird thing is that I don't know anybody who actually follows all those rules. I still haven't figured that part out.

If you're searching for the Torah in a synagogue, it'll look like a very special ancient handwritten scroll with these big carved wooden handles and a fancy velvet, embroidered jacket, and it'll be in a special cabinet—we call that the ark—probably up on a little stage—we call that a bimah. When the velvet jacket is off and the scroll is open and you can actually read it, the Torah is all Hebrew, just lines and lines of Hebrew all running together. Anywhere else, the Torah will look like a regular book, with English as well as Hebrew writing, so you can actually understand what it means (kind of). That's called a Chumash.

Anyway, the reason I had to tell you this now instead of later is that a few days after my first meeting with Rabbi Dan, I was sitting in the living room after school, eating popcorn and watching reruns of *The Office*, when my dad walked in with a gigantic book I'd never seen before. The cover was reddish maroon, with gold writing all over, and it looked ancient and special. Like something you might find in an attic. The book was dusty and shedding gross clumps of dirt all over my dad's white T-shirt, though he didn't seem to notice. Dad can be kind of absentminded.

"Hey, Zippy," he said. "Now that you're officially preparing for your bat mitzvah, what say we look up your parsha?"

"Um, okay," I said. "But what's *that*?"

"Your parsha?" asked Dad. "That's what we call your Torah reading for your big day."

"No," I said. "I mean, where'd you get that big book?"

Dad held it out to me. "It's the Chumash my grandfather gave me for *my* bar mitzvah," he said, pronouncing the "Ch" with extra spit. "My mother's father, your great-grandfather Sid. Man, he was a hoot! He gave me this when I was your age, and it's been in a trunk ever since. But I figured we could check it out today, together."

Now, I'm not sure I'd ever heard my dad mention his own bar mitzvah. And I definitely didn't know I had a great-grandfather Sid. But it was clear that Dad was on a roll, like he sometimes gets, and when that happens, there's no stopping him. So I didn't tell him that we could just look up the Torah portion online like everything else in the universe. Instead, I paused my show, Dwight's face freezing in a scowl at me, and said, "Cool."

One thing I should explain at this point is that while my dad's mom is Jewish, my dad's dad isn't. This probably seems like no big deal to you, whoever you are, but it can be weird if you're a Jewish kid who goes to visit your grandpa Bob for Christmas every year. I don't mind, since Grandpa Bob is awesome and he's from California and he thinks Christmas is all about Mexican food and carols on the beach, but it can be awkward when you mention to other kids that you're going to your grandpa's for Christmas and they're like, "Wait, I thought you were Jewish."

And I guess it was much harder on Dad, growing up. Dad says that when he was my age, it was a super big deal that his mom was Jewish and his dad wasn't. That he got teased at regular school for being Jewish and then teased at Hebrew school for having blue eyes and a Scottish last name. Sometimes it seems like Dad's still trying to make up for all that. Like naming me Zipporah Chava probably made him feel extra Jewy. And like with his big dusty book.

Anyway, Dad sat down beside me on the couch that day, laid the big heavy book on the coffee table, and began flipping around, like he knew what he was doing. Only he clearly didn't, and it took a long time just to find the right section. I watched as a clump of dust floated up to his floppy brown bangs and got stuck there.

At last he said, "Here it is: your portion, Mishpatim!," and he pointed to a word: מִשְׁפָּטִים. "Meeeeeshpahhteeeem," he said again more carefully, running a finger under the title of the portion of the Torah that I would be reading, like it was *his* big day we were getting ready for.

Now, I don't want there to be any confusion about this— my dad couldn't read Hebrew any better than I could. But when you have the English transliteration next to the Hebrew word (transliteration is when the Hebrew word gets written out like it sounds, with English letters), you can kind of follow along. Like מ is a letter called mem and it makes an "mmm" sound. And the little dot under it makes a sound like "ih"—the dots and dashes under the letters are the vowels—and then שׁ is a shin, and that makes a "shhh" sound. So, reading from right to left—that's how it goes in Hebrew—you can see that the word definitely starts out "mish." Got it? No kidding, Hebrew is *hard*. Maybe you can see why, at this point, I was feeling nervous about doing that in front of a roomful of people.

Anyway, that was where Dad's Hebrew reading stopped. After that, he slid his eyes over to the English side of the page and nudged the book my way so that it sat in front of me on the coffee table. I leaned over and tried to look interested as Dad read my parsha out loud in English.

At first, Mishpatim was what I expected: a bunch of rules God wanted everyone to follow as they were running around in the desert. And maybe because of that, I wasn't paying very close attention. Until Dad read out loud, "'. . . sell his daughter as a maidservant.'" Then I kind of woke up. Because what is *that*?

So I started reading more closely, and wow, is Mishpatim wackadoodle! All about putting people to death for hitting their parents and a bunch of random stuff about what to do if you dig a hole and someone's donkey falls into it. (I don't know about you, but nobody I know has a donkey.) Then I got to some super creepy stuff about people doing, well, *gross things* with animals and also what to do after you "seduce a virgin." I MEAN, COME ON!

But then I read a line that almost made me choke on my popcorn.

Thou shalt not tolerate a sorceress to live.

Huh?

I backed up and read it again.

THOU SHALT NOT TOLERATE A SORCERESS TO LIVE.

It truly said that. Right there in my parsha.

Now, I'm no Torah expert, but it seems to me that you don't have to tell people to kill witches if there aren't any witches around to kill, right? Which means that, as far as the people who wrote the Torah were concerned, witches were *real*. And apparently a big enough deal that they had to put them into their list of rules. If anyone had told me there were witches in the Torah, I might have been interested a lot sooner.

I glanced up at Dad to ask if he knew about any other parts of the Torah that talked about sorceresses, but he wasn't reading anymore. He was just sitting there, looking awkward. "Strange stuff, huh?" he said. "Turns out the Torah is a *little* freaky." He was shifting around in his seat, red-faced, and I guessed it was because of the seducing-virgins thing. I bet he'd had no idea what Meeeeeeshpahhhteeem was actually about when he dug out Grandpa Sid's book.

"Dad?" I asked.

"Hey," he said. "Look, Zip, I really want to do this together, but I just remembered I need to sort the recycling so I can take out the garbage tonight. Can we read it another time?"

I nodded. "Sure. Whatever."

Immediately, Dad scampered for the door. Dad's not usually very scampery, so either I was right about him being uncomfortable, or he was extra excited about the recycling that day.

But even once he was gone, I didn't close the book. Instead, I sat there, staring at that one line, reading it to myself over and over again. I looked at the Hebrew letters beside the English and wondered which word meant *sorceress*. As usual, the letters swam in front of my eyes, but for the first time ever, I really wanted to understand them. After a minute, I had a thought, and ran my finger over the line of text, as slowly as I possibly could. I did it again. And then I took a deep breath and tried again, but this time, I closed my eyes and muttered, "Reveal yourself."

Then it happened. I felt a faint prickle, a brief moment of magic. I stopped moving my finger and opened my eyes, looking down at the letters I barely recognized.

It was *the* word. I was sure of it. It looked like this: מְכַשֵּׁפָה
"Mmmm," I tried out slowly, sounding out the first letter, another mem. I didn't know the next letter, but there was a shin in there after that. "Mmmmm . . . Shhh . . ." That was as far as I got. So then I flipped over to the transliteration, and

found the word that had to be right, the only one in the line that had both a mem and a shin. *Mekhashepha.*

I closed my eyes and took a deep breath. "Mekhashepha," I said. But I didn't get the prickle this time, so I placed my finger back on the text, and tried once more. "Mekhashepha!" I shouted, staring down at the strange letters.

Suddenly the magic came on like a wave, so that my whole body was prickling, shimmering. I sat there, finger on the book, and let the sensation wash over me.

Definitely magic. *Jewish* magic? Was there such a thing? And in a bible that really didn't seem to love witches. I wasn't exactly sure what to make of it all.

That was when Mom popped her head in from the kitchen. "What's doing, kiddo?"

"Nothing," I said, and fell back onto the couch, away from the book. "I was . . . just . . . frustrated I couldn't read the Hebrew."

Mom smiled. "Well, it's nice to see you trying! And don't worry. We're only at the beginning. Before you know it, you'll be reading like a pro, and it'll be your big day, and you can invite all your friends from school to celebrate!"

"Ha," I said. "Yeah. All my friends from school. Sure."

"Oh, sweetie," said Mom with a sigh. "Don't be such a downer. Give it a chance." Which is just another way of saying, *Try to like it.*

"Fine," I said. "Whatever." But after she had left the room,

I touched the word again, whispered it. "Mekhashepha . . ."
Only this time, nothing happened. No prickle at all.

So I sat there, on the couch, in the quiet room, thinking
things over. But you know how there are different kinds of
quiet? That day, the quiet didn't feel like an everyday quiet.
It was the kind of quiet that feels like something is about to
happen. Like when you're waiting in a dark theater for a movie
to start. The kind of quiet that says, *Shhh, hold on, just wait a
second, let's see. . . .*

At last I closed the book, and looked down. I stared at
the big gilded cover on the coffee table, ran my hand over it
gently. I didn't get any more prickles, but for the first time, it
occurred to me that what it looked like, more than anything,
was a book of spells.

★☆ 5 ☆★

The Dating Thing

*O*kay, I know that most of the time in a book, each chapter follows the one before it in an orderly way, so that the story makes sense. Tuesday follows Monday, and Wednesday comes after that, and then—as you can probably guess—yep, it's Thursday!

As much as I really like things to be orderly, I don't think this is going to be that kind of book, because as you may have noticed, I keep coming up with different things I want to tell you about, and I'm not exactly sure where everything should go. Writing is hard! I know I'm supposed to "weave" my story together, with themes and stuff, but I don't exactly know what my themes are supposed to be, and I also don't know how to "weave." Instead, I'm just going to say the things I think to say when I think to say them. I hope you won't mind—whoever you are.

Right now, I feel like I need to mention dating. Because I might decide to talk about it later, though it makes me feel weird to even type the word "dating." It looks funny on my screen. Like something my grandma might ask about if she hadn't seen me for a year. *Are we dating anyone special, Zipporah?* Ugh. Honestly, I'd rather not talk about dating at all, but I swore this would be *The Truth*, and so here we are.

Maybe you are not in seventh grade, or maybe you are in seventh grade and things are different where you go, but where I go, seventh grade is when everyone suddenly starts "dating" each other all over the place, and it's super annoying. Honestly, I'm not even sure what dating people do when they're alone together. Do they actually kiss? Do they roll around, hugging? Do they stare at each other and wish they could roll around, hugging? It would be nice if there was someone to ask about this, but kissing is *not* a good thing to Google.

I know, in theory, that at some point in the future, I will probably want to roll around or whatever, but I can't imagine it at all and I can't imagine anyone wanting to roll around with me. It's like if someone said, *Tomorrow you are going to wake up and want to eat a bowl of live goldfish with a fork.* I just can't grasp it.

Like, *tongues.* People touch tongues. That's apparently a thing that perfectly normal people do. A thing they *want* to do. Do you get it? I don't get it at all. How do they know what to do with their tongues? And aren't tongues wet and slippery, and don't they taste like old food? I just don't understand. How do people know that their own tongues aren't grossing out their kissing partners? How do they know they aren't doing it wrong?

What I *do* understand is that, in the sixth grade, most of the kids in my class were still acting pretty normal, and then, suddenly, we all came back from summer vacation last August, and everyone started telling everyone who everyone else was going out with and asking everyone who they liked all around me. I could hear the whispers in the classroom and the cafeteria. I could hear people giggling about it in the bathroom whenever I went to pee.

Of course, I didn't *like* anyone at the start of seventh grade, and I didn't understand why everyone else was in such a hurry to date. I still have a shelf of dolls and stuffed animals in my bedroom, which I kind of think you are supposed to get rid of when you start being an actual teenager who wants to roll around and do adult hugging. Maybe that's not true, but it seems to me like it would be extra weird to touch tongues and adult-hug someone while a row of teddy bears stared at you. Or maybe not? There should be a handbook for middle school! It would be nice to have some clear rules about all this.

But don't worry, this is not going to be *that* kind of book, full of kissy-face stuff, any more than it's going to be a

Tuesday-following-Monday book. Because bigger things happened to me this year than walking to Morelli's for ice cream with someone goofy like Darius Genovese and maybe holding hands and gossiping about it afterward. Just because Darius happens to be taller than everyone else in our grade and has longish hair, everyone thinks he's so great. But I remember in pre-K when Darius picked his nose and saved the booger on a little piece of paper inside his desk. True story. *Tongues.* Can you imagine? Darius Genovese's tongue? Ugh.

Anyway, maybe you need to know that I had never kissed anybody and I had never really wanted to kiss anybody, and it felt like the whole world suddenly belonged to a club that I wasn't in. The whole dumb walking group and stupid Liv Randolph and even Bea. Especially Bea, I guess. It was like everyone had stepped into the next room together and left me behind. I didn't like that feeling, but I also didn't want to walk into the next room and join their club. Their club seemed gross to me.

Can that be a chapter? It isn't really long enough for a chapter, but I hope it's okay to leave it like this, because I don't want to talk about it anymore.

⭐ 6 ⭐

A Very Small Spell

It was funny how Great-Grandpa Sid's book changed things for me. Before Dad brought it into the living room, there was really no part of me that wanted to have a bat mitzvah. Then I found *Mekhashepha* and felt that wave of shimmering magic, and suddenly, I couldn't help being pretty curious. You know how sometimes you have an idea that won't go away, and whatever else you're thinking about, that thing is there, kind of floating around in your head too, making it hard to concentrate on the other stuff? Mekhashepha was like that for me. It made my heart flutter when I remembered it. It made me feel like maybe this was *supposed* to happen, the whole bat mitzvah experiment. Mekhashepha felt like a sign that I was on some kind of path. Which was a nice way to feel, since a lot of other things weren't going so great. Mekhashepha made it easier not to think so much about the not-great stuff.

I figured I might ask Rabbi Dan about witches in the Torah at our first bat mitzvah class, but that was still a week away, so one afternoon in Individuals and Societies, after I was finished with my classwork, I pulled up a search window and Googled "Mekhashepha." Unfortunately, that didn't give me anything useful. Just dictionary definitions and rabbis arguing about whether it should be translated as "witch" or "sorceress" or "diviner" or whatever.

So next I Googled "Jewish Magic," and I got a bajillion hits, but none of them made much sense to me. Most of the articles were hard to read, full of big words and footnotes, meant for college students or rabbis, I guessed. A lot of the links talked about golems—which were like big monsters made of clay—and dybbuks—which were some kind of ghost, it sounded like. I also learned about shedim, which were invisible demons that apparently swirl around us everywhere all the time. It turned out that Judaism is chock-full of strange creatures!

Eventually, I found some blogs and sites with actual spells on them, but the web pages looked super unreliable. Sometimes, with the internet, you can just tell. You know what I mean? We did a unit last year all about fake news and propaganda, how to cross-reference sources and check facts, and I wasn't going to fall for the winky purple letters of "Jewish

Becky's Magic and Mystery Corner Praise Yahweh AMEN."

But whether I was going to fall for it didn't matter, because just as I was finishing reading it over, I felt Mr. Norbert standing over me. And before I could close the screen, there he was, reading the words aloud to the whole class. And when I say aloud, I mean aloud LOUD. "'JEWISH BECKY'S MAGIC AND MYSTERY CORNER . . . ,'" he bellowed to the room. "'PRAISE YAHWEH AMEN!' Interesting, Zippy!" I closed my eyes as the classroom burst into painful laughter all around me. I waited for it to die down, but when I opened my eyes, Mr. Norbert was still standing over me. "So then, Zippy, you've picked out a research topic for your next current-event reflection, I see?" Another wave of laughter. I didn't close my eyes this time, but I stayed frozen, staring straight ahead. I didn't need to see their faces. I'd seen them all a million times before. I knew what *mean* looked like.

As he walked to the front of the room, Mr. Norbert called back over his shoulder at me. "As fascinating as I'm sure your pal Jewish Becky is, I'll expect you to come to school tomorrow with a hard-copy periodical from the library to work with and a research topic that has a little more to do with Upstanders and Changemakers, like everyone else in the class. Okay? And let's not use the internet for personal stuff during school hours either."

Back at the front of the room, he turned to face us, and I nodded. I could feel how red my face was. It was burning. I didn't know any magic that could fix *that*, but under my breath I whispered a tiny fortification spell. *I am me and all I need is I am me and all I need is I am me* . . . That helped a little, until Mr. Norbert said, "Oh, and this one's a group assignment, though maybe you were too engrossed with Jewish Becky to catch that part. You'll need a partner. Anyone not already paired up want to volunteer to work with Zippy?"

I turned and found Bea, since we always work on school projects together when we can. But that day, she wasn't looking at me.

Then came the silence. The worst kind. Have you ever heard it? For your sake, I hope you haven't. It was the kind of silence that happens when kids are afraid of drawing attention to themselves. You could hear the air-conditioning. You could hear a bird outside the window. A chair squeaked faintly.

Until at last there was a deep sigh. "I will," said Bea.

I turned back toward her. "Thank you," I mouthed.

But she wasn't looking my way.

"You didn't have to do that," I said as we walked along to the East Atlanta Library after school.

"I know I didn't," she said.

"Well, why did you?" I asked.

Bea was quiet for a second. "What kind of best friend would I be if I hadn't?"

I stared at my feet. "Well, you were pretty mean to me the

other day, for no reason. And you haven't talked to me since then. So I didn't know if . . ."

"I know," she said. "And I'm sorry, I guess, but can we please not make a big deal about it? Can we just call it even? Can we be done fighting and not talk about it anymore?"

"I guess so," I said after a moment. And I was grateful to be talking, even though I didn't feel *even*, exactly.

"Okay," said Bea. She walked a little faster, away, crossed the street as the light changed.

So I sped up too, and darted into the street after her. A moment later I caught up. It was hot that day, I remember, and her nose had tiny beads of sweat on it. Beads of sweat I'd been staring at all my life pretty much. I thought about the thousands of times we'd taken this same walk together. What had changed? When had things between us gotten so awkward? I wished I knew a spell to change Bea back, but I didn't. Maybe she was right. Maybe things would be better if I just pretended they were okay. Only I wasn't sure how to do that.

Suddenly, for no good reason, Bea shouted. "UGH!" she cried. "I can't take it. This weather is terrible. Do you maybe want to skip the library and go to the pool?"

"I wish we could," I said, feeling relieved for the change in conversation. "But we need to bring in our Upstanders and Changemakers periodicals tomorrow or we'll fail the class-work. The library closes at six."

Bea looked over at me. "Seriously? You have a perfect

grade in every class, Zippy. You always do. What will happen if you miss one dumb assignment?"

"I don't know," I said. "My mom would get mad."

That was a lie. We both knew my mom didn't care. In fact, knowing Mom, she'd probably say she was proud of me for taking a day to relax. The truth was it was me who didn't want to miss a classwork. *I'd* hate it. It would make me feel all itchy and twisty inside. I was feeling itchy and twisty just thinking about it.

Bea sighed. "Fine. Whatever. But let's hurry up and get this over with so I can go to the pool when we're done," and then she was running away, up the street, all the way to the library. I ran too, to keep up with her, but it felt weird, wrong. Like Bea was either running away from me, or I was chasing after her.

At last we burst into the chilly air of the library and it only took a minute to grab a copy of *Newsweek*. But as I was standing in line to check it out on my card, Bea announced that she had to use the restroom and hurried off.

I waited outside the bathroom—but not too close, since I didn't want to look like a creeper—but Bea didn't come out for a while. So then I kind of wandered around, staring at books I might like to read. After a minute, I spotted a sign I'd never noticed, in a corner of the big room, under a window. It said "Spirituality Section." One of the biggest books on the shelf there had a Star of David on the side, and so I stopped, knelt down, and pulled it out. The Star of David book turned out to be boring, but there was a cool book beside it with neat pictures, all about Hindu gods. And another about forest bathing, which sounded weird but in an interesting way.

Then I saw something else. Tucked into the very bottom shelf, there was a very small book. It was maybe four inches tall, and hidden, but the reason I noticed it was that its dark red cover was the same as Grandpa Sid's book at home, with the same gilded designs on it.

I reached for it, pulled it out, and held it in my hand. It was tied with a knotted silk ribbon, and it didn't look like anything I'd ever seen before. There wasn't even any bar code–sticker thingy that meant it belonged to the library. Had someone just stashed it here?

I started working at the knot, trying to untie it, and I was getting close when, suddenly, Bea ran up behind me.

"Zippy!" she shouted. "I need to go now. NOW."

About thirteen people shushed her, and I gave the one closest to us a dirty look. But when I glanced back at Bea, I saw that her face was panicked. All across the room, people were staring up at us from their desks.

"Are you okay?" I whispered. "What happened in the bathr—"

Before I could even finish my sentence, Bea turned and ran—*ran*—across the room and *zoomed* between the automatic glass doors out to the street. I didn't know what was going on, but I hopped up and followed her back into the blazing heat.

Outside, I didn't see Bea at first. She must have already sprinted off, heading for home. That's when I noticed that I still had the strange little book in my hand. I thought about going back in to return it, but I didn't know what was wrong with Bea. *I can bring it back later*, I thought, and shoving the book in my pocket, went running after her.

When I finally caught up, I reached out to grab her arm, and she shook off my hand, but when she glanced back at me, I couldn't figure out what to make of her expression. She looked a little like she'd been crying but also like she was excited. Maybe like someone looks after they come off a roller coaster they weren't sure about riding in the first place.

"What's going on?" I asked. "Are you all right?"

Bea whispered something but didn't stop walking.

"What did you say?" I called after her.

Now—at this point I need to confess that I'm a little bit unsure whether I should even tell this part of the story or not. It isn't exactly my story to tell because it isn't about me, so much. This part of the story belongs to Bea and it feels a little weird to share it. A little bit like gossip. For the record, even when we are in a fight, I do *not* gossip about Bea. When you have a best friend, you stay loyal, no matter what. Even if your friend runs away from you periodically.

The problem is that I'm also not sure how to connect all the pieces of the story without telling you Bea's secret. Because I never would have stolen the book if Bea hadn't dashed out of the library. Isn't it funny, how our lives overlap, how one event leads to the next? So even though this isn't *my* story to tell, I kind of can't tell my story without telling Bea's. I guess I'll just write this and hope Bea doesn't get mad. I can always cross it out later.

What happened was that she finally stopped speed-walking for a second at a red light on Glenwood, in front of a line of bars and shops. She stood there, panting, and catching her breath. Then she hissed at me, "Ugh, Zippy. I got my period at the library."

I didn't know what to say to that at all. I remember I looked around, as if someone might have heard her. I could feel myself blushing a little, though I desperately wanted to be *cool*, be *chill*, not *overdo* it.

"Really?" I asked.

"I'm a mess!" she cried. "My pants are full of bloody paper towels. I'm so embarrassed. Does it look funny?" She pivoted slightly so that I had a better view of her butt.

It looked the same as her butt usually did, so far as I could tell. I don't spend much time staring at butts. I shook my head and said, "No, not at all. You're fine."

"Okay, thanks," Bea said. "It totally feels like I'm wearing a diaper."

After that, we started walking again, at a more normal pace, side by side. But now I wasn't sure what else to say. I just followed along, trying not to stare at her paper-towel butt.

"Congratulations," was what I finally said. "Or I mean . . . how . . . is it? How do you feel?"

She shrugged. "I don't know. Weird. But also . . . not *too* weird. Different. I definitely feel different."

"Really?" I asked. "What kind of different?"

"I don't know. I can't explain it." Then she finally turned and gave me a strange look. "Maybe you'll understand, someday, when you get yours."

"Yeah," I said. "Maybe I will."

And that was it. She didn't even look at me again as we walked to her house. So I didn't look at her either. We both faced forward, marching together but apart. Is there anything more uncomfortable than walking in silence?

Not only wasn't I sure what to say, I wasn't sure how to feel. She was almost a year younger, but somehow, Bea had gone ahead of me, skipped past me again. There was nothing wrong with anything she'd said. But Bea *felt* different to me. Almost like . . . a stranger. It was like there was a space between us now, a chasm I couldn't jump over. I didn't exactly want to know more about her period. But I definitely didn't want the subject to be a wall between us either.

When we got to her house, Bea ran straight up to her room without a word, and I wasn't sure what to do. At any other time in our lives, I'd have followed her without an invitation, but that day I sat in the living room, on the couch, waiting. Wondering if maybe I shouldn't have come in at all.

After a moment I heard her shout, "Mom!" And then Mel walked past me and headed upstairs without even saying hi. Then neither of them came back down, and after a little while I heard laughing and whispers. Minutes passed. How long did it take to change your underpants?

At last I reached into my pocket for my phone, and that's when I found the little red book. In the rush of running and the drama of Bea's news, I'd forgotten all about it.

I stared down at the object in my hand. I stroked the silk ribbon with a finger. And then, because Bea and her mom were still upstairs doing whatever you do after you get your period for the first time, I used my teeth to untie the knotted ribbon from around the book—which I'll be honest, is a little gross, if you think about all the places that book had probably been, but I'm trying to tell *The Truth* here). When I finally opened it up, I discovered that the pages were old and yellowy and crumbly. They were also completely blank. I flipped through the book, inspecting every single page, but there was nothing inside but dust and the smell of old paper.

Why had it been shelved at the library? It was like something you'd find in a junk store. With a fingernail, I scratched at the surface of the cover, and then sniffed that. The tiny book was made of leather, I thought. I leafed through it one more time, and staring down at the empty pages, I remember I felt sad. Like everything in the world was as empty as that tiny book.

I felt lonely.

Suddenly, I couldn't sit there any longer. I shoved the book back in my pocket, got up off the couch, and left, without bothering to say anything to Bea. I figured she could call me later if she wanted to tell me about the secrets of her womanly new body and all its miraculous changes.

But I knew she probably wouldn't.

☆ 7 ☆

Not Much, Nothing at All

I feel like, in a book like this, I should probably tell you what happened *next*, but the truth is that I can't remember. See, this story took place last fall, and now it's March, and a lot of things happened in between—which I am about to tell you. I can remember some things clearly, and other things I can barely remember at all. Why is that? I remember the day I found the little red book and Bea got her period. But what happened the following day?

No clue.

Time passed, I guess.

I could make something up, but I have sworn that this will be *The Truth* and the truth is I don't remember much from the rest of that week. Probably I went to school and my parents were working—or pretending to work while actually staring at Facebook. Probably I watched TV or read in my room. Probably we ordered a pizza for dinner at least once from Grant Central. We eat a lot of pizza.

I only remember what *didn't* happen, and that was that even though we'd sort of made up, I didn't talk to Bea. I saw her in the hallways and in class, and I ate with her at lunch as usual, but that only made it stranger that we didn't talk. For the first time since kindergarten, we went a week without calling each other. A week without laughing. A week without whispers. I knew it was pointless to ask Bea about us not talking because she'd only have said, *Aren't we talking right this minute?* And I wouldn't have been able to argue with that. But it wasn't the same and I knew it. I just bit my tongue and felt a little worse each day.

Then one afternoon at lunch, when the cafeteria was all loud and buzzy and distracting and Bea and I were busy chewing and not talking about her period or the fact that things were so weird between us, Liv Randolph suddenly appeared beside our lunch table, all by herself.

"Hey," she said. She was talking to Bea. Definitely not to me.

This was unusual, since Liv usually traveled in a little herd of other eighth-grade girls I didn't know. They all looked pretty much alike, with very short shorts and shiny, beautiful hair. I'd never understood what made their hair so nice. My hair was even longer and thicker than theirs, but somehow it was always frizzy and it wouldn't stay brushed. Liv and her friends looked like shampoo ads.

"Hey!" said Bea, standing up really fast when she saw Liv. She turned away from me, so that I couldn't even see her face. "What's up?"

Liv shrugged. "Not much. But I'm leaving school early today, to go see my grandma."

"Oh, cool," said Bea.

It went on like that. I sat there the whole time while they literally talked over my head, eating my carrot sticks as quietly as possible, nibbling them like a rabbit. I didn't exactly want to chat with Liv, but I didn't like this either. I felt invisible. Like Liv didn't remember me, even. Like she'd never gone Slip-'N-Sliding in my backyard.

"Oh," said Liv as it started to sound like they were running out of boring things to talk about. "I wanted to give you this. You left it at my house the other day."

She had a purple phone charger in her hand.

"I wondered where it went!" said Bea, taking it. "You're the best! Thanks!"

I looked up at her when she said that. She didn't sound like herself. She sounded way too excited just to have a crappy phone charger back.

"No big," said Liv, tossing all her hair over one shoulder and twisting it with her hands. "See you, Bea. You too, Zippy the Witch!"

Then she turned and left, and Bea sat back down again, tucked the charger into the backpack at her feet, picked up her turkey sandwich, and started eating, like no big deal.

I ate too. Chewed my cheese sandwich as slowly as I could, trying to make it last until lunch was over, so that there could be an explanation for the silence. I tried hard to be *chill*, to *lighten up*. I didn't ask the question that was burning in my brain. I didn't say a word. I just chewed and tried to think of anything I could do that would feel right. But there was nothing.

It wasn't until we were walking down the hallway to class that I finally found some words to say. I tried hard to make my voice light, teasing. Tried not to *overdo* it. "Must be nice," I said.

"What?" asked Bea.

"Getting to leave school like that, just to hang out with your grandma. Bet they're getting manicures or something." I rolled my eyes. "Ladies who lunch."

Bea stopped walking then, right there in the hallway, and turned to me, so I stopped too. "Liv's grandma just had some big surgery, Zippy," Bea said. "She's in the hospital. There are limited visiting hours."

"Oh . . . ," I said.

"Yeah," said Bea. "*Oh*. She's super old and everyone is worried about her."

"I . . . I didn't know that . . . ," I said.

Bea stood a minute, staring at me. Then she frowned slightly and shook her head. "Zippy, there are a *lot* of things you don't know. Believe it or not."

"Bea—"

"No," she said. "No, Zippy. I'm really sick of this. Of you." She turned to walk away.

"Bea! I'm sorry," I called after her. But if she heard that part, she didn't reply. She was already gone.

I managed to get through the rest of school that day, using a series of calming incantations I happen to know. Though, honestly, I'm not sure the incantations accomplished much, since cleansing spells work best when you have sage to burn, which I can't do in school.

School finally ended, but things kept getting worse. About two minutes after I got out of the building, it started to pour, so I had to trudge home in that. Alone. By the end of the first block, I was already so wet my sneakers started squeaking and squishing and there was no point in even trying to run. I just trudged, head down, wet and sad.

By the time I got home, I only wanted to crawl into bed. Unfortunately, Mom followed me into my room with a laundry basket and a plan.

"Strip!" she commanded, and set the basket on the floor.

"What?" I asked.

"You're soaking wet!" said Mom. "You're a drowned cat. Strip! Take all those wet things off and change. Then grab your library books and I'll run you over to return them. I need to do errands today, and I'd like your company. If you sit in the car, I can double-park at the bank."

I tried not to groan. "Do I have to?" I asked. "I'm having a bad day, Mom. *Really* bad."

"I'm sorry about that, but we all have bad days, and your library books are not *my* job. You're not a little girl anymore and you need to learn a little personal responsibility, Miss Thing." Then she turned and left, closing the door behind her.

Letting out the groan I'd been holding, I started to peel off my wet pants. After I was dressed in new clothes, I went to get the magazine and the little red book out of my desk. But the moment I opened the drawer and touched the red leather cover, a prickle ran right down my spine. The truth is that I wasn't looking for magic at that particular moment. I wasn't looking for much of anything. But when magic calls, you have to answer. That's a rule. So I sat down at my desk, holding the book and wondering if maybe there was a secret to it I'd somehow missed. One only magic could reveal.

After a minute, I had a thought and reached to the back of my desk drawer, for the box of matches I'm not allowed to keep in my room. I felt pretty nervous, since you aren't supposed to damage library books, but it wasn't exactly a normal library book. In any case, I didn't feel bad enough to stop what I was doing, I guess, because before I could change my mind, I struck a match and lit my black candle. I set the candle down on the desk, held the first page of the book over the flame, and whispered these words: "Remove all shadows, bring to light, everything that's out of sight."

Then I waited.

And waited.

Nothing happened, so I turned to the second page, and tried again. I thought maybe I was holding the book too far away to reveal any secret messages, so I held it closer, and then the paper gave off a funny, hot-cracker smell, sort of like when the crumbs in the bottom of the toaster start to burn, but that was it. There were no invisible words or pictures. Nothing.

After that, I sat staring at the candle, and the book, frustrated. I turned the book over to look at the back, then flipped it around so I could see the spine. I fiddled with the ribbon. At last I gave up and stood, ready to go. But when I tried to retie the ribbon on the book, the funniest thing happened. The ribbon wouldn't tie. When I put the pieces together and pulled them tight, the knot slid loose again. For real. I tried again, and it happened again, over and over. Like the ribbons were snakes that didn't want to be tied together. I stood there in the room, feeling annoyed with the part of my brain that was trying to tie a knot and so sad about the horrible day I'd had.

But underneath all that was something else, a hum of hope, a hint of expectation.

I opened the book again. One by one, I flipped through the pages, examining each closely, and finding each the same as the last. I did this with every page in the book, until I reached the end.

Still—nothing.

Then—I'm not proud of this—I took a deep breath, screamed as loudly as I could possibly scream, and hurled the book.

SMACK.

It hit the wall, and dropped to the floor, where it bounced and fell open. It looked like I'd cracked the spine.

"That was your last chance," I growled at the limp collection of pages. "You stupid stupid book. Useless."

Of course, the book just sat there, broken, on the floor.

But then I said one last thing. I don't know why I did it, and I used a word I shouldn't have, but because this is *The Truth*, I will tell you what I said.

"Reveal. Your. Damn. Secrets," I whispered. (You should know that I don't swear a lot, but honestly, most kids in seventh grade swear way more than me, so you shouldn't be shocked.) Then I chanted, "Sign Argis." That's a spell to unlock doors I learned from a website, though I didn't have any lotus root to put under my tongue, which is how you're supposed to do it.

Anyway, whether it was power of *Damn* or *Sign Argis,* I'll never know, but at that very moment, the broken spine of the book shifted and something shook loose. A tiny scrap of paper. It was almost like the book had spit the scrap out at my very command, right onto my bedroom rug.

Holding my breath, I leaned over and reached down to pick them both up, the broken book and the bit of paper.

That's when the door flew open.

"What was that horrible noise?" shouted my mom. "Why on earth are you screaming? Did someone die?" Then she sniffed the air and glanced at my candle. "Also, stop playing with fire, Zippy. If I've told you once, I've told you a hundred times—"

"Sorry," I said. "I didn't mean to be so loud. I just . . . dropped this book on the floor. See?" I held out the little red book with one hand but kept the scrap of paper curled in the other. "That's all."

"That tiny thing made such a huge noise?" asked Mom, eyeing the red book "For Pete's sake. It sounded like a gunshot."

I shook my head. "Nope, no gunshot. It was nothing. Nothing at all."

Mom stared at me. "Then why did you scream?"

I shrugged. "Don't know. Like I told you, I had a bad day."

Mom rolled her eyes. "*Please* don't tell me you're turning

into an irrational teenager already? I'm not sure I have the energy for that right now. Can't you stay a little girl for another year or two?"

I shrugged again. "I thought the whole thing was that you wanted me to *become a Jewish woman?*"

"Touché," said Mom, rolling her eyes. "Now: Can you get your things together, please? If we're going to run to the library and make it to the grocery store and the bank, we need to go. We won't have time tomorrow, because of your Rabbi Dan meeting."

I nodded. "Okay, okay, I'm ready. I'll be there in one second."

Then Mom leaned over to collect my wet clothes, turned, and left. But once she was gone, I looked down into my cupped palm at the scrap of paper and felt another shiver down my spine.

I had totally lied. It wasn't *nothing at all*. It was *something for sure*. I could tell by the prickles. I definitely wasn't going to return the little red book.

Who needed Bea, or anyone else? I had magic.

Mumbo Jumbo

*B*efore you mess with magic, it's important to do your research. So when Mom and I got back from our errands that day, I really tried. But it's hard to look up something in a language you can't type on your computer.

The scrap of paper I'd found had some words on it, but the words weren't in English. They kind of looked like Hebrew, but the vowels were missing, and the writing was curvy and thick, with little doohickey things on top of the letters. If it was Hebrew, it was different from any Hebrew I'd seen before.

Because of what happened later on, I can't actually copy the exact words from the scrap here for you in my book, but I can show you sort of what they looked like, because I know more than I did back when this all happened. The words looked a little like this:

The paper was weird too, thick and stiff and yellowish, something like plastic. Or maybe like old Scotch tape that was stuck to something for years and years, and then fell off, if you know what I mean? I sat there, staring at the little scrap of paper that had fallen from the book, and then I had a thought.

I pulled out my red bat mitzvah folder, which had a sheet in it called "Hebrew Sight-Reading Review." One by one, I matched each of the funny letters on the scrap to one of the normal Hebrew letters on the sheet of paper, and made my own transliteration, making sure to read from right to left. After that, I tried to sound out the word. But even with my transliteration, it was hard without the dots and dashes. Like I think I already told you, in Hebrew, the dots and dashes are the vowels, and it's hard to read anything without vowels, even if you *do* speak the language. Lk cn y rd ths? t snt s sy!

So, even once I thought I'd figured out the letters, I still didn't have words. The first word was something like P-V-L-H, and the second word started with Ch and was very short.

How could I even pronounce that? Or look up an English translation?

Still, I was curious and excited. Between the small red book with the ribbon that wouldn't tie and the prickles down my spine and now this odd little hidden scrap of weird old plasticky-paper with its mysterious words, I could tell *something* was about to happen, something magical, but I thought I probably needed to at least figure out the words to get to the good part.

After a half hour of trying to figure it out, though, I got annoyed and impatient enough that I decided to try a spell anyway. As a rule, I don't like doing things in a careless way. I like to think things through, know everything I can before I attempt a brand-new incantation. But I was feeling impatient that day, so I went into my closet and dug out my WitchKit.

If you don't know what WitchKits are, that's understandable, since I'm pretty sure I invented the concept. Basically, when I was little, I started collecting things, like my pentacle and my black candle, that felt like they might have power. Cool feathers I found on walks, a robin's eggshell that was somehow whole but empty, that sort of thing. Just stuff that felt different and special to me. I have a penny that's entirely blue—but no idea how it got that way—and a genuine ancient scarab from Egypt that Bea's dad, Greg, brought me home from a work trip.

When I was little, I made up all my own spells. I made up goofy words like Spickelvixen and BlasterDisaster and taught them to the kids at school, so that we could all chant them together. As I got older, I started looking up real spells online and in library books and tweaking them or using them as models for my own incantations. I also began incorporating ingredients, learning about the properties of rocks and herbs, as well as the four elements. As my spells got trickier, I put all my gear together in a bag and hid it in my closet, and that's how the WitchKit came to be. Partly I did this so that I'd have my tools all together when I needed them, and partly I did this because some of the things used in spells are also things my parents kept taking from my room and returning to the kitchen to use for totally boring purposes. This was understandable and not entirely their fault, since a lot of witchcraft involves stuff like chamomile, which I had stolen from the tea cabinet, and my scrying bowl, which began its life as half of the mortar and pestle Dad uses to make his famous pesto.

So that day I pulled my WitchKit out of the back of the closet—I keep everything in an old Trader Joe's bag to avoid suspicion—and took it with me to Red's Farm.

If you don't know what Red's Farm is, I'll tell you. It's a special place near my house. It's not an actual farm, really, but there are raspberry bushes, and some people have a community garden on part of the property. The rest of it is pretty much wild. There's a creek full of frogs and minnows. There are hills covered in tall grasses, and there are big old trees with gigantic limbs that make creaky noises when the wind blows. Red's is a special place, but maybe the most special thing about it is that most of the time, nobody else is there. It's right in the middle of the city, but it feels still and quiet and like you could be anywhere at all—like in a forgotten meadow in Europe or something. When I'm at Red's I feel connected to the earth, which sounds like a goofy thing to say, but is a very big part of witchcraft. So are the four elements—earth and air and water and fire—and when I bring matches along, Red's Farm has all of those.

Like I expected, nobody was around when I arrived that day, so I walked down the hill to the creek and waded in the water until I got to the spot I like best of all, where there's a funny little overhang next to the creek bed. It's almost like a tiny beach of rocks and sand and dirt, where the kudzu hangs over and hides you. If someone was standing above you on the hill, they might not even know you were there. I like to wade in that spot when it's hot out, but it's important to watch for shards of glass and rusty bottle tops, since the water in the creek comes from the storm drains. If you ever go there, don't say I didn't warn you. Wear shoes!

On a big flat rock, I unpacked everything I thought I might need. My scrying bowl and a teensy shaker of salt I found in a hotel one time on vacation. Also of course my rosemary and fennel. I pulled out a purple scarf that used to belong to my mom until she lost it, and a box of matches. Last I pulled out my prize possession: a velvet drawstring bag full of stones.

Some of the stones in the bag were gems, from a store in East Atlanta that also sells wind chimes and tie-dyed T-shirts. Gems are important for spells, and you can learn all about that online if you want. They have different properties. Like black tourmaline will protect you, and hematite is good for self-esteem. But some were just regular old rocks and pebbles. See, I like to collect rocks whenever I go someplace that feels special to me. I don't know if that makes sense to you, but sometimes when I'm happy, I pick up a rock to remember the moment. Bea used to find rocks too, but I'm not sure she does anymore. There are probably twenty rocks in my bag, and I can tell you exactly where each one came from. When I roll them around together in my hands it feels like remembering, but with my fingers.

Rocks are amazing to me. They've been around for millions of years, but they're free. You can just take them, from wherever you want, even though they're ancient. As far as you know, people from thousands of years ago—maybe even witches from the past—used them as tools. It probably makes me a total weirdo, but I think rocks are cool. Free historical souvenirs, wherever you go.

So, anyway, enough about rocks. I got out all my stuff and laid it out in the exact right way that I always lay it all out—witchcraft is about a lot of things, but one of them is order. I set my scrying bowl on the edge of the flat rock so that it was basically hanging over the creek, and in the bottom of it, dead center, I placed a perfectly round gray pebble. Beside that, I placed a tiny jagged piece of white quartz. Then I covered the stones with some dried leaves and pine needles. I struck a match, lit the leaves on fire, and waited. After I was sure the fire had caught, I pulled two scraps of paper from my pocket: the plasticky one I'd found and the one I'd written my transliteration on. I took a deep breath.

For a minute, I sat down in front of the scrying bowl and watched the pine needles glow, watched the leaves catch fire one at a time. I love the way fire eats at the edges of a leaf, making little bits glimmer and then fade. After I'd added a few more leaves to the bowl, I looked down at the scraps of paper in my hand. Silently, I tried to make something that sounded like a word, shaping the syllables with my mouth and tongue, but being careful not to make an actual sound. The last thing a witch wants to do is accidentally speak words of power when she isn't ready. But that day, this was no easy task. Not only didn't I know what the words *meant*, but without the vowels, I was also just guessing at how they sounded. Like, was the first bit "POOVILHOO" or "PEEVLAH"? Was the second part "CHOO"?

Hmm . . .

When I thought I had the sounds worked out as best I could, I cleared my throat. Then I sat there, in front of the bowl, with its wisp of smoke rising above the creek bed, and tried to clear my thoughts. I closed my eyes, clutched the two scraps of paper in my hand, and held my fist out over the bowl. At last I opened my eyes, uncurled my fingers at the very same moment, and spoke in my deepest, calmest witch-voice. I *intoned* the words.

But just as I finished intoning, something strange happened. A gust of cool wind blew up from nowhere. And I mean nowhere. This was a hot, still September day in Georgia, and there wasn't a cloud in the sky, but here came this breeze, at the very wrong moment, and blew the scraps of paper out of my palm and up, up into the air above my head. It was as if the scraps were caught in a tiny tornado. I watched them swirl and lift just over my head, spinning and spinning, and then, as suddenly as the wind had risen, it died back down, and dropped the scraps into my scrying bowl, where they burst immediately into flame and vanished.

VANISHED.

Yeah. *That* happened.

What on earth had I *said?*

But what happened next was even crazier! Because the moment the scraps disappeared, I heard a strange noise above my head. A low long hoot, like "ooohhhhhhhhhhhh." It was a barred owl, flying around in the middle of the day. I heard his call, and then I looked straight up, just in time to see his huge wings stretched out above me. I screamed and jumped to my feet, but just then, something small and furry fell from his claws, straight down, and into my scrying bowl, which was still smoking at my feet.

"WHAT? NO!" I shouted.

I didn't even think, just moved. With my hand, I scooped the tiny gross thing out of my burning bowl, onto the flat rock beside it. It lay still, just a lump of gray-brown animal. It was a mouse, and dead, for sure, I thought. It had to be. So limp, and now a little bit burnt. What tiny creature can survive a fall like that, into a stone bowl full of burning leaves? Poor guy.

I leaned over the dead mouse, blew into the scrying bowl to check and make sure there weren't any hidden bits of flame, and when I was sure the ash was cool, stirred it with my finger. Not only didn't I find any Hebrew letters, but somehow the stones were missing too.

Weird, just like everything else that was happening.

I looked at the dead mouse on the rock. I looked at the scrying bowl. I looked up into the sky. The owl was gone. I felt . . . confused. On the one hand, something magical had definitely just happened to me, but on the other, I didn't know exactly what or why. Also, the words I'd spoken were gone now, and I'd never be able to get them back.

Had I ruined everything, done it all wrong? If this was magic, it was something I hadn't seen before, and I didn't seem able to control it, or understand it. I didn't know what to expect from it, and I didn't love that feeling.

Then something else happened. Right in front of my eyes, the mouse twitched. First it kicked a foot, and then its pink nose sniffed, rustling its whiskers. A moment later, it rolled over and popped up, onto all four feet. After that, it sat up on its haunches, and stared at me. IT STARED AT ME. The dead mouse stared at me.

What had I done, without meaning to? What had those Hebrew-ish words I'd read *been*? What had I said to animate this little zombie-mouse? Staring at the mouse, I moved my lips, rolled my tongue, trying and trying and trying to sound out the memory, to hold on to those words. Poovilhooh? Povilha? Choy? Chi? I couldn't quite remember.

I felt lost. I stared at the mouse, and he stared back, and finally, he ran off into the high grass up the hill, so I decided to do the same. Packed up my Witchkit and left. I wasn't sure what else to do with myself. For a split second, part of me wanted to call Bea and tell her what had happened. But I didn't. The story would sound wild, impossible, and I knew it. I figured she'd laugh and say, "Oh, Zippy, you're such a freak."

Or worse, she wouldn't answer the phone at all.

★ 9 ★

Judgment-Free Zone

The next day, I couldn't stop thinking about the mouse, the magic, and the little red book. I definitely wanted to get back to the farm and try the spell again, try to remember the words even without the paper. But that was the day of my next bat mitzvah class, and Mom picked me up the minute I walked out of the school building. She rolled up at the curb beside me and leaned out, waving like a maniac. "ZIPPY!" she screamed through her open window. "HERE I AM RIGHT HERE OVER HERE!" As if I wasn't standing there, staring at her, from three feet away.

Let me tell you, there are few things less cool than being picked up by your loud mom in her beat-up minivan covered in jokey political bumper stickers when all the other kids are walking home together, laughing and goofing around.

As we started up the street, we passed Bea, walking with Leah and Tess and Minnah and Lane. It sure looked like Bea had joined the walking group now, and through my smudged window I watched them chat and laugh. I didn't wave, but it wouldn't have mattered because nobody even saw me. It was like I wasn't there.

Meanwhile, Mom was busy listening to some boring podcast, so I did my best to push Bea from my thoughts. Instead, all the way to synagogue, I tried to come up with a way to ask Rabbi Dan about POOVILHOO CHOO or whatever it was. Maybe he could somehow help me figure out the real Hebrew words and write them down for me. I thought I might show him my little red book, ask what he had to say about its empty pages and worn ribbon. And I hoped that wouldn't make me sound completely nuts.

"Hey, Rabbi Dan!" I called out as I pushed open the door to his office. "Can I ask you about a Hebrew word that I—?"

But I broke off mid-sentence, because Rabbi Dan wasn't alone. In fact, I found myself facing three kids I'd never seen before.

"Oh," I said. "Hi."

The rabbi beckoned me into the room. "Zippy! We'll get to your question in a minute, but for now, welcome! Meet Ethan, Ari, and Sophie. You all have a b'nai mitzvah in the spring, so we're going to be spending a lot of time together. Guys, this is Zippy. She hasn't been in Hebrew school with you, but she's part of our community. I know you'll make her welcome."

Ethan and Ari (I wasn't sure which was which) just stared at me blankly. I was pretty certain neither of them wanted to be there either. Sophie glanced up from her phone, smiled quickly, but then went right back to scrolling. Silently, I recited an apathy incantation I like to use when I find myself in situations with new people. To ward off worry.

I made my way to an empty chair and fell clumsily into it as I wondered if Mom had known this meeting was going to involve other kids. I was pretty sure I'd have quit right away if anyone had warned me there'd be Ethans and Aris and Sophies joining us. But facing them, it was clearly too late to change my mind without looking like a scared baby.

Rabbi Dan, in his usual friendly way, directed us all to the stack of siddurs—that's what we call our prayer books—and asked us to turn to page 472. So I reached out and took a worn blue book from the stack, taking extra time to make sure I opened it up the right way, from the back—remember, everything in Hebrew goes from right to left—so I didn't look like an absolute idiot. Then, one by one, he asked us to read the prayer we found there. "Just to get a sense of where we each are with our Hebrew," he said. "So that we better understand the work that lies ahead."

"What?" I asked, without exactly meaning to. "But I

barely know any. . . ." I could feel my chest constricting, my face flushing.

Rabbi Dan just smiled. "No worries, Zippy. This is a judgment-free zone. We're all at different points in our Jewish journey, and I don't want anyone to feel bad about anything. This should be fun! Do I have a volunteer to go first?" He looked around at all of us.

It was the first time I had been angry at Rabbi Dan. I understood what he was trying to do, of course. I knew that he *wanted* it to be a judgment-free zone. The trouble was that there's no such thing as a judgment-free zone, at least not in seventh grade.

One by one, we took our turns. Sophie went first, chanting the prayer like it was no problem at all, before she returned to her phone. Then Ethan went—I knew it was Ethan because Rabbi Dan called on him. He did okay too. After that, Ari took a turn, or tried. He made it about three words before he burst out laughing, couldn't stop, snotted a little on himself, and had to be excused to the restroom until he calmed down. Gross.

When Ari had left the room, Rabbi Dan turned to me. "Zippy?" he asked. "Care to take a turn?"

"I . . . ummm . . . no," I said. "Or I mean . . . I don't think I can. I don't mean to be rude. I just . . . I've never done it before. I didn't prepare. I don't even know all my Hebrew letters or the tune . . . and I'm . . . a *really* bad singer." This was a true fact. I was so bad at music that when our combined drama/ music class had performed *Into the Woods* the previous year, I'd been moved out of the chorus to stage crew without anyone even consulting me.

Across the table from me, Sophie looked up from her phone long enough to glance at Ethan knowingly, and immediately I hated them both. It was just like school all over again. Some kids were born to smile knowingly at each other, and other kids were born to stammer awkwardly or snot on themselves.

Rabbi Dan made a gesture with his hand, patting the air as if smoothing something over. Then he said, "No need to worry. Just start with the transliteration. That's all the others are doing. You don't even need to sing it. Just read. We'll get to know the prayers this way, and then shift over to the actual Hebrew letters and the chanting later. All right?"

"Uh, okay," I said, looking down at the page, which said "Chatzi Kaddish" at the top, whatever that meant. I read those two words out loud. But as I tried to read further, the words swam. I took a breath. Then another. I could feel the seconds passing, swelling into minutes. The room froze.

Nobody else said a word until finally Ari came back into the room, banging the big wooden door. "Is she okay?" I heard him ask, though I didn't look up at him.

"Zippy?" asked Rabbi Dan. "Are you all right?"

I tried to say I was fine. But for some reason, my neck was refusing to raise my head, and my jaw was stuck. I sat there, gazing at the book on the table in front of me, staring down at the words I couldn't find a way to say, simply trying to breathe. More seconds passed. More minutes. I couldn't have told you how many.

Softly, Rabbi Dan said, "Hey, gang, how about we take the lesson into the other room and let Zippy have some time to study on her own in here. Okay?"

Then, as I sat there, chair legs scraped the floor all around me, and the others left, taking their pity with them. Of course, once they were gone, my neck worked again, and my mouth moved fine. I glanced around the room, and from out in the lobby, I could hear the others running through the prayer. But I didn't go in there. I didn't move until the building was silent. I just sat alone, like usual. Whispering my incantation for the soothing of troubled seas.

When at last I came out, I found Rabbi Dan sitting in the lobby, on a big red chair by the front door. I was worried he'd be mad, but he was his usual calm self.

"I'm so sorry, Zippy. That was poor decision-making on my part. I should have discussed this class with you before I asked you to read. You're so smart and studious, I just assumed this would be easy. But the others have been in Hebrew school together for a long time, and it didn't occur to me that it might be difficult for you to join them. Would you like me to make some audio files for you so you can work on everything at home?"

What I wanted to say was that I was quitting the whole dumb thing. But when I opened my mouth, all that slipped out was, "I can't read Hebrew."

"*Yet*," said Rabbi Dan. "You can't read Hebrew yet. I'll email your mom some links for good apps that might make this preparation easier, get you up to speed. Okay?"

I nodded silently.

Rabbi Dan stared at me a moment. His eyes were kind, but they couldn't soften me. I felt rigid, closed, angry. Why was I even doing this in the first place? I'd told Rabbi Dan I didn't feel welcome at the synagogue. Now the class had proved me right.

"You look like you want to say something that you aren't saying," Rabbi Dan said at last.

I shrugged.

"You look angry," said Rabbi Dan. "At me?"

I nodded. And when I finally opened my mouth, the voice that came out was louder than I intended. "I *don't* like surprises," I said. "I like to know what is going to happen, before it happens. I like to prepare myself, so I can do a good job and not get all flustered. But also, I don't want to be in a class like this. I *hate* group work. I'm better when I can work on my own."

"I hear you, Zippy," said Rabbi Dan. "I hated group work too as a kid. It's hard to let go of control. But there are reasons we come together in a place like this. There are reasons we do things in a group. Judaism is deeply rooted in the concept of minyan. There are prayers you *can't* say alone, that you need nine other people for. We all do need other people, sometimes."

"Well, maybe that's true," I said. "But minyan aside, that was . . . horrible."

Rabbi Dan folded his hands in his lap and stared at me. "Noted," he said. After that, he was silent for a minute. Just watching me intently. I could tell that it was *his* turn now, that he was thinking things he wasn't saying, but I wasn't sure what to do about that. If he'd been my mom, I'd have run away and slammed my door until she came to apologize and talk it out. If he was Bea, I'd probably have cried.

Just then, the bathroom door off the lobby burst open, and Sophie stuck her head out, looked at me. "Hey, Zippy, sorry to interrupt, but do you have a tampon or a pad?"

I turned from her, and felt myself blushing all over again. I couldn't believe she'd asked that in front of the rabbi. Even worse, I couldn't believe she'd been in that bathroom the whole time, listening to our conversation. Could this possibly get any more unbearable?

"No," I called. "Sorry. I . . . uh . . ."

She laughed. "No worries. I'll make do. Just thought I'd ask." Then she disappeared back into the bathroom, leaving me to wonder what on earth *make do* meant.

"Well," I said, glancing back at Rabbi Dan. "I guess I'll go wait outside for my mom now."

"That's fine," said Rabbi Dan as calmly as ever. "You do whatever you need to do to take care of yourself. That's important. But you *can* do this, you know. It's not as hard as it seems."

Which of course didn't help at all.

I headed for the door. "Bye," I said, without looking back.

But Rabbi Dan called after me, "Oh, Zippy! I almost forgot."

I stopped walking but didn't turn. I waited with my back to him, listening.

"When you showed up today," he said, "you wanted to ask a question about some Hebrew, didn't you? I wanted to be sure I answered you if I could."

Now I turned my head to look at him. "Right," I said. Yeah. But . . . it wasn't for my bat mitzvah. It's not your job to help."

"It's always my job to help," he said gently, "whenever possible."

I thought about the mouse, the little red book, and whether I really wanted to trust anyone with my secret. I stared at Rabbi Dan for a minute and decided I didn't. But I was also incredibly curious. At last I said, "It's just . . . I found a word, in Hebrew, without vowels . . . and I wanted to translate it, but I couldn't figure out the letters on my own."

"Oh," said Rabbi Dan. "Interesting, let's take a look."

I shook my head. "No. I don't have it anymore. I lost the scrap of paper. But I kind of remember the transliteration. The first part was something like poovilhee or pavelhah, maybe? It started with a 'pay.' And the second word started with a 'ch' and it was really short."

Rabbi Dan looked thoughtful for a second. Then he leaned over and scribbled something on the pad of paper in his lap, stared at it. "I can't know for certain with just that to go on," he said. "But it would help to know whether the V sound was a vav or a vet. If it was a vav, it might be operating as a vowel, something like an 'oh' sound, rather than a 'vv.' Does that make sense?"

Standing at the door, I nodded, though it didn't make sense at all.

He continued. "So, if, for instance, the word looked like 'pavelhah' to you, as you said, but the letter was a vav, the word might actually be 'paOHlha.' Get it? And the 'ch' word could be a lot of things, but one likely bet is chai."

"PaOHlha," I repeated after him. "PaOHlha chai. Got it. Thanks."

I guess I still looked confused, because Rabbi Dan suddenly stood up. "Come with me a moment," he said, and headed quickly for the sanctuary.

I followed, and found him standing up on the bimah, in front of the Torah scroll, which was open. He looked out at me. "I want to show you something," he said. "I should have done this sooner."

"Done what?" I felt nervous, walking up the three steps to join him on the bimah. Like I didn't belong in the empty sanctuary. Like I was an intruder. But I wasn't sure how to say no, and I did what he asked, joined him in front of the scroll.

There, he handed me something that looked like a magic wand. It was made of silver, encrusted with jewels, and at the very end was a silver hand with its pointer finger extended. I took the wand awkwardly.

"Don't worry, you won't drop it," said the rabbi. "Just think of it as a silver shish kebab skewer."

"I . . . ummm . . ." I didn't know what to say. The wand was heavy and old. I didn't get a prickle, exactly. But it felt . . . important. Special. Sort of like my pentacle. "What is it?" I asked.

"It's called a yad," said Rabbi Dan. "It means *hand* in Hebrew. We use it to follow along with the text of the Torah. We never touch the scroll with our skin."

"Why?" I asked, feeling my curiosity wake up, override my anger. "Because it's, like, holy?" Maybe I didn't believe in this stuff, but I had to admit it was pretty interesting. The scroll looked ancient. The yad too. Standing there, with Rabbi Dan, I felt a shiver run up my spine.

"Well, sure," he said. "But also because the oils on your skin will eat away at the parchment. Most of the rules we follow have both a sacred explanation and a practical one too."

"Oh," I said. "Okay."

Then the rabbi reached out, grasped the wooden handles in front of us, and heaved the Torah, flicking his wrists over and over to the right, so that the scroll rolled and moved on its handles. The whole time, his eyes stayed on the parchment as it shifted, and I could see he was reading it. At last he settled the Torah back down and pointed at a section. "Set the yad just there, where I'm pointing."

"Me?" I asked. "No, I don't want to do anything wrong."

He laughed. "Zippy. You won't. I promise. You're fine."

So, tentatively, I set the little silver finger down on a word and looked at it carefully for the first time. When I did, I couldn't help saying, "Oh!"

"Something interests you?" asked the rabbi.

"Well, it's just that it looks a little like the word I was asking you about. I mean, my word was different letters, I guess, but it had those same doohickeys on top of the letters, like all of these. And the vowels were missing like this."

"I thought that might be the case," said Rabbi Dan. "I wonder if your scrap of paper was perhaps made by a sofer—a scribe who makes these scrolls. It's an ancient Jewish art, and takes years of training. There's no prohibition against practicing calligraphy, so if you saw something like this on a small scrap of parchment, it might have been a bit of a practice text. Was the scrap made of regular paper? Or was it stiff and yellow like this parchment?"

"Like this!" I said. "Just like this. I thought maybe it was plastic." Then I looked down at the scroll. "What's it say, anyway, this part of the Torah?"

Rabbi Dan smiled. "That's *your* parsha," he said. "Mishpatim. I wanted you to see it, to get a feel for the scroll itself. And that word, the one you pointed to, is one of my favorites. It says 'mehkashepha.'"

"I know that one!" I said. "Sorceress! Witch. Diviner."

Rabbi Dan's eyes went a little wide. "Zippy! That's remarkable. I thought you said that you didn't know any Hebrew?"

"Well, I don't," I said. "Not really. Honestly, I mostly just know that one word. Because of what it means. It's . . . an interest of mine, you know. Witchcraft. Though I *don't* love what it says about it in my parsha. It sounds like they didn't like witches at all, back in Torah days. Still, I looked up that one word in Hebrew after my dad and I read over the parsha the other day in English. So I recognize it. And I . . . I like it, that word."

It took Rabbi Dan a moment to answer me, I remember. He stared at me thoughtfully for a while. Then he finally said, "Zippy, I want you to hear me when I say this. Are you listening closely?"

I nodded.

"*That*," he said, "that one word . . . is probably more than all the other kids understand put together."

"Huh?" I said. "No way, not Sophie. She was so good today."

He nodded. "Even Sophie. She's good at memorizing. But I bet she can't translate a single word of her parsha yet."

"But it's just one little word," I said.

"Yes," he replied, nodding. "But it's an important word, to you. You care about it. It has meaning. So you took the time to find it, to connect with the text. You have given it real thought and asked questions about it. Not only that, you're arguing with it too. *That* is Jewish learning, Zippy. *That* is meaning and understanding. And *that* . . . is impressive."

"It's just one word," I said again. But as I stared at the scroll, at the one word I knew, I realized that I'd never mistake it for any other word again. It belonged to me now, *mekhashepha*. It was mine. It didn't give me a prickle exactly. But I could feel it, making sense, inside me.

☆ 10 ☆

Happy Holidays

We were into September at that point and fall for real. When you're Jewish, fall means holidays. So maybe I need to put something in this book about the holidays, in case you don't know. Jewish holidays feel different from Christian holidays—or American holidays, or whatever you want to call Santa and the Easter Bunny and all that stuff.

I don't know how to explain this, exactly, but it seems like, for lots of people, holidays are mostly about having fun. With cookies and complicated desserts and special candies and of course vacation from school—which Jewish kids don't get, at least not where I live. Also at Christmas, there are parties full of themed sweaters and decorations and presents. Like I said, fun.

I know that a lot of non-Jewish kids think that Hanukkah is that way too. People always say they wouldn't mind eight days of presents, but in my experience, Hanukkah presents are mostly boring. Like, I'll get a book one night or a jacket I need because I outgrew my old one or art supplies (why do grown-ups love to give kids art supplies so much?). Also, we don't have parties at our house, because we don't know many other Jews. So it's me and Mom and Dad, alone.

In the spring there's Passover, which falls right around Easter. So when other kids are eating Cadbury Eggs and Peeps, I'm eating matzoh. At our house, we generally get about four days into Passover, forget we aren't supposed to have any bread, and order pizza by accident. Then Dad shrugs and says, "Well, we tried," as Mom groans and chews her crust. That's Passover.

But the fall holidays? The fall holidays are a whole other *thing*. I don't mean to say I don't like them, because I actually do. But they aren't what you'd call fun. It's just the three of us, as usual. But one time, Bea asked to go to synagogue with us for Yom Kippur, to see what all the fuss was about, and when it was over, she just couldn't stop talking about how terrible it was. "Interestingly terrible," she said. It hadn't occurred to her that we'd be there *all* day, and that since the rest of us would be fasting, she'd have to skip lunch too. And that then, on top of everything else, she'd have to make up her schoolwork the following day, the way I always have to. "Hungry-apology-day," she called it.

So yeah, our holidays aren't always a party. But in some ways, the rituals were the most interesting part about being Jewish. Even if we went only those few days every year, and even if I didn't know what anyone was saying or believe in any of it, I loved to look around at everyone in their beautiful white prayer shawls. I loved the music. And the prayers sounded a lot like spells to me. There's one on Yom Kippur where everyone pounds at their chests and recites this big, long list of regrets, and it feels . . . good. It reminds me of a thing I read that covens do on Samhain, where the witches all pound their chests three times to call on the ancestors.

Anyway, to get back to my story, about a week after I accidentally zombified the mouse and then Rabbi Dan showed me the Torah, things weren't any better with Bea. She still hadn't called me, and I was trying hard not to think about her. We'd had fights in the past, sure, but those had been brief screaming matches, not awkward silences. Somehow silence was worse. I felt so bad about it all that I'd stopped going to the cafeteria at lunch. Instead, I ate my sandwich in the library each day. I'd even started staying late a few minutes after school so that I didn't have to pass Bea and the rest of the walking group all heading home together, talking about the stupid Fall Fling. What all this added up to was that I was managing to go all day without talking to anyone.

Of course, I'd made myself a charm to ward off sadness, with a piece of rose quartz, lavender, and tears, all wrapped in a little square of fabric and tied with a string. I'd been carrying it everywhere in my pocket, and it helped a little. But I was still grateful for Rosh Hashanah when it came, since the holiday meant I could skip school. It's much easier to be lonely alone than it is to be lonely with people, and that's a fact.

In case you don't know, Rosh Hashanah is pretty much New Year's, but not in a champagne-and-fireworks-at-midnight way. Instead, Jews spend the day in synagogue, praying and being too hot for the dress clothes they inevitably wore because it's supposed to be fall but it's still ninety degrees in Atlanta. My shoes always pinch.

So, there I was at Rosh Hashanah services like usual, in my pinchy shoes and hot black dress, sitting with my parents in the back row. Some guy in the community choir was coughing a bunch, and people shuffled papers all around the room. Dad kept rearranging his long legs beside me, crossing and uncrossing them. But the thing is that, despite all that, I was sort of enjoying myself. It was a relief to be away from Bea, to stop pretending. It was a relief to be somewhere that wasn't school, somewhere different, lost in a crowd.

And even if I couldn't actually recite them, the prayers were beautiful and soaring but also somber and heavy in a way that felt right to me that day. It was like the music matched my insides. Plus, there was light was streaming in the window and shining on those wooden walls, and then someone was blowing the shofar, which is an actual ram's horn, and it makes a sound like nothing you've ever heard before. Sharp and loud but sort of full of light too. At some point I started to feel kind of loopy and full of light myself. Does that sound weird? It probably does, but still, it's *The Truth*.

Anyway, there I was, just sort of floating in the light and the music and the sounds of the shofar blasts, when Rabbi Dan got up to give his d'var—which is supposed to be a little speech that explains something funny or interesting about the parsha, though people get pretty creative, in my experience, and talk about all kinds of things. He tapped the mic and smiled. "Shalom, everyone," he said. "Welcome and L'shana Tova! Today . . . is the birthday of the world."

"L'shana Tova!" shouted the whole entire room.

I said it too, but quietly, in case I was pronouncing it wrong.

Rabbi Dan continued. "Today, the coming year is being written into the Book of Life. Today we begin the Days of Awe. May you all be inscribed for a sweet new year."

When he said that, I thought about the year ahead of me. I thought about a year of lunch in the library alone. I thought about Bea with the walking crew. Or with Liv Randolph. "Yeah, right," I muttered. "Sweet new year. I'm sure it'll be just perfect."

But do you know what happened right after that? Rabbi Dan stared out into the room, searching around with his eyes, until he found *me* sitting in my seat at the back. I know this sounds unlikely and kind of self-involved, but I swear it's true.

He sought me out with his eyes, and then he winked right in the middle of services, straight at me. Then, with his eyes still on me, he started talking. About something called tik-kun olam. And since I couldn't exactly look away without him noticing, I stared back and listened closely.

If you really want to understand tikkun olam, you should probably ask an expert, because there is no way I'm going to remember this or get it exactly right. But basically, from what Rabbi Dan said, when the world was created, everything was dark. Then God said, "Let there be light," and the light came forth in these ten amazing magical vessels. Like big, gigan-tic vases, I guess, floating around. The problem was that the light was some kind of miraculous, powerful God-light, and the vessels were too fragile to contain it, so they shattered. "Split asunder," said Rabbi Dan. I remember that part word for word.

Anyway, if the vessels had stayed intact, the world would have been a totally perfect place, but of course they didn't. Instead, all the teensy tiny little bits of light scattered and got blown around. Like sparks at a bonfire, maybe. They didn't get wherever they were going. So now we have this imperfect world, that needs to be fixed in a jillion ways. But even so, there are these little sparks everywhere.

You know how when you do a craft project, glitter gets scattered and onto everything, so that it's just impossible to ever find it all and put it back in the tube? I guess the God-light is supposed to be like glitter. Hidden in nooks and crannies, all over the world. Rabbi Dan said it's our job to look for it and gather it up. We're not just supposed to wander around in this imperfect world, uncaring. We're supposed to look for the light.

Then of course Rabbi Dan did that thing rabbis do where they turn a perfectly interesting story into a lesson. He said that now, at the holiday season, as we head into a new year, it can be useful to think about tikkun olam, to consider the shattered vessels as a metaphor. He said that it is everyone's job to gather the light and goodness—to repair the world—together.

Then Rabbi Dan was done, and he sat down and some opera-singer-sounding lady got up to lead us in a song, but I was still thinking about the God-glitter when my dad started poking me.

"Hey, what say we skip outta here?" he said.

Mom loud-whispered, "Hush, Gabe! The service isn't over yet," but she was already putting away her siddur and picking up her bag, so the next thing I knew, I was being shoved along the row of chairs, stepping on other people's purses and feet. Then we were out in the sunshine, and Dad was taking off his tie as we all walked to the car.

"Hey!" I yelled.

They turned to look at me.

I yelled some more. "You guys do that all the time, you

know. Just decide what we're doing. Did you even think about the fact that maybe I didn't want to leave?"

"You *really* wanted to stay for the rest of services?" asked Mom, looking puzzled.

Dad laughed. "Looks like Zippy's going frum on us, Emily," he said. "I guess those bat mitzvah classes are really sticking."

For the record, you shouldn't be embarrassed if you're reading this and you don't know what *frum* means. I wasn't one-hundred-percent sure what it meant when he said it that day either. But I looked it up online, and it just means super Jewish, like following all the rules and traditions and whatnot. However, I *did* know what his laugh meant, so I was angry anyway. "Stop laughing," I said. "I hate being laughed at."

"Oops, sorry," said Dad. But I could tell he didn't mean it.

"Great way to start the new year, Gabe," said Mom, punching him lightly in the arm. "Nice job repairing the world." But she was smiling too.

"I'm *not* going frum," I said. "And I may not exactly be repairing the world. But you know what? *I* thought that was interesting. All about the shattered vessels and the light. It was a nice story. You guys don't take anything seriously, ever. I just wanted to listen. What's so bad about that? Why do you have to make fun of me?"

"Oh, honey," said Mom. "We're sorry."

She didn't sound very convincing, but by that point we'd

gotten to the car, so I didn't reply. I just opened the door, which burned my finger when I touched the handle. We all got into the hot metal box, and I could barely breathe, so as soon as the car was on, I rolled down my window and stuck my head out, trying to ignore my parents and think about tikkun olam. Whether or not it was real, it was a nice idea. Sparks of something that should have been perfect, glitter all over the world. Something wondrous but invisible, waiting around every turn. A way to make things better.

A lot like magic.

I thought about that until we pulled into the driveway.

⋆☆ 11 ☆⋆

About Tashlich

O kay, so before I get to the next part of my story—which is where things get interesting—I probably need to explain about tashlich. Because it's going to sound strange if you don't know what it is.

Starting on Rosh Hashanah, Jewish people are supposed to think about all the things they've done wrong in the last year. Then we're supposed to go someplace with a stream or river and toss bread crumbs into the water. The crumbs disappear and take all those regrets with them, so we get a big do-over. Of course, throwing some crumbs around can't actually undo the bad stuff, but it feels nice. Like the water washes the year clean. Or anyway, it washes as well as creek water can wash anything, since we do tashlich at Red's Farm and, like I said, the creek isn't the cleanest.

When we got home from synagogue that day, I assumed that the farm would be our next stop, like usual, but Mom had other ideas.

"Do you mind if we skip it?" she said to me and Dad. "I really need to get some work done. The folks at AT&T aren't observing the holiday, I'm afraid, and I owe them a proposal."

"But it's Rosh Hashanah," I said. "And we already left services early."

"I'm with your mom," said Dad. "Maybe later, after I lie down with a book for a bit?" (Which is what he always says when he wants to take a nap.)

"Seriously?" I said, looking from Mom to Dad and back again. "We always do tashlich. We never skip it."

Mom sighed. "Honey, I think it's going to be okay if we miss one year."

"You still could have asked me before you just decided," I said. "I get tired of being bossed around all the time, you know!" I may have shouted that last bit, because my parents looked kind of surprised.

"Honey, I'm sorry. I didn't know you were so interested in tashlich," said Mom.

"Well, maybe I *am* turning frum!" I said, still shouting. "Or maybe you're the two laziest Jews in the world!"

"Okay, hang on—" Dad began.

"No, that's fine," I said. "It's okay by *me* if you don't care.

I guess you're only serious about Judaism when I have to do all the work and you get to have a big party and impress your friends."

"That's not true, Zippy," Mom said.

If I'm being honest, I can admit now that she was right. Mom is messy and disorganized and kind of nutty, but she doesn't do things to impress other people. I was just angry when I said that. But I wasn't going to back down either. "Forget it!" I shouted. "I'll do tashlich by myself. All alone. Like I do everything!"

"Hey, ease up, Zippy," said Dad. "It's not all or nothing. Be cool."

"Sure," I said. "I'll be *cool*. I don't care anyway. I'll just go out for a walk by myself. I don't need *anyone*."

Then I grabbed two packets of saltines from the soy-sauce-and-ketchup-packet-and-menu drawer in the kitchen and slammed the screen door on my way out. Behind me, I heard Mom mutter something about *life with hormones* as I stomped down the porch steps.

But as angry as I was when I left, I felt myself calming down by the end of my block. You know how, after you lose your temper, the anger burns off and you feel kind of good? Loose and empty? I felt like that. But also, it was nice just to take that walk. Even under annoying circumstances, it's interesting to be out of school when everyone else is trapped there. And it's interesting to walk past your school in your dressiest dress, looking in the windows at everyone else taking quizzes and reciting speeches and getting in trouble for leaving their phones on. It feels like you're breaking the rules, even though you aren't.

And do you know what's better than that? When you are just sitting by a creek in your black lace dress, crumbling saltine crackers into the water and dipping your toes in, trying to think about your biggest regret, but also not to think about it too much, because just whispering the word *Bea* makes you want to cry . . . when suddenly, there is a mouse sitting next to you, staring at the creek too.

It seemed impossible to me that this was my mouse. My magical zombie-rodent. But in another way, it seemed even more impossible that this was any other mouse in the world. After a minute, when he still hadn't left, I gave the mouse half a cracker, laid it in front of him. He picked it up with his little mousy hands and nibbled it.

And seeing him there made me remember the spell I'd done the last time I was at Red's Farm. I looked up above me, thinking about the owl. Then I stared at the water, at the cracker crumbs slowly sinking and being gobbled by minnows. I wished again that I hadn't burned up the scrap of paper with the Hebrew on it, so I could try one more time.

Finally, I closed my eyes, tried to recall the words. I mouthed them, silently, trying to pull them back from memory. Poovilho, was it? Or pavelha? Just in time, I remembered what Rabbi Dan had said about the letter vav. *PaOHlha*, I tried out the first word, silently. *Paoulha . . .*

At last I stopped mouthing the words and opened my eyes. The mouse was still there beside me, nibbling his cracker. He looked up at me but seemed totally unafraid, chewing away, whiskers twitching. He was, very clearly, a magical mouse. This wasn't like my usual spells. What I had done with the mouse was bigger. Usually, my magic didn't affect anyone much beyond me, but it had definitely changed his mousey life in a big way. If only I knew how that had happened . . .

I wanted so badly to know how to do more of *this* magic, to be stronger, more powerful. Then I could make Bea forgive me, make Liv vanish into thin air, make my parents less difficult to live with, make the Hebrew in my parsha as easy to read as this sentence. I glanced into the trees overhead, wishing the owl would reappear. Wishing for anything that might feel like a sign I hadn't blown everything.

"Do *you* know what the other word was?" I asked the mouse at last. "I bet you do, Magic-Mouse. Paolha what? Choy? Choo? Chay? Rabbi Dan said maybe chai."

The mouse didn't reply, but staring at him, I was filled with the oddest feeling that *I* knew what to say, deep inside myself, that if I opened my mouth, the right words would simply fly out. My brain didn't remember, but I felt like maybe my lips did, my tongue. It felt like the right words were inside me somewhere, ghosting around. Like the magic was waiting for me to remember it.

"What's the worst that could happen?" I said to the mouse. "Why shouldn't I at least try?"

The mouse wasn't looking at me, and of course he didn't respond. So I took a deep breath. I stretched my arms, and as I looked around at the creek and the kudzu choking the trees, I felt a tiny cool wind on my sweaty face, as hot as it was. And because the moment felt just-right, I spoke then, out loud. I swirled my hands over my head, opened my mouth, and let the words inside me tumble into the hot afternoon air.

"Paohlha," I called up into the trees, and as the word slipped past my lips, I suddenly felt a prickling, all over my face, rushing down my neck, throat.

The breeze picked up. Something was happening.

I closed my eyes and felt the wind in my hair. I felt the earth beneath me. I listened to the water shuffle by in the creek. All that was missing was fire.

"Paohlha chai!" I called out.

There was a strange silent beat after that, a moment of absolute calm. Like the creek had stopped moving. No crickets. No bees. Only silence.

And then, off in the distance, someone started screaming.

*☆*12*☆*

Something from a Dream

S creaming and screaming!
    I jumped up right away, jammed my wet feet back into my pinchy sandals, and dashed along the creek, then up the hill, slipping in the long grass.

"Hello? Hello?" I yelled as I ran. "Are you okay? Who's there?"

But by the time I came to the rise of the hill, the screaming had stopped. I looked all around me, turning in circles, and saw nothing. Just the empty green farm. Silent now except for the bees buzzing and the pounding of my own racing heartbeat.

"Hello?" I called again, panting.

Nothing.

I stared around me at the hot day, the cornstalks in the garden, a lizard by my foot, and tried to catch my breath. Until, out of the corner of my eye, off to the left, near the rope swing, I noticed a bush moving. An azalea, covered in pink flowers. It was rustling, just a little, but the leaves kept shaking, as if some animal was crawling around in there.

I turned and headed that way. "Hey!" I called out. "Is someone there?"

The shaking stopped.

"Hello?" I tried again. "Was that you? Are you all right?"

Nobody replied, so I continued making my way to the azalea. I stood for what felt like a long time, waiting, staring at the bush, and hoping that whoever was inside it hadn't dropped dead or fainted. Then the leaves shook again, and I heard a twig breaking.

"I can tell you're in there," I said. "I wondered if you needed help?"

"I . . . don't . . . know," said a soft raspy voice. A girl's voice. Almost a whisper.

"You don't know?"

"No," said the girl. "I don't know."

"Well . . . do you want me to go get someone? Are you hurt? What do you need?"

Silence.

Apparently the girl in the azalea didn't want to talk to me any more than anyone else did. I waited another moment before I tried one last time. "Look," I said. "If you don't need my help, I can go. I don't mean to intrude. I just came here for tashlich, but I'm done now."

The minute I said that, the azalea rustled again. "Tashlich?"

"Oh, uh, yeah, tashlich," I said. "It's a Jewish thing."

"A *Jewish* thing?" asked the voice. And this time, two pale thin arms emerged from the azalea, pulled the branches apart.

I stared awkwardly as a face appeared in the space between the two arms.

Now . . . I am going to tell you what I saw next, and you are never going to believe me. I know that. I know how bananas it sounds, this next thing I'm going to say. At the time, I wasn't even sure it was real. But that is exactly why I have to write it down. So that I can try to hold on to it, so that I can keep believing in my own memory. So that someday when I feel like, "Ahh, that was just some imaginary game I played when I was twelve," I can come back and read this, and remember *The Truth*. I need to tell you about the girl.

She stepped out slowly, carefully. Her eyes didn't leave me. She looked about my age but slightly taller and very thin. Her skin was pale. Not white-person pale but actually *white*. If you wanted to color her with a crayon, you'd choose a white one. Also, she was nearly transparent, if you can believe that. I could see through her. For real.

She wore a loose, sleeveless dress that fell all the way to

the grass, and her hair was even longer than mine, so blond it looked almost white, like the rest of her. Her face was beautiful, with huge dark eyes and a sharp jawline. Not regular-person pretty but beautiful in a way I'd never seen before.

None of that was the strangest part, though. The strangest part . . . was that she had wings.

Actual wings.

Long graceful wings. They were leathery, like bat wings, in a color I'd never seen. A gray-green-lavender, if you can imagine that. Kind of like old grape bubble gum you've chewed too long. When the girl walked toward me, the wings trembled, and when she stopped moving, she folded them neatly at her back, so that they almost disappeared behind her.

She stood in front of me and pulled an azalea sprig from her hair, tossing it down without blinking. Our faces were only a few feet apart, and I felt frozen as I tried to process what was happening, tried to take her in, make sense of her. She smelled like cinnamon and bonfire smoke. Like something from a dream.

The girl cleared her throat. "Hello?" she asked, like it was a question. Her eyes were a little bit lost in her face, disoriented. I remember thinking that they weren't black, as I'd initially thought, but dark purple.

I waited, unsure of what to do. "Where . . . ," I said, ". . . did you come from?"

The girl stared at me blankly, then shook her head. "I'm

not sure . . . ," she said again, but this time she sounded more normal, like any other girl who'd gotten lost. "I don't remember . . . anything. I don't think I came from anywhere."

"You had to come from somewhere," I said. "Unless . . ."

The girl looked at me expectantly.

I didn't know how to say it out loud, but at that moment, I had a feeling like I knew where she'd come from. I had a feeling that I'd conjured her. Was that possible? Could I have conjured this girl out of nothing with two mispronounced words in a language I didn't speak? If so, this was so much bigger than any magic I'd ever done before. *Worlds* bigger. I almost couldn't believe it. But then, this girl had wings. Clearly something magical was happening. And as far as I could tell, I was the only witch hanging around Red's Farm.

As I stood there in silence, the girl's eyes didn't leave my face. She gazed at me intently, so I stared back, and the moments passed slowly as she stood, unblinking, hands clasped in front of her. Like she was waiting for something to happen.

"Why . . . were you screaming?" I asked at last.

The girl shook her head gently from side to side then, as if trying to shake something loose, but when she spoke, her voice was calm. "Because of the pain."

"Pain?" I said. "What kind of pain? Are you better now??"

"No," she said. "I'm still in pain." And for the first time, she slowly closed her huge eyes and reopened them, taking a deep, shuddering breath.

"But you're not screaming anymore."

She shrugged. "It wasn't helping."

"Oh," I said. "I'm sorry. I wish I could do something."

The girl winced, visibly uncomfortable. "*Can't* you?" she asked. She reached out both hands to me, palms up, as though I might put something in them. But of course I couldn't think of anything that would help.

Then I remembered an incantation for the lessening of pain, which I sometimes used on myself if I stubbed my toe or skinned my knee. It wasn't much, but it was something.

"Actually, maybe I have an idea," I said.

I was supposed to use a bowl of water to work the spell, but I didn't have one. And while, as I've told you, the elements are important to spellcasting, and while I love all the cool stuff in my WitchKit, the truth is that the most important part of any spell is the words. Words matter more than anything else. Words are power.

So I simply cupped my hands as though they were a bowl of water. Then I closed my eyes, visualized all my power going into the imaginary water, and I chanted. "Your pain is gone and you are full of health," I said. "Your pain is gone and you are full of health. Your pain is gone and you are full of health. . . ." I said this ten times.

After that, I opened my eyes and poured the imaginary water over the girl's open palms, then pressed my hands down onto hers. I almost wondered if my fingers would pass right through, she was so ghostly. But that didn't happen. The girl's hands were cool to the touch, and they felt brittle, like dry sticks in winter.

"How's *this*?" I asked, pressing down harder.

Suddenly, together, we gasped as between our hands something sparked, burned. It was like a charge of electricity but not like anything I'd ever felt before. It was cold, like ice. Not painful but startling. I wasn't expecting it.

"Ahh!" called the girl as she grabbed at my fingers, clutched them, and the pulse grew stronger. Her eyes brightened, and two spots of pink appeared in her cheeks before she pulled her hands away, and I realized she wasn't transparent anymore. I could no longer see the trees beyond her. She was solid now.

"What . . . just . . . happened?" I asked.

"I don't know!" she said. "But oh, that's better! You *did* help! I'm not nearly so hungry."

"Hungry?' I asked.

The girl ignored my question. She stretched her long arms over her head and smiled. "*Thank* you," she said. "Oh, thank you so much."

I didn't know what to say to that. "You're welcome, I guess," I said as I clasped my hands together, feeling a sort of hum in them, a buzz. I was confused, but mostly I was excited. Something was happening.

"Now," said the girl, glancing around, "I need to go."

"Go?" I asked. "Go *where*? You just got here."

"I'm not exactly sure," she said. "I don't *know*, but I can *feel* it. All through me. I have a picture in my mind now that wasn't there before you healed me. There's a mountain, in the distance, somewhere." She looked up at the sky. "Yes," she said, nodding. "I need to go to it." And she leaped into the air, where her great wings burst open above her, unfolded, and beat once, twice, lifting her up.

"Oh! That feels good!" she called down at me, as if she'd never used her wings before and was only just discovering what they could do. "The wind is so sweet! Goodbye, now! And thank you!" With another pulse of her wings she lifted herself above the oak tree, and then flew off, disappeared above the canopy of trees. All that was left was the sound of her wings.

Whuff
whuff
whuff.

"Wait!" I called.

But the girl was gone.

✦ 13 ✦

Too Normal

After that, I just stood a little while in the middle of the farm. The whole place looked strange to me suddenly, too normal. The oak tree was just a tree. The grass was regular old grass. My black sandals were as scuffed as ever. Everything was usual and unchanged, but how was *that* possible after what had happened? The whole world seemed like a dream; the only real thing seemed to be the girl who had just flown away.

Had I really summoned her with my spell? As much as I'd been practicing all my life for a moment like this, it didn't seem likely that I'd managed to conjure a magical creature with a few misspoken words. But why else would she have appeared at Red's Farm at that particular moment? Also, it felt signifi-cant that I'd been able to heal her so easily. We seemed to be connected somehow. I wondered why.

"Your pain is gone and you are full of health," I whispered one last time. I glanced down at my hands, but they just looked like they always looked. Stubby, nails chewed. Then I noticed something at my feet. A spot of color, a branch of blooms, a few pink azalea flowers on a twig. I reached down, picked up the twig, and brought it to my cheek. I felt how soft and real they were, the azalea petals. They smelled faintly like smoke. If I had felt, even for a moment, that I had somehow imagined the girl, it was that azalea bloom that told me I hadn't. She was real.

I peered up into the sky and wondered what might happen to her now. Would she find her mountain, wherever it was? Would other people see her, flying over East Atlanta? What if she never came back? Did she really not need anything else from me?

That idea shook me, because even as I thought it, I real-ized I'd be devastated if I never saw the girl again. That felt funny, in a way, since I'd only met her a few minutes ear-lier. But if I *had* conjured her—and I felt pretty certain that I had—she was the best thing I'd ever done in my life. The greatest magic of all. She was mine. So she couldn't just . . . disappear. Could she?

Maybe, I thought, I could call her back to me, with the same words of power I had used before. It seemed worth a shot, at least. And so, standing right there at the farm, I closed my eyes to concentrate, began to weave my arms in the air above me. Just as I had done earlier by the creek, I opened my mouth to let out the words.

But before I could, I heard a voice nearby.

"Cookie! Cookie, come!"

I reopened my eyes and saw that there was a woman in a purple hat with a fat brown dog, walking in the garden.

Standing there with my arms over my head, I felt silly, goofy. Not like a powerful witch who could summon mysterious, magical creatures. Just like some girl playing nonsense in the middle of a hot September day. Magic can be funny like that. Sometimes it feels like the most natural thing in the world. But when it doesn't, it can be downright embarrassing. Like singing too loud in the shower, then realizing someone is listening.

So I dropped my arms, stopped what I was doing, and began walking quickly home, away from Cookie and her person. But as I hit the gravel road that led out of the farm, I had the strangest feeling my feet weren't the same anymore, like they were someone else's feet I was walking on, moving at a slightly different pace or speed. It wasn't a bad feeling, but it wasn't entirely comfortable either. Something was different about me. Something was new, though I wasn't sure what.

Then I turned onto the paved street and I had to pull myself together, because I was suddenly surrounded by a massive group of noisy kids all walking home from school. After the hour I'd just spent at the farm, that stampede around me felt like the loudest thing I'd ever heard. Someone was shouting about Pokémon, and someone else was throwing a notebook in the air, and of course, just my luck, right in the middle of them all was Bea. But she wasn't alone. She was with Liv Randolph.

The second Bea saw me, she glanced away, which I think was probably my cue to ignore her too, but for some reason, I couldn't do it. After so much silence and avoidance, I didn't want to run away from her or pretend. Standing there, I felt raw and brave. Nothing had changed in the actual world beyond the farm, but for some reason, something had shifted in me.

So I squared my shoulders and I stood in the middle of the sidewalk, waiting for her. I took a deep breath. And just as Bea was about to pass, I reached out, tugged on her backpack strap, and held on, so that she *had* to stop walking, couldn't look the other way.

"Hey!" I said, too loudly. "Hey, Bea. What's up?"

"Zippy," she said, looking back and forth between me and Liv. The flood of kids split, flowed past us. "What are you doing here? You weren't in school. I didn't expect to see you."

Beside her, Liv looked mildly annoyed. *Fine*, I thought. *Good.*

"It's a holiday," I said. "I was in synagogue, and then I was at Red's Farm. For . . . *something.*" There was no real way to explain my last hour.

"*Something?*" Bea repeated. "Are you okay, Zippy? You look strange."

"Thanks," I said. "Always good to hear."

She laughed awkwardly. "No, I just mean you seem different. I don't know what it is, exactly. Is today that hungry-holiday, where you don't eat?"

I shook my head. "No," I said. "No, that's in ten days. But I saw you and . . . well, just wanted to say hi. I . . . miss you, Bea." *I miss you?* I couldn't believe I was saying that in front of Liv. It sounded like someone else's voice. But it was the way I felt, and so I said it.

Bea didn't reply. She only shrugged. And I stood there a second, thinking about tikkun olam, and wishing for God-glitter, or whatever might help me repair my own little world. A spell that could fix things, make them the way they had been before. Or at least less awful. Our whole conversation felt uncomfortable, off-balance, but at least we were talking.

"Well, cool," said Bea. "Have a nice holiday, I guess. I need to get moving. Liv's dad is waiting for us."

"He's taking us shopping," Liv chimed in. "For Fall Fling dresses, and then out for boba."

"Boba?" I asked. "What's boba?"

"Are you kidding?" asked Liv. "Boba tea? Like, with the tapioca pearls in it? Everyone knows boba!"

I shook my head.

Bea gave me a funny look. "Stop messing with us, Zippy," she said. "You and I had boba tea, right before school started, weirdo. Remember?" She punched me on the arm, turned to leave.

"Oh. Uh. Sure," I said, nodding, even though I had no idea what she was talking about. But I didn't want to argue, and as they turned to leave, I somehow shouted after them, as cheerfully as I could, "Have a good shopping trip, Bea. You too, Liv."

They didn't turn back around, only walked off down Woodland together, so close their shoulders were touching, laughing about something that didn't have anything to do with me. Or laughing about something that *did* have to do with me.

Once the street was quiet, I began walking home alone. The not-myself feeling was gone now, a bubble burst by Bea and Liv and the noisy crowd of kids, but when I pushed that out of my mind and focused on my memory of the winged girl, I felt much better. So I tried hard to picture her in my head, and found that the more I thought about her, the faster I seemed to walk. And the faster I walked, the better I felt, until I was almost running, thinking about her dark eyes and white-blond hair, her raspy voice and the sound her wings made. *Whuff.*

⋆☆*14*☆⋆

Jewish Magic?

When I ran in the door, Dad was still taking a nap on the couch with a book on top of his face, snoring into the pages, so I tiptoed past him as quietly as I could, and then past Mom in the office, on my way to my room.

But Mom spotted me. "Hey there!" she called cheerfully. "How was tashlich? Are you a brand-new Zippy? All regrets washed away?"

Apparently, she'd decided to pretend we hadn't fought earlier, but for once that was fine with me. I had much more important things to think about now. "Oh yeah, sure," I said. "Totally. Brand-new Zippy, clean as a whistle!"

But that gave me an idea, and before she could say anything else, I headed to the bathroom and started a bath. I was sweaty and dusty from the walk and the farm, and a bubble bath sounded like a good idea. Just what I needed.

Here is the thing about baths: you can't do much anything else when you're in them. No phones or computers. No homework. I mean, you can read a book, I guess, but sometimes the pages get wet or your fingers get wet, and then you have to turn the pages with wet fingers. So baths are the one place where you just have to *be*. They're good thinking spots. Also, people have to respect your privacy in the bath, for obvious reasons.

And that day, in my bubble bath, all the things that had happened at the farm started swirling together in my head. I thought about the winged girl *whuffing* off into the sky, but also, I thought about the little mouse with his cracker, and all the smaller magic I'd done in my life leading up to that moment. Had it all been practice for this? I thought about how I'd conjured the winged girl, and I thought about how it had felt to heal her, if that's what I'd done, with my newly electric fingers. Could I heal other people too? Could my magic help the world? Most of all, I wondered where she had come from, and why she couldn't remember it. What *was* she? An elf? I didn't think elves had wings. An angel, maybe? She looked like an angel.

I thought about all of this, sitting in the bath, and it felt like too much. Too many mysteries I couldn't begin to guess at. It felt like I was drowning in questions, and I hated that feeling.

But thinking about *that* reminded me of what Rabbi Dan had said about questions. It was an awfully funny coincidence that if I *had* conjured the winged girl, I'd done so with a tiny scrap of Hebrew pulled from memory and probably mispronounced. What, I wondered, did that all mean? I sat up in the bath then, covered in bubbles, as a thought hit me.

Was this specifically *Jewish* magic? And if it was, was that why it was bigger, stronger, more? Had I unlocked some part of myself I'd never had access to, leveled up? "Mekhashepha," I whispered to myself, over the sound of the running water in the tap. "Mekhashepha, Mekhashepha, Mekhashepha." I felt prickles all over my skin as I turned off the water and leaped from the tub.

Back in my room, I pulled on clean clothes and plopped down at my desk, where I opened my laptop quickly. One thing that super annoys me is when some dumbbell in a book or movie has a mystery that could easily be solved with a Google search, but *conveniently* the character never even thinks to try. Well, I am not a dumbbell, and this is not that kind of book.

Right away I put in "Jewish angel" and fell down a rabbit hole of crazy-sounding things I didn't even know were part of my religion. Weird magic, even for a witch like me. Right away, I got all excited because it turned out there *were* Jewish angels: cherubim and Ishim and a bunch more. According to some guy named Maimonides, there were ten different categories of angels. At first, I figured my winged girl must be one of them, right? But the further I read, the more confused I became. It turned out that cherubim had four wings and bull hooves, so that wasn't right. And the Ishim were supposed to be closest to humans, but they were made of fire and snow, so that wasn't right either. In fact, none of the descriptions I found said anything about beautiful long-haired girls, though I hadn't managed to get through the whole list when Dad started shouting from the hallway about how it was time to help with dinner. I ignored him at first, but then the second time he yelled he sounded pretty annoyed, and I pulled myself away. I figured I could come back later.

Now, if you are reading this and you come from a more traditional Jewish family than me, you might be picturing Rosh Hashanah dinner with brisket or kugel or something, but even on holidays, we don't eat that stuff. Mostly, I think, because a lot of Jewish food involves putting a chunk of a cow or a whole chicken in the oven, and we're vegetarian and don't eat things with faces. So on Jewish holidays, instead of roasted mammals, our tradition is that everyone chooses the things they like best, and then we make them or order them for takeout, but eat them at the dining room table, with matching plates and cloth napkins and everything. Fancy! We also say a blessing over the candles and wine—the only prayers we all know by heart, because they're the same for every holiday including Shabbat, pretty much.

That night, we were making spicy veggie stew, steamed

artichokes with melted lemon butter, and mashed potatoes. Also, Mom was baking her grandmother's apple cake, which is the one really old-fashioned Jewish thing we eat. I love that cake, but it always means I need to peel a bunch of green apples, and so, while Mom and Dad did the other stuff, chopping and mixing and grating, I sat at the table and peeled and peeled and peeled, trying hard to keep the apple peel in one long strip, like I always do.

Of course, with nothing else to occupy me but the apples, my thoughts drifted back to the farm. I found myself remembering two arms reaching through the green leaves and pink blossoms. I could almost smell the cinnamon smoke over the scent of the apples in the bowl. I could hear the *whuff whuff whuff* of angel wings. It was strange, how close and real the memory felt to me that day. Like a movie I could watch by simply closing my eyes. Like the winged angel-girl was with me now wherever I went. Even if really, she was off searching for her mountain.

When I was done with the apples, Dad handed me a bowl of potatoes to peel too, and I groaned. "Really?" I asked. "Am I the only person in this house who knows how to use a peeler?"

Dad shook his head. "It's a hard life for you, Zippy. A hard, hard life. Want to hear about all the chores I did when I was your age? Want to talk about the standard of living in developing nations? Want to discuss life during the Industrial Revolution?"

"Umm, no thanks," I said, and went back to peeling.

But at some point, I must have started humming to myself, because Mom called out at me from her spot at the stove where she was frying onions in a pan, "Hey, Zip, what's that song? It sounds familiar, but I can't quite place it."

"Huh?" I looked up from my big silver bowl of potato peels. "What song?"

"That one," said Mom. "The one you were just humming."

"I didn't even notice I was humming," I said. "I guess maybe I made it up." I didn't usually hum, on account of *really* not being able to carry a tune and not wanting people to laugh at me.

Mom shook her head. "Nope, I've definitely heard it somewhere before." And then she turned her back to me, to mix something in a bowl on the counter, and I heard her humming it too but louder, with some wordless words tossed in. Hum hum hummmm . . . Yai-dye-dye-dye . . . Hummm . . ." Like that.

After dinner and after the apple cake, and the teensy little glass of wine I'm allowed on holidays, and after the dishes were cleared to the counter, I sat on the couch for a minute, to wait for the candles to burn down the rest of the way. I always like to watch the candles go out. I like the burnt oily smell they leave in the room right after they fitz. And I guess I must have fallen asleep sitting there like that, because when I woke up, the room was dark, and there was a blanket spread neatly over me.

I sat up, looked around, and felt confused, in the way dreams you don't remember can make you confused. All alone in the darkness. Across the room, the curtains were drawn, but the moon was shining brightly, casting a thick beam of white light so that it fell across the old rocker in the corner and the out-of-tune piano that nobody ever played.

I stood up, walked over to the piano. I stared at the beam of light, and off in the street, I heard a sudden rustle, the sound of something lifting, as if a lot of little birds were taking off in the night. I peered out, searched the sky, but saw no birds. Then, for some reason, I sat down at the piano, put one finger on a dusty key, and pressed down.

The first note startled me. It hung in the air in the dark room, trembling. But when nobody woke up, I pressed down again, this time on a few keys at once, still as softly as possible. Under my breath, I found I was humming the tune I'd been humming in the kitchen. So, with my fingers I searched for it now, that song, tried to match my humming with the notes on the old piano. I wasn't sure why I was doing it, except that the song was stuck in my head. I also wasn't sure exactly *how* I was doing it. I'd never had any musical ability before in my life. But I kept going, quietly, carefully, in that beam of moonlight. Note after note. As I did, I somehow felt less confused, less alone, like the dream was falling away with the music. Like the song was keeping me company.

I'm not sure how long I sat that way, but at some point, I

heard a cough and turned. Mom was standing in the hallway, watching me. Her arms were folded, and she leaned against the wall. She looked tired, but she was smiling. "Hey, you," she said in a hushed nighttime voice. "It's late, but that's beautiful."

"Oh, thanks," I said. "I just woke up on the couch, and the moon was on the piano, and I don't know why, but I thought I'd try to play it."

"Well, you're doing a lovely job," whispered Mom. "But I think it's time to go to bed now. If you don't plan to go back to synagogue for the second day of Rosh Hashanah, you'll need to get up in time for school."

"Oh yeah, sure," I said. I stood up and walked across the room.

Mom gave me a quick kiss on the cheek. "Good night," she said. "And l'shana tova, my love. I hope this year will be a sweet one for you. A little easier, maybe."

I kissed her cheek too, then smiled. "You know, I have a feeling it's going to be a good one. Interesting, at least."

"That's wonderful to hear," said Mom. Then, as she turned toward her room, she added, "By the way, I remembered where I've heard that song before."

"Really?" I said.

She nodded. "Yep, my grandfather used to sing it to me at bedtime, though I hadn't heard it in decades. He loved those old melodies, those nigunim." She sighed.

"Nigunim?"

"Improvisational songs," she explained. "Old Jewish tunes. But I've never sung that one to you, so I wonder where you picked it up."

"Oh," I said. "Yeah . . . I wonder too. . . ."

Before I could think about that too much, Mom yawned and turned away, down the hallway and to her own room. As she walked off, she whispered, "Also, I have to say, you're good on that piano. Your music teacher at school must be fantastic. I didn't even know you were taking an instrument!"

"Yeah. Thanks," I said as she disappeared into her room.

I didn't go to bed right away, though. Instead, I turned around one last time, to stare back into the living room, at the piano in its moonbeam. I looked down, at my own two hands, pale in the darkness. My healing hands. My electric hands. Suddenly full of surprises. I held them up in front of my face, wondering at what else they might be able to do.

Because the thing is, I *wasn't* taking piano at school. In fact, I'd never played the piano in my life.

★☆ *15* ☆★

Almost Human

The next morning, I woke up even before my alarm went off. My parents weren't up yet, so the house was silent, and I just lay there for a while, going over what had happened the day before, and feeling jittery and excited, even though I really didn't understand what was happening. Had I dreamed the angel-girl? I was sure I hadn't, but now that she had flown away, how would I ever find her again? I turned the problem over and over, but eventually, the alarm went off, so I hopped out of bed. And reached for my tarot deck.

I should probably explain that I don't always trust tarot, and maybe you shouldn't either. Fortune-telling isn't real witchcraft, and a lot of the time the cards are inaccurate. You can kind of make them say whatever you want. But for some reason, it felt like a good idea that morning. Standing in front of my desk, I held the cards tightly and asked one single question: "Where will I find the angel-girl?"

Then I pulled three cards. One at a time. First came the Fool, and I wasn't sure what to do with that. The Fool can mean different things, but most of all, it suggests that something unexpected is happening, a new adventure or journey. That was fine, of course. But I knew that much already, and it wasn't very helpful in answering my question. Then I looked at my other two cards and gasped. Both the Seven, and the Nine of Pentacles! Two garden cards. Now, the tarot isn't usually so specific in its advice. Normally, you have to interpret what it's trying to tell you. But in this case, I stared at the gardens on each card and felt like I'd have to be an idiot not to get their message. So I pulled on my clothes, washed my face, and brushed my hair. I didn't even shower (I *always* shower), just bolted, closing the door carefully behind me so that it didn't slam, and ran down the steps.

As I ran, I could feel how exhausted I was from my late night and early morning. My eyes were tired and my leg muscles didn't want to move. But despite all that, my heart was racing and my mind was jumbled with new thoughts as I sped down our street, my backpack bumping against my butt.

When I got to the farm, I set down my backpack and water bottle next to the oak tree and glanced around. "Hello?" I called, trying to make my voice loud enough that she'd hear me, without shouting like a maniac, in case anyone else was out for an early walk.

There was no answer. Just morning birds chirping and chittering. So I walked over to peer inside the azalea bush where I'd found the girl the day before, but it was empty. After that, I walked around the farm, looking everywhere. I headed down the hill to the kudzu-tangled creek but everything was quiet. I wandered into the garden and stared at the bright red tomatoes. Back at the oak tree, I found nothing, but I tried calling for her anyway. "Hello?" I shouted again, a little louder this time. "Hello?"

The minutes ticked by as I waited for something to happen. But nothing did, and I began to feel very sad. Things had been so hard the last few weeks, with Bea. So stuck and silent. Now, for the first time in forever, something exciting had happened. But that only made it harder to imagine that the angel-girl had already flown away.

"Stupid tarot cards," I muttered, and kicked the tree, hard. It hurt, so I yelped and shouted a very bad word, which I am not going to write here. You can use your imagination.

I knew I needed to get to school, but I couldn't stand to give up just yet, so I gave her one last chance. I took a deep breath and shouted, "PLEASE?" And a minute later, "PLEASE! I HAVE TO GO TO SCHOOL NOW! ARE YOU HERE? PLEASE BE HERE? HELLLLOOOOOOO, ANGEL-GIRL?"

There was a pause, a beat.

I leaned to pick up my backpack.

I stood up.

And then . . .

Whuff.

I looked above me, and there she was. Stepping off a branch far above my head, stepping out into the sky as if she could walk on it. Only she didn't walk. She flew.

Whuff

whuff

whuff.

Her wings beat the air in great gusts I could feel as wind on the ground. She flew a ways off, circled back, and began to glide down. She slowed, and as she reached the patch of grass where I was standing, her feet seemed to dance, scramble, to keep up with the rest of her. As graceful as she'd been in the sky, she stumbled and fell when she reached the ground, landing in a heap at my feet.

"Oof! Hello!" she said cheerfully, looking up at me. "It's you! I'm so glad! I was hoping you'd come back."

"You were?" I asked.

"Of course!" she said. "You're the only person I know in the world, after all."

Since she was still sitting on the grass, I reached down a hand to help her up, but when she put her fingers in mine, it happened again, just as it had the day before. I felt the stir of my magic waking up, a prickle between us.

Her eyes widened. "Ohh," she said with a grin. I gave a jerk on her arm and she rose in a swift motion, almost a jump. Then we let go.

"Oh! That was . . . *something*!" she said. "Will it happen every time we touch our hands?"

"I don't know," I said. "It doesn't hurt you?"

She shook her head emphatically. "I'm always in pain," she said. "It's like a kind of hunger. But somehow, when *that* happens, it's better. Easier. For a while."

"Weird," I said. When I held out a hand, the girl immediately reached out, and the magic crackled between us.

"How did you learn to do that?" she asked, staring at our clasped hands in wonder.

"I don't know," I said as I felt the current build between us, humming and buzzing until it almost stung. "I've never done magic quite like this before. It's new."

"Is magic something you do a lot?" she asked. "Is magic how you brought me here?"

"I . . ." I tried to answer her, but I didn't know what to say, and my hand was starting to really hurt. So I just let go and said, "*Maybe*. Maybe it is."

The girl smiled at me. "Well, thank you!" she said. "I feel *much* better now."

"Good," I said. "You know, I've never shared my magic with anyone. Not like this."

"Really?" said the girl. "It's wonderful! It helps me *see* things. When we touch. Does it do that for you too? Do you see new things?"

"I don't think so," I said. "But what do you mean? What do you see?"

"In my mind," she said. "Things I couldn't see before." The girl closed her eyes for a moment, as if concentrating. "It's as if . . . I see a picture, the moment after we let go. But you don't?" She opened her eyes again.

"I have lots of pictures in my mind," I said. "Tons of them. Too many."

"I don't," said the girl. "When I met you, my mind was like the sky, blank and bare. I didn't have *any* pictures."

I tried to imagine what that might feel like, but I couldn't. "None at all?" I asked.

She shook her head. "It's better now, though. Because I have all this." She gestured around at the garden, the hill, the oak tree. "And you! Also, I have pictures of all the things I saw yesterday, flying. Buildings and people. Trees and roads. I flew over a horse, even. But . . . when we touch, I find *other* things in my mind. New ones. Like the mountain, yesterday. And now today, this time, I saw water. Lots and lots of water. It was beautiful. Cold and dark, full of ice."

"Like a lake?" I said. "Or an ocean?"

She shrugged. "I'm not certain. There was mist on it and a giant creature like a hill, rising up, and there were cliffs in the distance. But I don't know any more than that. I suppose it might be only a picture my mind made up, something to do with your magic."

"Maybe," I said. "Or maybe you're just slowly remembering things? From where you came from, before this?"

"Oh yes," said the girl, nodding. "That . . . makes sense too."

"You really don't remember anything else? No family, even?"

"No," she said. "There's nobody. There's nothing. I don't remember anything at all. Just me, here, alone. And you."

"Is that scary?" I asked. "To not remember? To feel empty like that?"

The girl was silent for a moment. Then she said, "No. I don't think so. The emptiness just *is*. But when I do remember something, it's better."

Then she leaned over and brushed damp grass from her dress. The fabric was stained green where she'd landed on her knees. I remember thinking that she seemed different that morning than she had the day before. She looked more real. Almost human. Her hair was tangled now, and there was a scratch on her cheek.

I thought about the strange descriptions of angels I'd read the day before, and wondered where such creatures lived. Would they even *have* families? I pictured a wild, empty world of mountains and water and mist. I'd need to go back and finish reading about the ten categories. Surely she was in there somewhere.

"Well, you aren't alone anymore," I said. "You have me. And I'm glad you came back. After you flew off yesterday, I was afraid I wouldn't see you again."

The girl laughed. "Of course I came back! This"—she gestured around her at the farm—"is the only place I have to come back to! This is my home now, I suppose."

I was thinking about what that might feel like when the alarm on my phone suddenly went off, which meant I had exactly five minutes to run all the way to school.

"Oh! I have to go," I said. "But I'll come back, as soon as I can."

She smiled.

"And in the meantime, I'm Zippy. That's my name. What's yours?"

The girl shrugged. "I don't think I have one. If I ever did, I don't remember."

"Right," I said. "Well, do you want one? For now, at least?"

The girl nodded. "Please."

"Okay. Let's see . . ."

I don't know where it came from, but a second later, the name rose up from inside me. It felt very right, and sort of automatic, the way it appeared in my thoughts. Like another part of the magic. "I know," I said. "I'll call you Miriam.

That's your name. How's that?"

"Miriam?" she said softly, like she was asking herself permission for something. Then, suddenly, she nodded, and her face split into a huge smile. Her eyes crinkled at the edges, and she laughed. "I like it. *Miriam.*"

I turned to go. I was going to be late for school for the first time ever in my life. I'd get in trouble, but it was totally worth it. "I'll come back," I said. "I promise. Just as soon as I can."

⋆☆ 16 ☆⋆

Never Not Hungry

That whole day at school I was a mess. I was exhausted and excited and I couldn't seem to pay attention to anything at all. After second period, when I got a blue slip for falling asleep on my desk, I went to the bathroom and tried casting a spell for calm and concentration. I made sure nobody else was in the bathroom, and then I sat on the toilet lid and breathed in for six seconds and out for six seconds. In for six and out for six, over and over, ten times. I know this just sounds like a regular breathing exercise, but it's not. Because each time I finished breathing out, I spoke these words: *Calm the thoughts that roil like seas, bring forth focus, inner peace.*

It's a good spell, and it works a lot of the time, but that day I think I was too distracted to breathe properly or something, because it didn't do much. I still zoned out and drew a total blank on the pop quiz in science. Then, I was distracted in Language and Literature, just doodling on my paper instead of doing my persuasive writing assignment, and Ms. Marty, in front of the whole class, said, "*What's* going on with you today, Zippy McConnell? Wake up! You don't seem like yourself at all."

When that happened, Bea looked at me and mouthed, "Hey, are you all right?"

Unlike the day before, she actually seemed like she was asking for real. But I just mouthed back, "I'm fine." I didn't need her concern that day. For once, I wasn't thinking about Bea. My mind was elsewhere. On more important things.

Then Ms. Marty called my name again and told me to stop whispering and keep my eyes on my paper, so I looked down right away. That's when I saw what I'd been doodling. In the margin of my paper was the same set of letters scribbled in pencil, over and over. But they were letters I hadn't known I was even capable of writing. Letters I definitely hadn't been able to recognize the last time I met with my bat mitzvah class. The words read:

צִפּוֹרָה חַוָּה מיקונל
צִפּוֹרָה חַוָּה מיקונל
צִפּוֹרָה חַוָּה מיקונל

Even stranger than the fact that my own hand had written these Hebrew letters was the fact that I knew, immediately, what they meant. It wasn't just that I could read them, but that I didn't have to sound them out or anything. Like the way you don't really read a Stop sign so much as recognize it. *Zipporah Chava McConnell*, said the words. *Zipporah Chava McConnell*, *Zipporah Chava McConnell*, *Zipporah Chava McConnell*, over and over again, in my own messy handwriting. Mine but not mine, at the same time.

I erased the words and tried to look like I was listening to the class share their samples of persuasive writing. But I don't remember anything anybody said that whole entire hour. Not a word. *What is happening to me?* Had one little word on a scrap of paper really been powerful enough to change me in all these ways? Woken up some sort of latent Jewish power? And if it had been, what might happen next?

"Mekhashepha," I whispered under my breath.

By the time the bell rang at the end of the day, I was more than ready to run back to the farm and Miriam, as fast as possible, just like I'd promised. But when I stepped out onto the sidewalk, squinting into the sun, I found Mom waiting for me *again* in the car-rider line, waving her arms and shouting.

"Hop in," she said. "Chik chak! Pick up the pace, kitten!"

"No!" I shouted back at her through the open window. "I have important things to do. Go away. I'll walk home."

Mom shook her head. "Sorry, Zippy, I guess I didn't remind

you this morning. You're getting that cavity filled. Come on. We're already late."

Grumbling, I climbed into the car and slammed the door. "You are the least organized mom of all the moms in the history of moms."

"It's true," said Mom cheerfully. "But I compensate by being both hilarious and beautiful, right?"

I groaned and rolled my eyes. "Not funny," I said.

She laughed. "Eh, I'll make it up to you with ice cream after."

"What are you even talking about?" I grouched. "I can't have ice cream after a filling, Mom. Isn't that, like, a basic parenting rule?"

"Oh, shoot," said Mom as she turned the key in the ignition. "I guess you're right about that. I'll need to revisit the Basic Parenting Book of Rules. Too bad. I was having a mint-chip craving." Then she almost ran a stop sign as we drove away from the school.

About an hour later I was back in the car with a mouth full of Novocain and a T-shirt covered in drool. Even so, I was trying to think of an excuse to ask Mom to drop me at the farm, but when we turned onto our street, she suddenly pointed and said, "Hark! Who's *that*?"

I harked. We were still a block away, but it wasn't hard to

spot the pale figure against the blue siding of our house.

There, right in the middle of our front yard, stood Miriam. With her white hair and long dress, she looked almost like a sculpture, a statue in a cemetery.

"Oh!" I said. "That's . . . umm . . . Miriam." There was no time to think up explanations. All I could hope was that Mom would think the wings were a costume, maybe, the way some girls at school wore cat ears.

"Miriam?" said Mom, rolling to a stop in front of the house. "My. She's . . . striking."

"Striking?" I asked.

"Sure!" said Mom. "With all that hair, so thin and tall. She looks like a model or something. Not a regular kid."

I eyed my mom carefully. "Yeah, she's . . . different," I said. "I like her."

Mom nodded. "Sure! I just didn't know you had a new friend. Where did you meet?" She turned the car off and reached for her purse. By now, Miriam had noticed us and turned to wave.

"Uh," I said. "Just around the neighborhood. She doesn't go to our school. She's . . . ummm . . . homeschooled. Her parents are like, hippies, I think."

Mom opened her car door. "Well, let's go say hey." Then she paused. "Though, you know, it's a shame. . . ."

"What's a shame?"

Mom sighed deeply. "That we can't offer her some nice mint-chip ice cream. A catastrophe, really."

I rolled my eyes and climbed down from the car. "Miriam!" I called.

"Zippy!" shouted Miriam. "You're here. I thought you might be."

I hoped Mom would go inside right away, but of course she didn't. She lingered on the porch, grinning momishly at Miriam. "Don't I get to meet your new friend, Zippy?"

"Uh," I said. "Sure. Mom, this is Miriam. Miriam, Mom."

Mom waved cheerfully and turned to unlock the front door. "So nice to meet you, Miriam! You can call me Emily. And Zippy, just let me know if you girls want something to eat."

Before Mom even had the door open, Miriam shouted out, "Oh yes!"

Mom turned back, confused. "Yes?" she repeated. "Yes what?"

"Yes!" said Miriam once more, nodding vigorously. "I *do* want something to eat."

Mom looked back at Miriam and nodded. "Well, great! Just come inside when you're hungry."

"But I'm never not hungry," she responded. One thing about Miriam: she said what she was thinking. It was like she wasn't human enough to be embarrassed about manners.

For once I was glad my mom wasn't the kind of polite,

normal mom I'd always wanted. She stared at Miriam a moment, like she was trying to figure something out and said, "Well, then I suppose you should probably come on in and eat." She went inside.

As we walked up the path to the front porch, I turned to Miriam. "How did you find me? I mean, I'm glad you came, and I'm sorry I was late. But how did you know to come here?"

"I'm not certain," said Miriam, shaking her head. "I think I just felt it. Where you'd be. I let my wings bring me to where they wanted to go. I listened to them, and they came right here, to you."

"Wait," I said. "You *flew* here? Just zipped along in the air, in broad daylight?"

Miriam nodded. "Of course. How else would I have come?"

I didn't know how to answer that. But I tried. "Umm. I think maybe from now on, you should try walking."

"Why?" Miriam asked.

"Well, it's just that nobody else I've ever met in my life has wings, except you. So folks aren't used to seeing them, and it might freak people out. People don't have wings. People can't fly."

"*None* of them?" Miriam looked perplexed.

I was nervous about how Miriam would manage with her wings in the house, but it turned out that I didn't need to worry at all. They looked fragile, like they might tear or break, but they were actually sort of bendy and tough, and she leaned against them comfortably on the couch. She sat there happily beside me, peering around at every little thing. Like she was studying the room for a test or something.

Just like in the yard, Mom didn't seem to notice the wings at all. Anyway, she didn't say anything to us. She was being extra nice, bringing us in a platter of cut-up veggies and fruit slices like she used to do for me and Bea when we were little, and she set it down with an unopened bag of pretzels on the coffee table. Then she came back with two glasses of iced tea and lemon. I reached for mine and took a big gulp. Miriam watched me and did the exact same thing, like a mirror image, one second behind me.

"Mmmm," she said, licking her lips.

I took a pretzel, and so did she. Then she took another and another.

Mom hovered, watching. "Well, what are you girls going to do?" she asked. "Watch a movie? I could dig out a board game, maybe Catan!"

"It's fine, Mom," I said. "You don't need to entertain us. I'm not a baby."

"Okay, okay," said Mom. "You just haven't had a friend over in so long." To Miriam she added, "I don't know if Zippy told you, but she and her best friend have had a fight."

"Mom!" I said. "Please stop. Just . . . go away." I glared at her until she sighed dramatically and left.

Miriam turned to me. "Is it true? You had a fight with your friend?"

I shrugged. "Yeah, that's true, kind of. It's complicated."

"What happened?" asked Miriam, shoving pretzels into her face and chewing with her mouth open. Which was funny to me, for some reason. Someone so beautiful and graceful, eating like a dog with a mouth of kibble.

"I'm not sure," I said. "Things are just weird. Bea's changing, I guess. She's different than she used to be. Which is fine, but it's like she seems embarrassed of me. Or annoyed. I'm not sure. It feels like she's outgrown me, and now she's sort of . . . done."

I looked at Miriam then but had trouble meeting her eyes. I hadn't told anyone this before, not even Mom. I hadn't ever talked to anyone about Bea. Because really, Bea was the only person I ever talked to.

Miriam took a slow sip of her tea and set down the glass. "That sounds hard," she said. "To have something so dear to you and then to lose it."

"Yeah," I said. "It is. I hate it. She just doesn't seem to care."

"I don't know very much about anything," said Miriam thoughtfully. "But to me it sounds like maybe she *does* care."

"Huh?" I said.

"I mean that, if *you* are her past and she is changing, or trying to, then maybe it's hard for her to do so when you're there. Maybe you, and her memories of you, are making the changing more difficult. Could that be it?"

I considered it for a moment. "I don't know. What made you think about it like that?"

Miriam looked at me solemnly with her big dark eyes. "I had *no* memories when I flew away yesterday. But then when you didn't come back, I was worried, for the very first time. And I realized it was because now I had *something*—you. And I didn't want to lose it. Do you see? In a way, it was easier when I didn't have anything at all. It was easier to fly away when I had no reason to return."

"I . . . guess that makes sense," I said. "Kind of." I had the strangest feeling that I only understood the very edges of what Miriam was saying. It was a slippery idea. I'd need to think about that some more. I wondered what it was I might be afraid to lose.

Just then Miriam laid a hand gently on top of my arm and raised her eyebrows to me as the prickles began. "Is it . . . all right?" she asked.

I nodded. But it wouldn't have mattered. By that point, my skin was already alive with tiny points of light. My arm was humming and pulsing, and Miriam's eyes had gone wide. She gasped, and her cheeks flushed.

She pulled her hand away, and I asked her, "Did you get another memory? Something new?"

She nodded. "I did. But it wasn't a nice one this time. There was a dark room. Someone was crying."

When Mom came into the room a little later, I had turned on *The Office* as usual, but Miriam didn't seem interested in the TV. Instead, she was wandering the room, looking at the pictures on the mantel and bookshelves. She paused for a long while in front of the picture of my parents' wedding, the two of them so young and smiling, under the chuppah.

"It reminds me of something," she said. "Only I don't know what." She stared at it for a long time. Then she stopped in front of another frame. "What's this? It's beautiful too but in a different way. It reminds me of something as well. . . ."

Mom peered over Miriam's shoulder. "Oh, that's Kodiak!" she said. "It was wonderful. You should go if you ever get the chance. Remember that, Zippy?"

"Kodiak?" I said, looking up from where I sat on the couch. "Where's that?"

Mom laughed. "Alaska, silly. Our cruise? That day of whale watching? And the stars from the boat, over the glacier. What a trip! Anyway, it was until you caught that terrible cold."

"Oh, right," I said, though I couldn't remember that trip at all. I stood up to look at the picture from across the room. Sure enough, there I was on the deck of a boat, staring out at the ocean, cliffs in the distance wreathed in mist. Tiny Zippy, gazing out at the water. "I was pretty little, I guess." Staring at the picture in its frame, I found I couldn't remember that moment at all, that boat or the cliffs in the distance. Nothing. It was as though I'd never been there in my life. And even as though I'd never seen the picture before, though it was coated in dust and had clearly been sitting there on its shelf for years.

Mom elbowed me. "Well, I'll leave you two to hang out. But I have to say, I'm so glad we spent thousands of dollars to give you such a memorable childhood, rich with interesting travel experiences." She rolled her eyes, turned, and left the room.

Miriam was still staring at the picture of Alaska, with her back to me. When she turned around, she looked upset. "Zippy?"

"Yeah?"

She gestured at the mantel. "I've been thinking."

"About what?" I asked.

"About all of these pictures. They make me wonder . . . what *I've* left behind."

"What do you mean?" I asked.

She sighed. "It's just that . . . watching you and your mother, your home, all these moments—the more I realize I must have left people behind, somewhere. Don't you think? I might have a world too. And someone who misses me?"

"Sure," I said. Though I wasn't sure I thought that at all. Where *did* angels come from? Or whatever Miriam was? Were there angel-moms?" "I guess that's probably true. But you're getting those memories back, right?"

"I am," she said, nodding. "But they aren't enough. I can't add them together and make anything from them yet. There's just a mountain. Some water. A dark room. They're pictures like these, here." She turned and gestured at the mantel. "But I don't know how to connect them, turn them into a world or a story. It's not enough, Zippy."

"Not yet, maybe," I said. "But you've only been here a day. I'm sure, once you have more memories, you'll have a better idea of where you came from. Don't you think?"

"I hope so," she said.

"I'll help you," I said. "Or I'll try my hardest, anyway."

"Really?" asked Miriam. "Can your powers do that? Do you think?"

"I don't know," I said. "I guess we'll find out."

That night, after dinner, I went to my room and tried again. But this time I searched for "Jewish girl angel." And I found one.

"Laila," I whispered as I leaned in to read.

According to the site, Laila was the angel of conception, who whispered to unborn babies, told them everything their soul needed to know. Then, just before birth, Laila apparently tapped everyone in the face and knocked all their memories out so that they were born empty, knowing nothing, and ready to relearn everything they'd just forgotten. The site said that that's why we all have a little groove above our upper lips, where Laila's finger left a mark.

I remember I sat there, with my finger above my upper lip, feeling the soft hollow, and staring at my computer. Could Miriam be Laila? On the one hand, it made a kind of sense that someone whose job it was to make everyone forget everything they knew might somehow end up forgetting everything she knew. That seemed like a sensible sort of karma. But if that was the case, if Miriam was really some actual "angel of the Lord," what on earth could I possibly do to help her? And how would I explain any of this to Miriam herself? It felt like too much. Where would I begin?

I turned off the light and climbed into bed. I didn't think I believed that babies got any memories knocked out of them right before birth. That sounded bonkers to me. Like I'd told Rabbi Dan, I didn't think I believed in bible stories or any of that stuff. It just all felt too impossible. But what if it was all true? What if it was real?

Anyway, even if it was, Miriam would just have to do what the babies did, I supposed. The ones who got their memories knocked out of them. She'd need to recover what she'd lost, wait for more of her pictures to return. But also, she'd have to start over, fresh.

That night in the darkness of my bedroom, I turned my pillow over to the cool side, snuggled down, and closed my eyes.

Whatever sort of angel she was, I'd be happy to help Miriam. Like Rabbi Dan had said, we were all supposed to repair the world. Right? Maybe together, Miriam and I could repair her world, her life. We'd recover her lost memories, but also, we'd make new ones. We'd start right away, in the morning.

☆ 17 ☆

Dumpling Shabbat

That was another blur of a time, that week after Rosh Hasha-nah. I wish now that I'd taken notes so that I could include more here, in this book that I'm writing. Each day, I went to school, and somehow it wasn't nearly so terrible to pass Bea in the hallways anymore. We'd wave vaguely at each other, and once, she asked to copy my math homework, and I let her. I don't know exactly why, but I did. Maybe just to hear her say, "Thanks, Zip!" Maybe because I couldn't let go.

In the cafeteria, Bea had started sitting alone with Liv, so I'd just get my milk to take it to the library. I can't pretend that didn't hurt. But somehow, the pain was quieter now that I had other things to think about. Now that I had Miriam.

Each day I did my homework at lunch, so that I wouldn't

have to think about it after dismissal. Then I'd race out of school and run right over to find Miriam at Red's Farm. She was weakest then, in the afternoons. Each day, when I got to the oak tree and she flew down to me, she looked pale and a little shaky. But we'd sit together a minute, and I'd lay a hand on her hand and feel the prickle of my magic working, the jolt of something happening that I didn't quite understand. Until I heard Miriam whisper, "Thank you." Then she'd be solid again, her cheeks flushed.

How lucky I was, I thought, to have been granted this gift. This magic. This power. But also, to be able to help her. To have something to give, and someone to give it to. Whatever else she was, Miriam was mine, and I was the only person she cared about. The only person she needed. Just then, after everything that had happened with Bea, that felt a bit like magic too.

Unfortunately, there were things I couldn't seem to figure out how to do with my new powers—like helping Miriam figure out where she came from. I did my best—like the time I attempted an incantation for the return of memories, burning a branch of rosemary and waving it all around, inhaling the smoke and chanting, "Return return return." But the smoke only blew in our faces and made us both cough. Miriam didn't say anything, but I could tell she was disappointed.

On Wednesday at lunch, after some digging, I found something online about a super-ancient Jewish codex called the Tree of Knowledge. The site said that the author, Elisha, had copied spells and wisdom from an older text found in Venice, locked away. There were even scans from the book. But though there was mention of a memory spell, I couldn't test it out, because there were pages missing, and also I didn't have any powdered snakeskin. Still, when I saw those old images, those words written in Hebrew, I couldn't help thinking that I *would* find the answer for Miriam, somewhere. Jews had been working magic for centuries, I knew now. They'd unlocked secrets I could only dream about. I wasn't alone. I was part of a tradition, and I just needed to keep looking. . . .

But I needed to figure it out soon. For Miriam, each failure took a toll. She'd be so hopeful as I laid out my ingredients, took a deep breath, gathered my magic, began to chant. But then, each time after I was done, she would shake her head sadly. "No good," she'd say. "Nothing. I'm just the same. Still empty." Each day Miriam seemed more interested in recovering her story, and each day, we got no further.

Of course, she was still retrieving scraps of memory, what she called her *pictures*, each time we touched. But none of them seemed significant. They were all just random moments, snapshots and details, nothing that anchored her to any specific time or place, or gave her what she seemed to long for most of all: a sense of where she'd come from, a family. I couldn't help wondering if maybe this wasn't because angels don't have families, but I never said that.

Besides, she *did* have memories, or so it seemed. They were just so random! One day she recalled a small man walking in sand. Another time it was a slice of orange melon, sprinkled in pepper. There was a falling-down building in a snowstorm, and a garden full of glass. But when she told me these stories, it was like she was reading a book out of order, without any characters in it. The only thing her memories had in common was that none of them sounded the least bit familiar to me. I had hoped that finding Miriam here in Atlanta meant that the things she was remembering were connected to the city around us. But if that was true, it was impossible to know.

Then on Thursday afternoon, when we were picking wild raspberries from a bush at the farm, I looked over and found her staring down at her own two hands with her brow furrowed.

"What's wrong?" I asked her. "Did you get a pricker?"

Miriam looked up at me and shook her head fiercely, then held up her hands for me to see. "No," she said. "It's just that . . . I should recognize them, shouldn't I?"

"Recognize what?" I asked.

"My own hands?" she said, pointing to one of her palms. "I should have memories of where these scars came from, at least. They should be familiar to me. Even if I never had a home or a mother or father like yours or a life in the world. Despite all that, *these* are my hands, and there must be a story of where they've been, don't you think? Shouldn't my body remember *itself*, even if it has always been alone, as I am now? What happened to me, Zippy? Why don't I remember anything, not even myself?"

She thrust her hand in my face, and I noticed her scars for the first time. The thick, shiny white markings looked like they'd been made by fire or a hot knife.

I nodded. "I get it. But you're *not* alone, Miriam. Not now anyway. You have me."

"I do have you," said Miriam, nodding slowly. "And I'm grateful. But you don't know what I am any better than I do. You can't help me, really, in the end. Magic or not."

I didn't know how to answer that. I just nodded, because she was right. There was so much I didn't understand about Miriam! Even if I had conjured her with magic, I still had no real clue how she had arrived, or even what word had conjured her, exactly. Poovilhoo or pavelhee or whatever it was I'd said. It drove me nuts, of course, that I didn't know what she was or where she had come from. I didn't know why no one else could see her wings or what the prickles meant when we touched. I didn't know why she looked a little more human each day, her skin tanner, hair more tangled. But as frustrating as those unanswered questions were, I was still glad to have Miriam in my life. The only thing I knew for sure was that she was my friend. I wanted that to be enough.

That was what I clung to, as I tried to help Miriam make

new memories. As I distracted her with delicious foods and stories from school. As we watched movies and listened to music. As we bought sunflower seeds at the Big M Mart and sat on a curb in the sunshine, spitting the shells in the street. One day it stormed and stormed, and after that, we took a long walk to the little meadow beside the creek. There, we found that the rain had filled the creek so high it overflowed its banks, and as we wandered around barefoot, squelching and splashing in the flooded fields, we discovered the grass was full of minnows. They swarmed us, tickled and nibbled our toes. Miriam laughed and laughed and it was the most joyful sound I'd ever heard.

But in the end, did that help anything? It didn't seem to, for her anyway. Everything was more fun for me with Miriam around, but she seemed to be slipping into sadness herself. Thinking about who we had been when we first met, it was almost like we were trading places. On the outside, she was getting stronger, better, more human. But on the inside, she seemed to be fading a little more each day.

Then it was Friday, and Miriam and I were on my front porch, eating lime Popsicles, when Mom came out, slammed the screen door.

"Zipporah Chava!" she shouted. "I hereby declare that tonight is Dumpling Shabbat. We will be eating delicious food from Gu's and saying the blessings at the proper time."

"Okay," I said, slurping my Popsicle. "No objection to dumplings. But why this week?"

"Why not?" repeated Mom. "Because I feel like it!" She turned and went back inside.

Miriam, beside me, was silent. She finished her Popsicle quietly and laid the stick on the arm of her chair. "What are dumplings?" she asked.

"Oh! They're like . . . little balls of food? With filling? I don't know how to explain them. Sort of like noodles, with stuff inside. They're spicy. Chinese. Delicious little bites. A treat for Shabbat."

"Oh," said Miriam. Then she added, "Yes. *Shabbat . . .*"

"It's a Jewish thing," I started to say. "A day of rest. See, you're supposed to not do any work and you have a special meal and . . ."

But I stopped explaining because Miriam had a funny sort of dreamy look on her face. She closed her eyes. "*Shabbat . . . ,*" she said again. "Are there . . . candles? On Shabbat?"

"Yes!" I shouted. "Yes, we *do* light candles. Also, we drink wine and say prayers. Well, sometimes, anyway. Mom forgets most weeks. But are you . . . remembering something?"

"*Something,*" said Miriam, opening her eyes and nodding. "Maybe something. Just the faintest bit of something. When you say that word, I can picture lights, shining."

"Wow," I said. "That's amazing." Then I had a thought.

"Hey—Miriam. Do you maybe want to stay for dumplings and Shabbat? See the candles yourself? I bet Mom wouldn't mind."

Miriam nodded right away. "Oh yes!" she said breathlessly. "Yes, please. I'd love to see the candles and taste the little bits of deliciousness."

"Great!" I said.

Then Miriam frowned. "I hate night in the tree, Zippy. It's hungry and the bats are everywhere."

That was when I realized: I hadn't thought about what happened when I left to go home to dinner and my comfortable bed and Miriam stayed behind at the farm. "I'm sorry I never asked before: Would you also like to sleep over? It's a thing people do, have guests stay. Bea used to. . . ."

I trailed off at that, but Miriam's smile widened. "Yes, Zippy. I *would* like that. I think so, at least . . . never having slept anywhere but the tree." She laid her fingers on my arm gently. "Thank you."

"You'll like the dumplings," I said, and closed my eyes to wait, feel the prickle, the hum that connected us. "Everyone likes dumplings."

Of course, Miriam loved the dumplings. Everyone loves dumplings! But the thing that happened at dinner that night, the thing I remember best, happened before the Gu's delivery arrived. What I remember is the candles.

Have you ever said the blessings for Shabbat? It's nice because it's easy, simple. It's not like a big religious service but more like a tiny spell. It's just a little bit of specialness in your house, your dinner, your regular life, and it only takes a minute. How it works is that you light these two candles, and then you kind of swish the light from them toward your face, and cover your eyes a minute and say a blessing that goes: *Baruch ata Adonai, Eloheinu melech ha-olam, asher kidshanu b'mitzvotav vitzivanu l'hadlik ner shel Shabbat.*

That's it, easy peasy. Then you sip some wine and say another little prayer, and then you do almost the same thing with a piece of bread. After that, it's time to eat!

But that night, the night Miriam came for dumplings, a weird thing happened. When we got to the blessing over the wine, we said the words together, *"Baruch ata Adonai, Eloheinu melech ha-olam, borei p'ri hagafen."* But then, I couldn't stop singing. I kept going and going and going, and said, *"Baruch ata Adonai, Eloheinu melech ha-olam, asher kid'shanu b'mitzvotav v'ratza vanu, v'shabbat kod'sho b'ahava uv'ratzon hinchilanu, zikaron l'ma'aseh b'reishit. Ki hu yom t'chila l'mikra-ay kodesh, zaycher l'tziat mitzrayim. Ki vanu vacharta v'otanu kidashta mikol ha'amim. V'shabbat kod-shi-cha b'ahava uv'ratzon hinchal tanu. Baruch ata Adonai, mi'kadesh ha Shabbat."*

I didn't even know I was doing it until I was done. Inside my head, it just felt normal, like what we were all doing. Have you ever been asked to read aloud in class, and then you're concentrating on not messing up so hard that you go too far, past where the teacher wanted you to stop, and when you look up, everyone is staring at you? It was sort of like that. I finished, said, "Amen," and when I looked up, Mom and Dad were staring at me like I had an eyeball in the middle of my forehead.

"Wow," said Dad. "That was . . . something else, Zip."

"That was fantastic!" said Mom. "You must really be studying your Hebrew, huh? You've only had one bat mitzvah class. Are you just working on your own, at night?"

"I . . . uh, yeah . . . ," I stammered. "I've been practicing. Thanks."

Then, thank goodness there was a knock at the door, and the dumplings and noodles and green beans arrived, so we all got busy eating, and nobody said anything more about my amazing new abilities. But even though we talked about other things, I couldn't stop thinking about the blessing. About how random my new powers were. And wondering what might happen next.

After dinner, we played poker with my parents for gummy bears instead of money, which is not a traditional Shabbat ritual, in case you're wondering, but is a fun thing to do any day of the week. Miriam had a hard time following the rules, but even that didn't really matter, because we were having such a good time.

Then it was late, so we got down the pile of blankets and

sleeping bags and made up our beds on the floor in my room. Miriam lay down and folded her wings around herself.

"Do you want something else to sleep in?" I asked, reaching for my own pajamas.

"What do you mean?"

I looked down at her stained dress then. I'd gotten so used to it that I hardly registered it anymore, especially since, like the wings, Mom and Dad didn't seem to notice it. Grown-ups can be like that sometimes, selectively blind, especially where kids are concerned. Like they live on one layer of the world, and we live on another.

"It's just that here, where we live, in Atlanta, people usually wear different clothes to sleep in than they do during the day," I explained. "And also, they wash their clothes. Sometimes."

"Why?" asked Miriam.

"Because clothes get dirty," I said. "So, if you borrow something of mine, I can wash your dress for you, if you want."

Miriam sat a minute, thinking about that. "Is dirt bad?" she asked, touching the old stains on her skirt.

"I mean, I don't think it'll kill you to wear a dirty dress. But other people won't like it, and they might not be nice about that or want to be around you."

She thought about this. "Do you think your mom might not like my dirty dress?"

I shrugged. "Mom is unpredictable."

"Then we'll wash my dress," she said. "All right?"

I nodded, smiling.

It took me a minute to find something that worked with her wings, but once she'd changed into a clean sundress and was sitting back on her sleeping bag, Miriam laid a hand on my arm. "Zippy," she said.

"Yes?" I felt the prickles begin.

Then we sat like usual and felt the energy between us buzz and swell, more intense each moment. I watched her eyes this time, in the dim room, as they glazed over. As she seemed to lose focus and her eyelids fluttered.

Then, suddenly, it wasn't nice at all anymore. It hurt.

"Miriam, stop," I hissed. "That's too much." But her eyes were closed and her grip was firm. "Miriam, no!" I said, and I tried to pull away, but I couldn't. Her hold was too strong, or I was too weak.

Finally I felt her hand loosen and I jerked my hand free. She snapped back. Her eyes rolled open.

"I'm . . . . sorry," she said breathlessly. "It was . . . different this time. I couldn't stop. I don't know why."

"You can't do that again," I said with tears in my eyes. "Not like that. Okay?"

Miriam nodded. "I understand," she said, looking frightened. "I'm sorry, Zippy. I'm so sorry. I won't ever do that again. But Zippy?"

"Yeah?"

"This time I . . . I saw something new."

"What?" I asked, clutching my sore hand, which buzzed now, as if it had fallen asleep. "What did you see this time?"

"I saw a place," she said. "A place with a statue."

"What kind of statue?" I asked.

"A lion," she said, "made of stone. And he looked like he was sleeping, and very sad. He was up above me, in the sky." She glanced up at my ceiling as if expecting to find the lion there.

The next thing I knew, I was scrambling out of my blankets, switching on my laptop. Most of the things Miriam saw—mountains, water, screaming—were too vague to be searchable, but this was different.

"What's *that*?" asked Miriam.

"This," I said, "is a computer."

"What does it do?"

"It's like . . . a box full of pictures and stories and information. The whole world is in here, pretty much. Like a gigantic library."

"How wonderful!" said Miriam as she rose and came to stand behind me. "It can tell you everything? It can show you anything at all?"

"Mostly," I said. "The trick is that you have to ask it just the right questions." I opened up Google and typed into the search bar: "Stone Lion Sleeping Sad Statue Sky."

"That's all you have to do to find my memory?" asked Miriam. "Is it magic?"

I laughed. "No," I said. "Not really, but sometimes it feels that way."

And this was sort of one of those times, because when I hit Enter and a bunch of images popped up on the screen, Miriam shouted, "That's IT! *That's* my picture. The box *did* do magic, Zippy. It found him, right there. Just like in my mind."

"Which one?"

Miriam pointed a long, thin finger at the screen. "*This* one," she said. "Oh, he's so sad, Zippy. Look at him."

I'd never seen the statue before, but when I clicked on the link, I discovered something even more magical. "It's here, Miriam!" I said. "What are the chances? It's here in Atlanta, only two miles away. At Oakland Cemetery. I've been there a million times, on field trips and with my parents. I've never noticed that statue before, but we can *go* there. *This* memory we can find! And maybe it will tell us something about who you are or where you came from. Maybe it will lead us somewhere else. Like a clue."

Beside me, Miriam's face lit up with a smile I'd never seen on her before. She looked, for the first time, hopeful.

⋆☆ 18 ☆⋆

What It Feels Like to Fly

"When?" Miriam asked. "When can we go there? Now?"

"Not *now*. It's really late, and my parents won't let us. I'm definitely not allowed to go roaming around in the darkness."

Miriam's face fell. It was like someone had flipped a light switch off. "I see."

"But I bet my parents will drive us over there in the morning," I offered.

Miriam looked like she might cry. I wasn't sure what to do. I wasn't allowed to walk that far by myself, not even during the daytime. "Anyway," I added, "I'm sure the cemetery gates are locked for the night and also the wall is super high. We wouldn't even be able to get in if we went there now."

Miriam stared at me with her big dark eyes. "*I* would," she whispered.

"What do you mean?"

"I could fly right in," she said. "I could fly all the way there, right now. Both of us could!"

I stared at her then, just stared, for what felt like a full minute.

On the one hand, the thought of wandering off into the darkness of Atlanta at midnight terrified me.

On the other hand, Miriam had been feeling increasingly lost and sad. Now, for the first time, she was hopeful, eager. She had a clue, at last. It made sense she wanted to follow it. It felt like fate almost, like we needed to.

On the one hand, my parents would kill me and ground me and I'd never be allowed to see Miriam again if I got busted in the cemetery after dark, miles from home.

On the other hand, I was a witch, with my powers increasing, and what kind of a witch worries about getting grounded?

On the one hand, what if someone saw us flying? What would they do? Could we get arrested?

I was mulling all that over and probably could have argued with myself for hours, but Miriam asked, "Zippy?"

And I replied, "Yes?"

Then she asked me a question I'd asked myself a million times before. A question I could answer with certainty. "Don't you want to know . . . ," she said, "what it feels like to fly?"

"Yes, of course!" I said. "But . . ."

And suddenly, in my mind there was a picture, of a witch swirling her arms in the darkness and shooting up into a purple sky. A glittery witch, flying wild in the night. All my life, I'd wanted to fly. I'd tried for years, but none of my spells had come close to working. When I was little, I used to work really hard at dreaming about flying. I'd lie there in bed, with my tongue pressed between my teeth, concentrating, and picture my own wings, in hopes that when sleep came, I might get to try them out. As if I could will a dream into being.

"Okay," I said, meeting Miriam's gaze. I nodded. "Let's do it."

At last Mom and Dad were in their room, and the light under their door winked out. Then we tiptoed as quietly as we could through the dark house, slipped out the back door, and into the weeds and wildflowers of the yard. Our lawn is overgrown like you wouldn't believe. Once in a while, Mom nags Dad to cut it, and Dad refuses and says that lawns are a vestige of snooty British aristocracy and class oppression and also that it's better for the bees and the butterflies to just let the lawn become a prairie. Mom argues that if that's true, the glorious revolution will probably die of Lyme disease and rat bites, because you can't have a prairie in a major urban metropolis. And she might be right, but the truth is that I like the yard.

Except maybe when I need to wade through it at midnight. There are an awful lot of prickers. Still, we managed to get through them without too much fuss that night. Then Miriam unfolded her wings. And surrounded by weeds and moonlight, with her arms extended to me, she really did look like an angel. An angel who had borrowed my sundress.

I wish I could explain in this book what ran through my head in that moment. But I can't because it was *all the things*. Mostly, despite how long I'd wanted to do this, I was terrified.

"Wait!" I said, standing in the middle of the yard. "Wait, Miriam."

"What?" she asked. "Don't you trust me?"

"Of course," I said. "I don't know how to explain it. I just . . . worry. That's all."

Lighten up, echoed Bea's voice in my head. *Try to like it.*

Miriam smiled. "I won't let you fall, Zippy. I've never fallen, not once." Then she walked toward me with her arms held out and reached them around me, wrapped her arms around my middle. "I've got you."

And then . . .

Whuff.

There was a lift and a lurch as I felt my feet leave the ground, dangling in their sandals, waving beneath me, kicking the air. The wind was suddenly all in my hair and blowing my nightshirt and we were in the sky and we *were* the sky. Above us, I could feel the whole world shift each time Miriam beat her wings, as the house dropped far away beneath me.

A minute later, everything was blurring with the dark sky

and the tears the wind brought to my eyes. So I closed them and tried to feel safe. Safe on the *inside*. I had no control of anything, could only feel Miriam's arms around my middle and the whole world swirling around me. I was lost in the night, powerless and bewildered. I could have been upside down.

"How do you know where to go?" I shouted to Miriam after a few minutes, with my eyes still shut.

"I don't," said Miriam into my ear. "I've told you. I don't *know* things. I only feel them."

I didn't say anything more after that. I just tried to be like Miriam. Stop worrying. Stop thinking. Just *feel*. Which worked, I guess, because a few minutes later, we were landing gently on the neatly clipped grass of the cemetery.

By the time I'd caught my breath, Miriam was already setting off through the graves, and so I followed. Even though I was the one who'd been to Oakland so many times before, I let her lead the way along the familiar brick walking paths as she *felt* her way toward her lion.

In case you don't know it, Oakland Cemetery is famous. A lot of important people are buried there, though I couldn't tell you who, really. I don't remember their names. We took a class trip in the fourth grade and learned all about the dead authors and dead Civil Rights leaders and dead soldiers and dead enslaved people too. There's a big Jewish section, full of graves with Stars of David on them instead of crosses. When I was little, Mom and Dad sometimes used to take me to Oakland for picnics, which might sound weird, but it's really more like a park, with beautiful trees and gardens. Like any good witch, I've whispered my share of spells in the cemetery too, among the mausoleums and old statues. It feels haunted and you can just tell there's power all over the place. It was even more that way at night, with the darkness and moonlight, the aloneness.

Before long, Miriam gasped and came to a halt in front of me. "There it is," she said.

I turned to look where she was pointing, and sure enough, there was the lion. He was huge, bigger than any of the other statues nearby. He was sprawled and sad, like Miriam had said, and honestly, he looked kind of dead.

"Wow!" I said. "He's really something."

"Yes," said Miriam. "He is." She walked over and placed a hand delicately on his haunch.

We stood and stared for a minute. Then I asked, "Why do you think you remembered him? What do you think he means?"

Miriam paused, staring at him. She tilted her head to one side. "I . . . don't know."

"Well," I said, "at the very least, he means you're from here, from Atlanta. Right?"

"That *sounds* right," she said slowly. "Or how I have ever seen him before, to remember him? How could I have the picture in my mind?"

"Exactly," I said. "And since what you remember is *here*,

in a graveyard, I wonder if maybe you know someone buried here? Either that, or maybe you're a—" I cut myself off. I couldn't finish the sentence. I had started without thinking, spoken too quickly.

"What?" asked Miriam, turning to look at me. "Possible that I'm a what?"

"Nothing," I said.

"No, say it."

"It doesn't matter."

"Say it," she said again. "What do you think I am, Zippy?"

"I mean, it's just a thought, but you *could* be a . . . a ghost."

"A ghost . . . ," whispered Miriam. "Do you think? I don't *feel* dead."

"Maybe," I said. "I was thinking you were an angel, but now I don't know . . . because if you're a ghost, that might explain what happened to your memories. Maybe these pictures you recall when we touch, those are memories from when you were alive, and when you died, they kind of . . . fizzled."

"Oh," she said. "I see." She didn't look happy about the idea.

"But maybe not," I said quickly. "You could have remembered the lion for some other reason, right? You could have been, like, a groundskeeper in the past who time-traveled here? Or maybe you're descended from the person who made the statue, and so you feel a connection to it. That happens in books, sometimes."

Miriam stared a little longer at the lion before she said, "I don't think groundskeepers have wings."

"It's funny," I said, searching for a way to change the subject. "I've been here so many times before, but I don't remember ever seeing this statue." I wonder how I could have missed him.

Miriam didn't respond. I walked up closer to look at the lion. I liked his sad face and felt sort of sorry for him. But when I got up close enough to read the words carved into the stone beneath him, my stomach turned over.

"Ugh," I said.

"What?" asked Miriam, joining me. "What is it?"

"Nothing," I said. "Never mind."

Unknown Confederate Dead, the words read.

"What does it mean?" asked Miriam with a worried look on her face.

I started to answer her, then paused. Stopped myself. Because if she was actually a ghost, and this statue was important to her, what did *that* mean about who Miriam might have been, when she was living?

"It's . . . from a war," I said. "A really bad one. And people died in the war. I guess the statue is to commemorate that." I shivered. "War is terrible."

"People die," said Miriam simply. "All around us. Everywhere. Today. Always. People are dying this very moment. *You'll* die too. Is a war worse than other kinds of dying?"

"I'm . . . not sure," I said. Suddenly, the whole night seemed to be heading in the wrong direction. What if we *didn't* want to know where Miriam came from? Better she should be an angel, for sure. "Maybe it's time to go."

Miriam nodded distractedly, then held out her arms. I stepped to her, and she folded me back into that very strong hug. A moment later, with a hop and a beat of her beautiful wings, we were up in the air again.

Whuff.

This time, I opened my eyes wide, looked around, and craned my neck to watch the cemetery grow smaller and smaller below my dangling feet. I felt my stomach lurch, but I didn't close my eyes. Instead, I tried to make out the specific things I knew around me. Not just Miriam's face, which looked distant now, distracted. But also the towers of the old cotton mill lofts in the distance, the sign from the Publix glowing small and green at our dizzying height. And all over and everywhere, spread out across the city, tiny bursts of light from homes and yards, glittering in the darkness. *Shattered vessels,* I thought to myself, as we flew over the highway and the park. Then, just as we were nearing the house . . .

I slipped.

I don't know what happened. I'll never know what happened. One moment I was wrapped firmly in Miriam's arms, and I could feel her breath on my ear, her hair tickling my neck. The next, I felt myself sliding, slipping free, her arms loosening. The world suddenly tilted. "Miriam!" I cried.

"Zippy!" she screamed, and I felt her hands grasping for me, her fingers raking the thin fabric of my nightgown as our bodies came apart. But she was too late. She was still flying, and I was falling now. Falling, falling, free in the air, and then dropping. Heavy and hurtling through the night like a stone.

I don't know what happened then. I can't know. I was only a body in that moment, falling through the sky. The only things holding me were darkness and wind. There was nothing I could do, nothing I could fix or try or choose or think. It was the strangest thing of all. Like my mind disappeared and once it was gone I didn't flail or reach or worry or anything else. I closed my eyes, beyond worry. I could only fall and fall.

An object.

Hurtling.

Until suddenly, I felt a sharp smack, a crush of my body into *something*. I felt my bones shudder and my teeth crash. My eyes flew open, and only after that, I realized something was holding me. I hadn't hit the ground.

I'd hit Miriam!

She'd somehow turned midair, and rushed for me, raced me to the ground, caught me from below. Now she was clutching me in her arms and flying skyward again. Never in my life had I felt so much at once. I felt the pain in my teeth and jaw, the windburn and welcome tears in my eyes. The relief and pounding heartbeat in my chest and the thrum in my limbs, radiating out, warming me and echoing in my ears.

I let myself be carried, limp and safe.

Until, after a few moments . . . I felt something else. Miriam's hands, her bare fingers gripping my bare legs. At first, the prickle warmed me, buzzed and hummed, comforted and soothed me.

At first.

Then it began to burn.

"Miriam?" I tried to say.

"Shh," said Miriam. "We'll be home soon. Almost there, Zippy."

But the longer she held me, the more it burned. The prickle became something else. A wave of electricity, a current that overrode my thoughts. It zapped my brain and body, froze my tongue so that I couldn't speak. I couldn't spit out the words in the back on my throat, couldn't scream. *It's too much*, I wanted to shout, *too much too much too much*, as we flew through the night.

I don't know what happened after that. Until I woke up, sprawled in my dark, wild yard, surrounded by the weeds and the high grass.

Everything hurt. Everything felt heavy and bruised. Also, I couldn't see. Why couldn't I see?

"Zippy?" I heard Miriam say, as if through a wall of static. "Zippy, I didn't mean to. I was upset. I wasn't being careful, and then——"

A light came on, a door banged open on the porch.

"Zippy!" I heard my mom shout. "Is that you? Girls? What's going on? What was that crash?"

It took me a minute, but in the end, I managed to sit up and wave limply. "Just me," I said. "Just me and Miriam."

"Zipporah Chava McConnell! What on earth are you doing out here at this hour?"

If I answered, I don't remember what I said. I don't remember anything until morning.

19

What's a Dybbuk?

*A*ll during breakfast the next morning, Mom tried and failed to act normal. The thing is that Mom isn't great at normal even on a normal day, so nobody was fooled. We all just shoveled in our pancakes, gulped our juice, and tried to get through it. Dad barely looked up from the book he was reading.

When Miriam had finished her last bite, Mom abruptly said, "Well, now, I think it's probably a good time for Miriam to go. We have a busy day ahead, don't we, Zippy?"

"Uhh, do we?" I asked.

But Miriam took the hint and got up from her chair. "I'll go," she said meekly, her head bowed. "Bye, Zippy." She looked back at me, and I could see the apology in her eyes, but I didn't know what to do.

"We'll see you around," Mom called vaguely from her seat at the table.

As she turned to open the door, Miriam looked so alone to me. So alone and worried. I felt like I should say something, but I was still so foggy-headed myself. I was scared and confused and needed some time to think about things. I wasn't sure what was happening at all anymore. The magic at work here was too big, too bewildering. Everything was changing, and it was more than I could take.

Once Miriam was gone, Mom leaned forward across the table and glared at me. "Zippy McConnell," she said. "What on earth happened last night? Do I need to ground you? I've never had to ground you before, but you aren't supposed to be wandering around outside at one in the morning."

"You never told me that," I said. "Now I know. I won't do it again. How's that?"

Mom crossed her arms and frowned. "I don't like this new attitude of yours, kiddo. And I should not have to tell you that once we lock up the house for the night, you need to stay inside it. You *clearly* snuck out, which means you clearly knew that what you were doing was wrong. Right? Back me up here, Gabe?" She looked over at my dad for support.

In response, Dad just ate some cold pancake off the serving plate with his fingers. I don't know about your dad, but mine doesn't like confrontation. He leaves that stuff to Mom.

"I guess so," I said. "Anyway, I won't do it again. I promise."

"Well," said Mom with a sigh. "I suppose this can be a warning. But I can't help thinking that maybe Miriam isn't a great influence on you. In any case, no more sleepovers anytime soon. Okay?"

I got up to clear the dishes without being asked.

Then out of nowhere, Mom suddenly called out in an overly cheerful voice, "Hey! I've got an idea! What say we give Bea a call? Maybe she'd like to go roller-skating later."

"Roller-skating?" I asked, turning from the sink. I really just wanted to go back to bed. I was sore all over. I felt like I'd been tossed by a million waves. But I couldn't tell Mom that, because then I'd have to explain why. "When have I ever roller-skated?" I said. "When has Bea ever roller-skated? Who roller-skates?"

"Well, I don't know what kids do these days," said Mom. "Shoot me, why don't you, for suggesting something fun. I just miss Bea. That's all."

I stared at her. "*You* miss Bea?"

"Sure," said Mom. "She's like family. It's weird not having her around."

I blinked. "Are you seriously suggesting that *I* don't miss her?"

Mom paused a moment, then said, "How should I know what you're feeling, Zippy? You don't tell me anything anymore, and you've been spending so much time with Miriam. We've barely seen you the last week or so, and I thought that maybe——"

"Bea and I didn't just have a fight, Mom," I said. "She has *new* friends now."

Her expression softened then, and she opened her mouth like she was going to say something—something I didn't want to hear.

"And so do I," I rushed to say. "Miriam is the only person in the world who doesn't make me feel like a weirdo. The only person I can be myself around."

"Now, Zippy," Mom said. "I'm sure that's not true. You have wonderful classmates, sweet friends all over the neighborhood."

That was when it hit me that my mom really didn't know me at all. She didn't understand any of what went on at school, or inside me either. *Of course* she thought I'd love to have a bat mitzvah and a fun party with all my many friends. *Of course* she thought Bea and I should go roller-skating. She was so clueless.

I stared at her. "Mom," I said. "I eat lunch in the library."

"What?" she asked. "What's that got to do with anything?"

"Alone," I said. "I eat lunch alone. In the library. Because it's easier that way. Did you know that? I'm *that* kid."

"Oh," said Mom. "No. I didn't know. . . ."

"Right," I said. "You *didn't*. You don't know what it's like to be me. You don't understand at all. When did anyone last invite me to a birthday party?"

"Oh, Zippy," she said in a sympathetic voice that made me want to cry. "I didn't think you cared much about things like that. You go out of your way to, well . . . be your own person. Like you don't need anyone else."

I didn't know what to say. I didn't know what she wanted. "Mom. I don't go *out* of my way. I just . . . *am* this way. I'm me, and people don't like me, especially. So it's just better to be by myself, most of the time. Rather than pretend to be someone else. Someone who has friends."

"But everyone needs friends," said Mom. "We all need our people."

"Well, now I have Miriam," I said. "She's all I need. Miriam likes me the way I am."

Mom didn't say anything after that, and I was glad. I went to my room, lay there in my bed, thinking about how quickly things in my life had changed. I wasn't sure why or how, or even exactly what had happened. But things were different inside and outside. I could tell Mom felt bad after our conversation, but I was too tired and drained to care much that day. Honestly, it had felt good to say all that, to let it out. I hadn't known I was holding it all in until I suddenly wasn't anymore.

For the rest of the weekend, Mom and Dad were busy cleaning out the basement. I ignored them, mostly, and stayed in my room. In the back of my mind, I knew I needed to walk down to Red's Farm and check on Miriam, but somehow I slept most of Saturday. Then it rained on Sunday, so I just hung around home, waiting for the rain to stop, until somehow the day was over. I know that sounds bad, and it is, but do you know how sometimes, the world is just too much? It's funny how being sad or worried can make you kind of selfish. I wasn't exactly sure what I'd say to Miriam—about my fall, or about the idea that maybe she wasn't an angel like I'd thought. Somehow, it felt right to stay quiet and safe for a little while. So I reread *The Witches of Worm*, start to finish. I made a beaded necklace with an old jewelry-making kit. I folded all the clothes in my drawers. I listened to music. I polished the stones in my WitchKit. That was enough for a rainy Sunday.

By Monday morning, the memory of Friday night had faded a bit, even if I hadn't figured everything out. I wasn't exactly excited to go to school, but I was bored of being at home and ready for things to feel normal again—to walk out the door like normal. To sit in my assigned seat in class like normal. To eat my normal cheese sandwich in my normal spot at the library. I was fine to listen to my teachers say the same things over and over again. *Eyes on your own paper, Ella. Yes, Sam, you can have a hall pass, but be quick about it.* And by the time Mom picked me up for bat mitzvah class, I felt more or less like myself. Time does that, I guess, if you let it.

I hadn't been back to bat mitzvah class since I'd made such

a fool of myself, but for once in my life, I wasn't stressed out too much. I'd been so distracted by Miriam all week, I hadn't had any time to waste worrying about Sophies and Ethans and Aris, or thinking much about my bat mitzvah. But in the car on the way over, I flipped open my red folder and began scanning over the printouts of the prayers. That's when I found that whatever magic made me able to doodle my name in Hebrew and sing the long prayer over the wine on Shabbat had another effect. Not only could I read the Hebrew fluently, but I knew all the prayers by heart. The tunes were just there, in my mind, when I scanned over the text. Suddenly, I was almost excited to get to the synagogue.

But when I sat down at the table with Rabbi Dan and Sophie and Ethan and Ari and pulled out my red folder, I realized everyone was staring at me.

"Zippy?" said Rabbi Dan, in the kind of soft questioning voice that you know means someone is being gentle with you. A voice that sounded like he was petting me on the head like an old dog. Like he was concerned. And I could tell from their phony, over-friendly smiles that Sophie and Ethan and Ari had been prepped for me to join them today. They were probably worried I'd cry or something. But I knew better. So many things had happened since the last class. So many more important things. It was almost funny to me now that I'd gotten so upset last time. As if it mattered what they all thought.

"I hope you won't be upset by this," Rabbi Dan went on,

"but I discussed your situation with the others before you got here, and we all just want you to know that if you need to be a passive participant and listen until you've caught up, that's fine. We all have different modes of learning, and it might really help you to hear the others practice. We don't want you to feel pressured to—"

That was when I burst out laughing. Like, for-real laughing. Out loud. I wasn't sure where the laugh came from or why it happened, and in some part of my brain, I knew I should be embarrassed and apologize, but I didn't. I only kept laughing.

Rabbi Dan was startled.

Ari and Ethan were weirded out.

Sophie . . . grinned.

I clapped my hand over my mouth and tried to stop. But it took a minute, and even after that, I had to sort of massage my cheeks to stop them from smiling. "I'm sorry," I said, still grinning through my hand. "I really am. I don't know why I did that. I've . . . had a pretty bizarre week. I'd almost forgotten about what happened last time, and when you reminded me, it seemed . . . funny. But I'm okay now. I really am."

Rabbi Dan furrowed his eyebrows, but all he said was, "I'm glad to hear you laughing, Zippy, whatever the reason. In the Torah, Sarah laughs and doesn't understand her own laughter either."

"Uhh, okay," I said, not sure what that had to do with anything.

"So, then if we all have our giggles out, let's proceed," he said. "If I could have a volunteer to review the Chatzi Kaddish?"

"I'll do it," I said right away. "To make up for last time."

"Sure!" said Rabbi Dan, sounding optimistic and unconvinced as I opened my siddur, riffled around, and found the page.

Do you want to know what's a great feeling? When you've absolutely bombed at something one week, but you come back the next week and totally kill it! That was something I learned that day, because when I chanted that Chatzi Kaddish, I didn't miss a beat. I got to sing those words and watch everyone's mouths drop open. It felt so strange, like I was someone else entirely, someone confident. Someone who knew things would turn out fine. And someone who could sing.

Do you know something else? It wasn't just that I chanted that day. I actually *understood* the prayer. I wasn't even reading the transliteration! I read straight from the Hebrew side of the page. I read the letters, and I guess because of my new magical powers, the words just formed themselves and flowed into my brain the way English would have. It was incredible. I still didn't exactly know what I believed about God, or that he needed to be *extolled*, *adored*, *glorified*, and all that other stuff that was in the prayer, but for the first time I realized how much more interesting synagogue might be if I could at least follow along.

"Whoa," said Ari when I was done.

"Yeah," said Sophie, looking impressed. "You totally *slayed* that."

Rabbi Dan sat back, smiling. The confused look was gone from his face. "Yes, Sophie, she did," he said. "Zippy did indeed *slay* the Chatzi Kaddish."

When we were done with class and everyone was packing up to go, Rabbi Dan pulled me aside. "Zippy, I'd love to know: How did you get over your fear of chanting in the group? That was a truly remarkable improvement this week. I've never seen anything like it."

Ethan and Ari headed for the door, but I noticed that Sophie hung back, listening.

How was I supposed to explain that I'd magically become fluent in Hebrew? I eyed Sophie nervously. But then I decided to just tell the truth. Nothing could ever be as embarrassing as the last class had been, and I'd gotten over that, right?

I pulled back my shoulders and said, "As you know, Rabbi Dan, I'm a *witch*."

I waited for Sophie to laugh, but she didn't. She looked interested.

"Yes, I remember that you're curious about the occult," said Rabbi Dan gently. "But I don't understand how that affected your anxiety."

"It didn't affect my *anxiety*," I said. "It affected my ability. I did a spell, with that scrap of Hebrew I found. The one I asked you about last time? You explained about the vav, remember, that it wasn't povilha but poahlha? Or whatever?"

He nodded hesitantly. "I remember that conversation."

"Well, I didn't plan it this way, but a side effect of the spell is that I'm now fluent in Hebrew. Also, I know all the prayers and tunes and everything. Like, I'm done. Pretty much."

Rabbi Dan, for once, didn't seem to know what to say.

But beside him, Sophie grinned. "Coooool," she said. "Can you show me?"

"No," I said, shaking my head. "Not that I wouldn't. I just lost the spell. Trust me, I really wish I remembered it."

I'm not sure if Sophie believed me or not, but that seemed to be enough for her. "Too bad," she said with a shrug as she leaned over to pack up her bag. I waited for her to go, but she was moving slowly.

For the hour we'd been in class, I'd managed to not think much about Miriam, about all the things that had been happening all week, but now that we were talking about magic, I knew that this was my chance. If anyone could help me, it was Rabbi Dan. So even though Sophie was still there, I took a deep breath, and said, "Hey, Rabbi Dan? Speaking of witchcraft, can I ask you a question? It isn't about my bat mitzvah."

"Of course," he said. "You can always ask me anything."

"I just wondered if you know anything about ghosts," I said. "Jewish ones, I mean."

"Ghosts?"

Across the table, Sophie looked up, interested. She shouldered her bag but still didn't leave.

"Yeah, *probably* ghosts," I said to Rabbi Dan. "And probably Jewish. Have you ever heard of a Jewish spirit that is pale, even a little transparent? With wings?"

Rabbi Dan rubbed his forehead. "I know quite a bit of Jewish folklore, yes. We have texts about shedim, demons. And also angels—"

I shook my head. "No," I said. "Not angels. I looked up about angels. Laila. Maimonides and all. And according to everything I read, Jewish angels aren't supposed to look so much like regular people. But the creature I'm thinking of, she definitely does. Oh, and also, she's always hungry?"

"Hungry?" asked Sophie.

"Yes," I said. "Hungry, all the time. She gets tired, this creature, but then when she, like, touches other people, she kind of sucks something out of them and fuels up, feels better. It's hard to explain."

Rabbi Dan stood stroking his beard and thinking. I stood waiting across from him. At last he spoke. "There's nothing quite like that," he said. "Nothing I can think of."

"Well, couldn't it maybe be some kind of . . . dybbuk?" interrupted Sophie.

"A dybbuk?" I asked. I thought that I'd read that word before, but I couldn't remember exactly what it was. I was impressed Sophie knew anything about Jewish magic.

"Hmmm," said Rabbi Dan. "It's certainly not the standard definition of a dybbuk, but folklore evolves, and there are probably alternate ideas about what exactly a dybbuk should be, from different periods of Jewish history. I'm certainly no expert. Here, let's look. . . ." He walked over to a bookshelf and began to search for something.

"But aren't dybbuks . . . bad?" I asked.

"They are," called Rabbi Dan over his shoulder. "Traditionally they are without souls. They are a kind of wicked spirit that lives in between life and death."

"Oh," I said. "And they can't ever be . . . kind? Or helpful?"

"Why do you want to know?" asked Sophie.

"I'm just . . . uhh . . . doing a project," I lied. "For school. I'm writing a story."

"Your school sounds way more fun than mine."

"It's okay," I said with a shrug.

At that, Rabbi Dan turned and held out a book to me. "*This* might interest you," he said. "It's a scholarly text, not exactly light reading. But if you're interested in Jewish folklore, this is a good place to begin."

"Thanks!" I said, taking the book and scanning over the cover. *Worlds Beyond: Demons and Other Creatures*, it read. It wasn't old and gilded like the little red book or Great-Grandpa Sid's chumash. It was a regular paperback like you'd find anywhere. "Well," I added. "I guess I need to go now. My mom will be waiting for me. She's been in a *mood* lately."

"Okay, Zippy," said Rabbi Dan. "Next week, then!"

"Yep." I turned to go, hurrying for the door.

But outside, just as I was reaching Mom's car, I felt a tug at my sleeve.

When I turned back, I found Sophie standing there.

"Hey!" she said, smiling.

"Oh, hey," I said, pausing a moment. "Did you . . . umm, need something?"

She shook her head. "Nope," she said. "I guess I just wanted to say that I think you ask good questions."

"Well, thanks," I said. "I, uh, guess I'll see you next class."

"See you next class," said Sophie.

20

People Who Need People

As soon as I climbed into the car, I opened the book and began to read. Right away, I learned that shedim and mazzikim were demons and ruhot were spirits, and they were different. I learned that dybbuks were not demons but clinging spirits, creatures that could not leave this world entirely, but instead sought out hosts, living people they could attach themselves to. The book said that there had been many ways of understanding dybbuks over the centuries, and that while all the old rabbis disagreed about pretty much everything, they all seemed to agree that dybbuks were malevolent spirits, dislocated beings, who sought refuge in a living person. Clinging to them. Possessing them.

When I read that part, I closed the book right away. It was too much already, too much to take in. There was no way this was what Miriam was, was there? She wasn't malevolent. She didn't *cling* any more than two friends ever clung to each other. Plus, I was still here. It wasn't like I was disappearing. I think I'd have known if I was possessed, right?

I set the book on the floor at my feet and looked over at Mom. She was staring at me intently, her brow wrinkled. "How about a bagel for dinner? Seems appropriate after bat mitzvah class, no?"

"Sure," I said.

She pulled into a parking space outside Emerald City Bagels and shut off the car. But she didn't get out.

"This silence is killing me, kiddo," she said. "I'm sorry that we fought this weekend. I know it's hard to be your age. Boy, do I remember. And I know you didn't mean to do anything that would worry me, that you were just . . . exploring. Seeing what it would be like to sneak out. Think you can maybe give your old mom a do-over?"

"It's okay," I said. "I'm not mad anymore." And the thing was, I found I really wasn't. I'd been too busy thinking about Miriam to care much about the fight with Mom.

"Well, even if you aren't mad, you've been awfully silent," she said. "And . . . I miss you."

I shook my head. "It isn't about *you*, Mom. There are

things. . . . Sometimes I'm just thinking my own thoughts. And I don't want to share them."

"That makes sense," she said like she was trying not to sound sad. "All the parenting books said this would happen in middle school. I suppose I'm just not used to it. But I hope you know that you don't have to be a closed box all the time. I want to help you, and I feel like I can't if you don't tell me things."

I glanced down briefly at the book on the floor. "I can try, but I can't tell you everything. You wouldn't understand if I did." What, I wondered, would Mom do if she really knew about Miriam? Her wings, her lack of memories? What happened when we touched? I was pretty sure Mom didn't want to hear about any of that.

"Ugh," said Mom. "Things were simpler before. All this stuff with Bea sounds so hard."

Oh yeah. I thought. *Bea.* "She and I just aren't friends the way we used to be."

"But why?" said Mom. "I'd really like to understand."

I shrugged. "She wants friends who aren't me, I guess. Like, friends who are *specifically* not me. People like Liv Randolph. Older kids, who want to talk about lipstick, I guess. I don't know. I'm just not enough anymore." I hated to say those words, hated to feel them coming out of my mouth. But the minute I said them, I knew they were true.

"That's hard," said Mom. "Gosh, I'm sorry, Zippy. Well, I

guess it's good you met Miriam, huh?"

"Yeah," I said. "She's interesting."

"She *is* interesting, that's for sure," said Mom.

For some reason, the way she said it felt different from the way I had. "You don't like her, do you?"

"Oh no!" said Mom. "Of course I like her. She just seems . . . unusual. Her clothes and the way she talks. I can't put my finger on it, but she doesn't feel like any other kid I've known."

"Exactly," I said. "I *hate* most of the kids I know."

Mom sighed. "Yeah, I know you do. And I get that. I just wish things were easier for you, Zippy. I always had a hard time socially myself, until I got to college, so maybe—"

"Mom!" I said. "Why do you need to say things like that? You make me feel terrible. I feel enough like a loser without you telling me I won't have friends until college."

"Sorry," said Mom. "I love you and think you're wonderful. You know that. You're my favorite twelve-year-old in the world. But I just sometimes feel like maybe things would be easier for you if you tried to fit in a little more. You know? Maybe not wear black all the time? Maybe talk a little less about all the magic stuff? It's hard to see you lonely."

"It's hard to *be* lonely," I said. "But that doesn't mean I want to fake it to fit in. Anyway, it wouldn't work."

"I'm not saying you should become a mindless drone,

Zippy. I just think maybe you don't need to work so hard at standing out."

I opened my car door. "I love you, Mom. But I don't want to talk about this anymore." Then I climbed out and slammed the door shut.

If you don't already know this, *I love you* is the one phrase that can get you out of any conversation you don't want to have with your mom. It may not technically be magic, but those three words have power, for sure.

"I love you too, kid," she said with a sigh, as she got out of the car out on her side. "Yeah. Let's nosh."

The conversation was over.

But there's one more thing you need to know about the trip home from that bat mitzvah class. It probably won't sound important, but it was. It was a clue, though I didn't know it yet.

Standing in front of the counter at Emerald City, I looked down into the case, at all the deli things I'd found so completely revolting all my life. All the weird fish stuff. The lox and the pickled herring and the whitefish salad. And suddenly, my mouth started to water. I tried to look away, but the craving overpowered me. I could actually taste the fish on my tongue, salty and rich, as though I'd eaten it a million times before. I could taste it in a way that defied my powers of imagination. My tongue felt big in my mouth.

"Mom," I asked, "can I . . . try some of that salmon? Maybe?"

She turned to stare. "Seriously? Is this some hormonal, puberty thing I don't know about? You've never had fish in your life, Zippy! We don't eat meat."

"I know," I said. But my mouth disagreed. My mouth felt like it was chewing on a memory.

And even though I'd never tasted smoked salmon before, when I bit into my sesame bagel with scallion cream cheese and the thick, salty piece of lox, I found it was exactly as good as I remembered.

When we got home that day, I walked straight down to Red's Farm. I'd waited too long already to visit Miriam, and I knew it. I felt bad, and talking about her with Sophie and Rabbi Dan had only made me feel worse.

"Miriam?" I called, scanning the top of the oak tree. "Where are you?" There was no reply, so I sat down in the grass to wait. After what must have been fifteen minutes, I decided to walk around, look for her.

It was nice, I remember, that walk along the creek. I was full of bagel and egg cream, and the sun was almost about to set, so the light was golden, filtering down through the kudzu along the bank. There were cicadas starting to hum and chirp, and everything felt green and yellow.

Until I saw Miriam.

She was slumped, sprawled on the big flat rock. My rock. She was barely there now, transparent in a way I hadn't seen her since our first day together.

"Miriam!" I shouted as I ran, splashing, toward her. "Miriam, are you okay?"

She didn't answer. When I reached her, I laid a hand on one of her leathery wings and felt her tremble. I wrapped my arms around her middle then and lifted her, pulled her off the rock, and dragged her up toward the grassy bank. It was like she weighed almost nothing. Through her dress I could feel the bones of her, the hard edges of her rib cage and spine. But she was breathing. She was alive. Or anyway, she wasn't *gone*.

I laid her as gently as I could on the grass. Her hair was matted, knotted. Her mouth was stained green. I looked down at her and felt sick. What had she been doing the last few days that I'd been away? Who was Miriam when she wasn't with me?

I sat beside her and put my hands on her cheeks, which were so cold, even though the day was warm. I cupped her face in my hands. "Come on," I said.

But nothing happened. No prickle of magic. If anything, her breathing grew shallower.

She shuddered again, seized. "Stop it," I said with my eyes closed, like I was working a spell. "Stop!"

The shuddering stopped then, and she went limp.

"Oh no," I said. I pulled my hands away from her face. Then I leaned over and laid my forehead against hers, draped her with my hair, and reached my hands beneath her, lifted her up. She felt like a bundle of sticks.

It was my fault, mine. I pressed my face into her neck, my bare arms against her bare arms. "Oh please oh please oh please oh please," I whispered.

Then slowly, slowly, on every bit of skin that was touching her skin, I began to feel something. That slow heat, that faint humming, that prickle. She was drawing energy from me and I could feel it, but I couldn't worry about that. I held on as hard as I could in the warm grass, and the sensation swelled, built, grew and grew so that my brain was buzzing, until just when I thought I couldn't take it any longer, I heard a great gasp, a rush of air, an intake of breath.

I sat back and watched her dark eyes flutter open. "Zippy!" she cried as her body woke. As she came alive. She sat up right away, blinked.

"You're okay," I said weakly. My own vision was blurry now. I was stunned but grateful, relieved. I let myself slump over.

But in the back of my mind there was a voice, whispering. *Malevolent spirit. Refuge in a living person. Dybbuk.*

Miriam reached out a hand and laid it on my foot. "Thank you, Zippy," she said. Her hand on my bare skin was searing now, burning.

"I . . ." I tried to speak, but my voice was fading, my own

breath shallow. "Miriam," I whispered. "*No* . . . no more." But she didn't stop, and I was too weak to push her away.

I don't know how long we stayed like that. I don't know what time was in that moment. There was nothing beyond us, Miriam and I. Connected. The whole universe was just the two of us, prickling and humming and locked together, her hand resting on my foot. In that moment, it was all I could think of, all I could feel in the world. We were only the humming, the buzzing, the painful magic of something I didn't understand but couldn't stop.

When I woke up, sore and faint, Miriam was sitting beside me. We had switched places. She was no longer translucent, but her hair was still tangled and her mouth was still stained. "Zippy . . . ," she said sadly. "It was too much. I took too much again. I'm so sorry. I couldn't help it. This time, I was almost . . . It was as if I was almost gone."

I sat up weakly. "I know. I shouldn't have stayed away so long. I didn't know you needed me like *that*." And that was almost the truth.

"I promise to be more careful," she said.

I nodded. "Why is your mouth green?" I asked.

She leaned over and picked a handful of grass from the ground beside her, let the torn blades fall limply through her fingers. "Only this. There was nothing else. I waited and waited, and it rained, and I was cold and empty. So hungry."

"You should have gone to the garden!" I said. "There are

berries, tomatoes. Or you should have come to my house and knocked."

She shook her head. "I didn't want to steal from anyone. And your mother didn't want me at the house anymore. I could tell."

"Maybe," I admitted. "But people can't eat grass, Miriam."

She looked at me sadly then. "Perhaps. But then, I'm not *people*. Am I?"

I didn't answer her.

"Maybe I *am* a ghost," she said sadly.

"No," I said. "I don't think that anymore. Not exactly. I did some reading, and I think . . . I might know now, what you are."

Her eyes lit up. "Really?"

I nodded. "I think you're something called a dybbuk."

"A *dybbuk*?" She rolled the word on her tongue. "Dybbuk. What does it mean?"

I couldn't answer her. Or anyway, I didn't want to. I needed more information. So I stood. "I'll explain tomorrow," I said. "Right now, I need to go home."

Miriam stood up too, and when she spoke, her voice was angry, in a way I'd never heard it before. "You are *always* leaving. You are *always* going home. What am I supposed to do, when I have no home to go to? Where is *my* home, Zippy? Why did you ever bring me here?"

"I . . . I don't know," I said. Which didn't feel even close to enough, but it was the only truth I could come up with. At that moment, as terrible as it feels to admit it now, in the pages of this book, I just wanted to leave, to run home and crawl into bed and pull the covers over my head. I was scared. I was weak and tired, and lost. I didn't know what to do.

☆21☆

Malevolent Spirits

The next day when I woke up, I thought immediately about Miriam, alone at the farm and hungry. I thought about her stained mouth and her words. *You are* always *leaving*. So I got up before my parents could emerge from their room and filled a cooler, with bananas and carrots, a jar of peanut butter, a loaf of bread, a box of raisins, and four string cheeses. Whatever else happened, I wouldn't leave her hungry again.

But when I got to the farm, for the first time ever, I didn't call to Miriam. I didn't know what I'd say, and so I simply left the cooler at the foot of the old oak tree and slipped away again as quietly as I could.

I'll come back later, I told myself as I walked to school along the gravel road that led away from the farm. And as I walked, I wondered: Could Miriam really be a dybbuk? We were linked in some deep way, and she was *clinging* to me, for sure. But she was also still herself, still fully Miriam, when the book made it sound like a dybbuk should be trying to *inhabit* me, take over my actual body. Miriam wasn't trying to do any of that. She stayed at the farm and ate grass rather than come look for me. She didn't want to be anyone but herself—all she wanted to know was who that was. Shouldn't a malevolent spirit feel less . . . sad?

The thing was that it also made a kind of sense, I thought as I kicked at the gravel. That I'd summoned some sort of Jewish creature, with those mysterious Hebrew words I only sort of remembered. That on Rosh Hashanah, one of the holiest days of the year, I'd somehow worked a kind of special Jewish magic and ended up with a Jewish spirit.

That day, I barely did anything in school. Instead, I read the book Rabbi Dan had given me. I read and I read and I learned a lot of new information, and got confused by most of it. There was so much I didn't understand! The thing is that the book wasn't actually a guide to dybbuks. It was a kind of history of what people thought about spirits and demons and dybbuks going back hundreds, even thousands of years. But the trick was that whoever put the book together clearly didn't *believe* in dybbuks. And even if some of the old rabbis and scholars did, they never seemed to agree with each other. Some said "dybbuks of the Jewish folkloric tradition" were always men, but then some said they could be women too. Some of the rabbis said that dybbuks had done something evil in life and were condemned as a result; others thought that dybbuks had been harmed in their lives and returned for vengeance. Some thought dybbuks could eat and drink, and others said that wasn't possible, that they didn't have any physical form. The only thing that everyone seemed to have in common was that NONE OF THEM HAD EVER MET A DYBBUK. Which meant that if Miriam was a dybbuk, I knew at least as much as the experts.

Even more important, Miriam clearly needed help, but none of the old rabbis and scholars seemed to want to help dybbuks. They just wanted to destroy them. Most of them used a word that gave me the shivers: *exorcism*. According to one paragraph, what I really needed was some fancy kind of rabbi who was trained in expelling spirits and could send Miriam on to the place she was supposed to have gone when she first died, or to wherever evil spirits live or whatever. The Sitra Achra. I didn't know what that was, but it didn't sound good. Anyway, I didn't have access to any fancy old rabbis, and I didn't think I wanted to send Miriam to the Sitra Achra.

By the end of morning classes, I was kind of losing my mind. How could I concentrate on my awful "expressionist project" in art class when I had potentially unleashed a dybbuk on the neighborhood? Even if it was a nice dybbuk who hadn't really hurt anyone, at least not on purpose? I needed more information, and so I didn't even stop by the cafeteria for my usual milk that day, just ran through the hallways to the library, where I sank into a chair at one of the computers and typed "Dybbuk Exorcism."

But I never even got to read the search results, because a moment later, I heard my name.

"Zippy?"

It was Bea, standing in the doorway.

"Hey," I said. "What's up?"

"Not much," she said. "I just saw you flying down the hall and wondered if everything was okay."

"Oh," I said. "I'm fine. Thanks for asking, though."

I was going to turn back to the computer, but Bea didn't go away. "We . . . haven't talked in a minute, huh?" she said.

"Nope," I said. "We haven't." And when I said that, I felt something happen inside me. A funny little click. Suddenly, I didn't want to work so hard anymore to keep Bea as a friend. It was lonely and exhausting, and I didn't need to feel any of that. "Wasn't that how you wanted it?"

Bea's eyes went wide. "No! Of course not. . . ." But almost immediately, something changed in her expression. After a moment, she added, "Well, maybe a little bit, for a minute. I don't know. I wanted a break, I guess. I wanted to see what it was like to hang out with other people, since you never wanted to do that. I felt bored, I guess. But now it all just feels so . . . sad."

"*You're* sad?" I said. "You seem just fine to me."

"What do you mean?"

I felt strangely hot then, wild. My face was still flushed from my run through the hallways, but that wasn't all it was. I was bewildered by Bea. I was worried about Miriam. I was lost and trapped and so many other things. I didn't know how to fix myself or anything else and I was feeling so *much*. I guess I let it all come flying out.

"I mean," I said, "you don't need *me*! You have Liv now. And she knows how to *lighten up*, right? She's not a *baby* like me. Plus, you have the walking group. Why are you even here? What do you want? Why can't you leave me alone?"

She shook her head. "Zippy, it's not like that. It's not like I'm not your friend anymore—"

"That's sure what it feels like," I spat.

"No way," said Bea. "No way. You're like my sister or something. I miss you. But things are different. It's . . . hard to explain. Complicated."

"I don't think it's complicated at all," I said. "It feels pretty obvious. You dumped me, Bea. You're a bad friend."

"No!" said Bea. It almost looked like I'd slapped her. "That's not it."

"You got bored of me," I said. "Me and my baby games, my magic." In that moment, I wished it *was* baby magic. Bea couldn't possibly know what I'd gotten myself into. And that made me even more mad, for some reason. "You *outgrew* me, Bea. Just admit it."

"Fine," she said sadly. "Maybe that's sort of true. But it's also not that simple, Zippy."

I scowled. "If it isn't so simple, why don't you *tell* me what you're feeling? You know, the way you used to tell me things? You could text me. You could eat lunch with me again. Just talk to me in school, even."

"What do you think I'm doing right now?" she asked, her voice rising. "Why do you think I'm here?"

I couldn't really argue with that, but I also wasn't in a mood to give in. I was in a mood to fight. "Too little too late," I said, standing up. "And, you know, I'm actually kind of grateful you turned out to be such a terrible friend, Bea. It makes it easier to stop caring. So thanks for that, I guess."

"Zippy, wait!" she said. But I was already leaving the library, and I didn't turn back. I was too busy hexing her. I hexed her and hexed her, all the way to the bathroom, where I slammed the stall door. Hard.

Then, I cried. But I wasn't even sure what I was crying about. Everything, I guess. Still, it had felt good to say all that to Bea, to tell her the truth of what it felt like to be me. The truth I'd been holding inside for so long.

I managed to make it through the rest of the day without running into Bea again, and when the bell rang for dismissal, I was the first person out of my seat. I ran through the hallways, and I was almost clear when Bea came chasing after me.

"Zippy," she called as I stepped out into the sunshine. "Please, stop. Can we talk a minute?"

I looked over my shoulder. She was by herself; I didn't see Liv or the walking group anywhere. She was just standing alone in the doorway. For a minute, I wondered what she might say.

But then I thought about Miriam, waiting. So I shook my head and started walking.

A minute later, when my phone buzzed in my pocket, I looked down and saw that it was a text from Bea.

EXORCISM?????

She must have seen what I was searching for in the library. But I wasn't going to answer her. I didn't owe her anything. I turned the phone off.

When I got home that day, I found Miriam there ahead of me, sitting in a rocker on our front porch, staring out at the street. As I got closer, I could see that her jaw was clenched, her arms folded, as she rocked back and forth, hard.

"What's wrong?" I asked as I walked up the porch steps.

"You avoided me," said Miriam. "You didn't even talk to me. Why?"

"When?" I asked. But of course I knew exactly what she

meant. I was lying, and we both knew it. "You mean this morning?" I added. "I was just in a hurry. But I brought you food. I didn't want you to be hungry. You were the first thing I thought about when I woke up."

"You said you would *tell* me today," said Miriam. "But then you were scared and ran away. Are you scared of me, Zippy?"

"No," I said. "I just . . . I needed a little break."

"From me?" asked Miriam.

"From everything," I said.

"I'm part of everything," said Miriam.

I nodded. "I'm sorry."

Miriam stopped rocking. "You *promised* you'd figure out how to help me. But I'm only getting worse, Zippy. I've hurt you and hurt you. I have no idea what I am or how I got here—"

"I *will* help you," I said. "I still haven't finished the book, and I—"

Miriam grabbed my arm and held it, tightly, so that I could feel the electricity wake up under my skin. She must have felt it too because she dropped my arm just as quickly. "*No*. Zippy, I *need* to know. It's too much, to wonder. It's worse than the hunger, even. To sit alone, not knowing what I am. To hurt you when we touch. You said yesterday that you thought I was a dybbuk. But what does that mean? I need to know more. You *have* to tell me what you know."

"I don't even know if it's true!" I said.

"Tell me what it is you *don't* know, then," said Miriam, looking somehow taller, older. "It doesn't have to be perfect. You don't have to be sure. You can be uncertain. Just tell me what you *think*."

I shook my head and felt the tears building, hot in my eyes. I was crying but just a little. "You really want to hear this?" I said.

She nodded.

"I think you used to be a regular person," I said. "I have no idea who, exactly, but I think you died and got lost, became a dybbuk. Then, somehow I brought you here, so you're clinging to me. Half a person. Not quite here, not quite gone. Doesn't that sound nuts? It can't be true. It's crazy."

Miriam stared at me a moment, looking sadder than I'd ever seen her. She shook her head softly. "Oh, Zippy," she said. "I wish it did sound crazy. But that's exactly what it feels like to be me, on the inside. I *don't* belong here. I *am* clinging to you. I am . . . lost. Not quite gone. That's exactly it. And it gets worse each day. I was happier in the beginning, when I was barely here at all, when I couldn't remember anything, when I didn't spend all day wondering who I am. Is there something you can do? Is there really no way to send me back to where I came from, before it gets even worse?"

I wiped my face with the back of my hand. "The thing is, we don't know where you came from. Your pictures, they don't tell me enough. Even when we found that statue you remembered, it didn't help. Maybe when you have more memories, we could find a way to send you back to where you came from. But honestly, I'm not sure how. There's only one spell I've found, and it's . . ." I thought about the descriptions in Rabbi Dan's book and shivered.

"What?" asked Miriam. "It's what?"

I shook my head. "It's called an exorcism. And I think it will send you someplace terrible, Miriam. Not home. Or it will simply end you. You'll be gone from the world forever. Anyway, I'm not sure I know how to do that kind of magic."

Miriam was trembling now. She looked uncontrolled, unruly. "And there's no other magic you can think of? For someone who's lost?"

"Someone who's lost . . . ," I repeated after her. And staring at her there on the porch, I suddenly had an idea.

"Wait. Hold on. Come inside," I said.

"Why? What are you going to do?" asked Miriam.

"Magic," I said. "Or anyway, I'm going to try."

In my room, Miriam sat on the bed and watched me closely while I got out my WitchKit and made a Ward for the Settling of Lost Souls.

If you don't know what a Ward is, I'll tell you. It's a kind of spell for safety, a way of casting a circle of protection around something or someone. I didn't know exactly how to fix the specific situation Miriam was in, but I'd memorized this Ward years before, and without any other options, I thought it might be worth a try.

First, I put the ingredients for the Ward inside the jar. I dropped in three cloves, a sprinkle of basil, two branches of rosemary, a burnt match, a chunk of hematite, and a pinch of salt, and then I spit ten times. I whispered Miriam's name into the jar. With that, I put the lid on it, screwed it tight. Then I set it down on my desk beside my black candle. I drew a pentagram with my finger on the lid of the jar, lit the candle, and began to whisper the words of power.

They went like this:

When darkness threatens, shed a light,
And promise stars for every night.
When winter's cold, bring warmest wool.
When hunger yawns, keep bellies full.
The world's a bridge on which we all
Walk timidly, afraid to fall.
But from now on, we shall be freed
From endless hunger, fear, and need.
Provide a salve for every burn,
And settle now these souls that yearn.

After I was done, I picked up the jar and held it out to Miriam. She gripped it, with wide dark eyes that never left mine, and I laid my hands on top of hers. We stood that way for a few minutes, with our hands overlapping on the jar, our fingers prickling as usual.

"Is it working?" asked Miriam.

I was feeling hopeful, but nothing seemed to happen, except that we heard a door slamming, and then the sound of Mom's keys hitting the coffee table in the next room. "I'm home, everybody!" she shouted, as loud as usual.

"Zippy?" Miriam whispered to me. "I don't feel any different. Do you think it's working?" Her eyes were downcast. She set the jar slowly down on my desk again.

"No," I said. "I don't think so. Though some spells take time . . ."

Miriam didn't reply to that. She suddenly looked very tired. "I'll go back to the farm now. I don't think your mom will want to find me here."

That's not true, I wanted to say. But of course she was right. So I nodded and opened the bedroom window as quietly as I could. Miriam slipped away, and I'd be lying if I didn't feel a small breath of relief to have her gone.

After that, I sat for a minute, thinking about my new powers, all the ways I'd grown stronger since Miriam had arrived. The fact that I'd been able to call her from some far-away place, and the fact that I pretty much kept her alive. I thought about how I'd been able to learn Hebrew, overnight, and then there was the piano. So why hadn't I been able to do the Ward? It seemed wrong, unfair.

I was thinking about all of that when I leaned over to blow out the candle on my desk. But the wick had gotten too long and the flame was high and my hair was so loose and messy. I must have leaned into the candle without meaning to, because suddenly, I was on fire. Hot quick flames were leaping all around my face. It happened so quickly I only had time to panic, to flutter. Silently, I beat at my hair, beat it with my hands, and before I knew it, the fire was miraculously out, but my hands were red and burnt and my heart was beating so fast I thought I might die.

I didn't die, but when I looked down, I saw that the bottom half of my long brown hair was badly singed. Whole chunks in the front were missing, now no longer than my chin. I held a strand up to my face and sniffed. It smelled like rotten eggs and scorched plastic. It made me gag, and once I was done gagging, I found there were tears in my eyes, which spilled over and fell, streamed down my face. It was all I could do not to sob too loudly. The last thing I needed was Mom's attention at that moment.

My hair. It had taken me all these years to grow it out. I had the longest hair of any kid in my grade, and I knew it looked bad sometimes, but my hair was part of me, who I was. Throughout history, witches have worn their hair long and loose because other people didn't, or couldn't. Because women were supposed to be nice and tidy and well-behaved, and witches didn't care what other people thought or didn't need to fit in. I felt ashamed that my hair mattered so much to me, but the truth was it did.

Or anyway, it always had before.

★☆22☆★

Blades of Any Kind

efore I had too much time to think, I grabbed some big
metal scissors out of my desk drawer and ducked into my
little bathroom, where I stood awhile, staring at myself, thinking about how ugly I was, uglier than usual, even. And about
how it was my own dumb fault.

I remember Ms. Marty told us once that it's a cheap trick
authors do in books sometimes, to have a character stare into
a mirror just so that the reader can know what the character
looks like. So maybe I shouldn't include this part of the story.
But it's an actual thing that happened, in my real life. I definitely stared in the mirror that day. I looked at the charred,
uneven chunks of my hair in the front, the funny gap on the

side over my ear, and the rest of the hair all long and tangled down my back like usual. I stared at my blotchy, tear-streaked face. And then, before I could chicken out, I took a deep breath and raised the scissors.

I began to cut. Snipped one of the long, burnt strands, watched it fall sadly into the sink. And I didn't stop. I kept going. Snipping one strand after another, all the way around the back of my head, to make everything mostly the same length. Or I tried, anyway. I watched and felt the layers fall away from my hair, felt the weight disappear. I kept at it, leaned close to the mirror, and continued snipping hair all around my head, trying to get it all about chin-length. "Goodbye," I said to the girl in the mirror, who already looked completely different.

I started crying again. Not just quiet tears this time but out-loud sobs. I couldn't help it, couldn't stop. I wasn't just sad. I was something else too. Almost angry but not quite. What was it I was feeling? *Lost*, Miriam had said. She felt lost. What did I feel? I didn't even know.

Suddenly, there was a sharp knock at the bathroom door. "Just a minute!" I called out, sniffing back snot and tears and trying to sound cheerful. I don't know what I thought a minute was going to do for me. It wasn't like I knew a spell to grow my hair back.

"Zippy?" said Mom in a gentle voice that meant she could

tell I was crying. "You okay? What's up, kiddo?"

"Uhh, nothing," I said. "I'm just . . . doing something."

"Yeah?" said Mom. "What kind of something?"

"I'm . . . giving myself a makeover, I guess," I said. "Only it isn't going very well."

There was silence for a good long while before Mom said gently, "Honey? You aren't *piercing* anything, are you? Or *tattooing* anything? Nothing involving needles or blades of any kind?"

I looked down at the scissors in my hand. "Not *exactly*," I said. "Do scissors count?"

That was when the door swung open.

"I look *terrible*, Mom," I said before she could say anything. "Something happened, and I had to cut my hair, but now I'm a mess. I'm even uglier than I was before." I set the shears on the edge of the sink and began to sob again.

"Oh, honey," she said, lifting a strand of hair from my face and letting it fall. "You're beautiful. You're *always* beautiful. But sometimes, even beautiful people need some help. That's why God invented Sephora. Now, come on, let's get out of here."

"Get out of here?" I asked, glancing back at my hideous reflection.

"Just trust me," said Mom.

* * *

Twenty minutes later, I was in East Atlanta Village, in a big leather salon chair, with a Sprite in my hand and my head soaking in a sink as some lady named Sandy rubbed amazing-smelling goo into my scalp.

"What do you want to do about this?" she asked my mom. "Pixie cut? That patch on the side is too short for a bob."

Mom shook her head. "That's up to Zippy. It's her hair, after all. I'm just support staff."

I smiled up at her. My face still felt like it might cry at any moment, but I'd gotten to that funny peaceful feeling that comes after a real cry. You know what I mean? When the heaving is done and you're all worn out? To Sandy I said, "I don't know what to do. I've always had long hair. Can you really fix it? It's pretty bad, huh?"

Sandy laughed. "Sugar, I can work magic, *real* magic. You'll be gorgeous, I swear it. You won't even recognize yourself. Just let me ask one question. How adventurous are you?"

"I don't know," I said. "What do you mean by adventurous?"

"I mean," said Sandy, "how important is it to you to look like everyone else?"

"Oh," I said. "Not very, I guess. Though I've never thought of that as adventurous."

Beside me, Mom laughed.

After that, I closed my eyes and gave myself over to Sandy's magic fingers, the fruity smell of the shampoo, and the warm suds. I think I even fell asleep for a minute.

When we were done with the washing and massage, Sandy said, "Allez-oop!" really cheerfully, like I wasn't an idiot with jacked-up hair that smelled like death. Then I was in a different chair, and Sandy quickly started pinning up sections of hair, then snipping and slicing with a razor. I waited to see what she was going to do. I couldn't even imagine what I'd look like. I only knew I wouldn't look like myself. I'd look different. Normally, that would have made me crazy, but for some reason, it was kind of exciting.

Then Sandy was putting some other kind of goop in my hair and drying it and brushing it, and her arms were moving all around me super fast, and she was smiling and nodding and talking, though I couldn't hear a word she said. After that, she shut off the hair dryer and swirled my chair around so I could see myself in the mirror and . . .

Whoa.

I sat staring at a girl I'd never met before. I didn't recognize her. I didn't know who she was, this girl. She looked a bit like me but different too. Her eyes were somehow bigger, fringed with a layered bang that slanted across her forehead. On one side, my hair fell into a neat point, just below my chin. On the other side, it was clipped short, close to my scalp, almost shaved. It looked lopsided but not in a bad way. When I shook my head, I felt everything fall into place. Just so.

I tilted my head. "I don't look like me at all."

"Yes," said Mom. "You *do*. You look like a new version of you."

I stared at her. "Well, I don't look like the me I *know*," I said.

"*Yet*," said my mom. "You don't know her yet. And if this version isn't quite right and you want to look like a different you tomorrow, you can try that version on too. We'll get you some headbands if you want, maybe even a little makeup. You can play with your new look. The thing is that you can be any version of you that you want to be. You always think your dad and I want to change you, and you seem so scared of that. But you know what? *I* think you're wonderful and just want you to be open to *all* the ways you can be wonderful. All the Zippys inside you. I want you to trust that whatever you try on or try out, it will be fine."

I wasn't so sure, but she wanted an answer, so I said, "I guess."

"And maybe we could go shopping too," she said. "Get some new duds to go with your new haircut. It might even be *fun*. Remember fun? We used to have fun."

"But aren't you mad at me?" I asked. "Even a little bit? For cutting my hair?"

"Oh, absolutely," said Mom. "You're a big dummy and I'm furious, but I also love you and want you to feel beautiful and happy. I'm sure I can find a good reason to scream at you later for something. How does that sound?"

"It sounds okay," I said. "But you know you're a very weird mom, right?"

"Definitely," she said, with a smile.

⋆☆ *23* ☆⋆

New Old Information

I'm sort of embarrassed to write this down, but the next day, despite everything that had happened with Miriam, I was actually kind of excited. To go to school, I mean. I didn't want to get my hopes up or anything, but I sort of thought I looked a little bit . . . pretty. Or, if not pretty, at least interesting. I didn't look like anyone else at school, that was for sure. And with Mom's lip gloss and my one pair of dangly earrings, I looked older too. I stood staring at myself in the mirror again before school, swinging my earrings back and forth and fussing my slanty bangs with my fingers. All those years with my witch-hair, and yet somehow I still felt like me, on the inside. It was like this new self had been waiting for me to find her. Not like I'd put anything on but more like I'd taken something off. Like a snake—like I'd stripped away an old layer of Zippy and found a fresh one underneath. Anyway, it was nice to forget about magic for a minute, to be distracted by the real world for a change.

Of course, the nearer I got to the school building, the less certain I felt. My feet moved slower that last block, and I began to wonder if maybe I should have brought a hat along. I remember thinking that maybe I should take off the earrings, at least, so that nobody thought I was trying too hard or thinking I was anything special. In my head I could hear Bea's voice, saying, *The main thing, Zippy, is that you don't want to* overdo *it. Because that's the kiss of death.* But I took a deep, brave breath and blurred myself into the crowd of kids heading in through the main doors of the building.

I walked quickly through the halls, managed to keep my head down and avoid eye contact with anyone at all, until I was sitting in my Advisory, where Ms. Marty, taking attendance, looked up and out into the classroom and called my name. "Zippy McConnell?" I watched her eyes scan the room for me several times without finding me, before finally connecting. Her eyes lit up. "Zippy!" she shouted. "Oh my gosh, look at you. You look H-O-T, girl. HOT. That haircut is *everything!*"

I felt myself blushing right away, and sinking down into my chair, but also, I couldn't seem to wipe the silly grin off my face. I didn't know how to feel. I was sure that nobody had ever, in my whole entire life, used that word about me. *Hot*, really?

Now, all around me, chairs were scraping the floor and heads were turning to look. I glanced down at my hands on top of my notebook and felt my earrings shift and settle. I licked the gloss on my lips and waited for the moment to end.

"Zippy does legit look nice," said Hank Thomas behind me.

"Yeah. Looking good, Zipster!" said Ellie Johnston, over near the window.

"Anyway, better than you, Ellie," called Darius Genovese.

Then there was laughing all around me, but somehow it didn't sound mean. Everyone was just joking and messing around, like they would with anyone else. So I peered up, searching for Ms. Marty again, since she seemed the safest place to settle my gaze. She smiled, winked at me, and continued with attendance.

And do you know what? The whole day was mostly like that. People kept telling me how nice I looked. Ms. Jenkins, the principal, said I looked like I belonged in a punk band, which I'm pretty sure was a compliment, coming from her. Mr. Norbert wanted to know if I'd gotten taller, which seemed like a very weird thing to say, but I guess he meant it to be nice. Mr. Norbert never seems to know the right thing to say to anyone. You almost have to feel sorry for him.

At lunch, I decided if there was ever going to be a day to venture back into the cafeteria, this might be it. So I took a deep breath, walked into that loud, spaghetti-smelling room, and glanced around, searching for Bea. When I saw that she was sitting alone, I made my way over. Slowly.

"Um, hi?" I said, standing beside her table.

"Hi," said Bea, taking a sip of her milk. She didn't ask me to sit down, so I didn't.

"I got a haircut," I said. Which felt stupid the second it was out of my mouth. "I mean, obviously, I guess."

"Yep, you sure did," said Bea as she popped a grape into her mouth and chewed.

After that, I wasn't sure what to say, and we just stared at each other for a minute until Bea had swallowed her grape.

"How's Liv?" I asked at last.

"I don't know," she said, shaking her head. "I'm not in charge of Liv. How's your *exorcism*?"

"Oh," I said. "That." And suddenly, all my cheerful confidence was gone. I'd spent the whole day avoiding thinking about Miriam. But with that one word, Bea brought everything into a terrible focus. For some reason, I found myself reaching up to touch the prickly hair at the nape of my neck. "Can I . . . ummm . . . can I sit down?" I asked. "With you?"

"It's a free country," Bea said with a shrug.

I set my lunch on the table and sat down. "The truth is," I said, "I made a mess of things, if you really want to know."

"Sucks to be you, I guess," said Bea coldly.

"Sometimes," I said. "Sometimes it super does."

"Yeah?" said Bea. "Well, do you want to know something?

Sometimes it sucks to be all of us, Zippy. For instance, it sucks to be *me* when I'm trying to talk to a friend in the library and she literally runs away like a baby."

"Stop!" I hissed. "Stop calling me a baby. I hate when you do that. Just because I'm not obsessed with makeup and boys doesn't mean I'm a baby. Also, it wasn't personal. It wasn't about you. I had things to deal with yesterday."

She nodded. "Yuh-huh," she said. "Important things like haircuts? Or pretend exorcisms?" She rolled her eyes. "And I'm not obsessed with boys. But you know, Zippy? I'm glad it worked out the way it did. I needed that reminder. You can go play witch all alone, and I'll just figure out how to get along without you, I guess."

"I'm not *playing* witch," I said.

"Well, then, what are you doing?"

For a moment, I thought about how it would feel to tell her the whole story, the whole big mess of it. She wouldn't have believed me, but it might have been a relief, to not be alone with my secrets. I missed her. Even after everything the last few weeks, I missed Bea. I did.

"I'm not playing witch," was all I said, again.

Bea's face looked serious. "Look, I really wanted to tell you something yesterday, Zippy. I needed to talk to . . . a *real* friend. I tried twice. But you know what? Sometimes you're pretty selfish."

I wasn't expecting that. "I was just in a hurry," I said.

"Clearly," she said, rising from the table. "I guess there are more important things than your best friend when she needs to talk."

"Well, do you want to tell me now, instead?" I asked, looking up at her.

"No," she said, shaking her head. "Not anymore." She lifted her tray to leave. "Well, maybe someday. I don't know. Try me tomorrow."

"Tomorrow I won't be here," I said. "It's Jewish hungry-apology day. You remember how that is?" I faked a smile.

"Oh well, then," said Bea. She didn't smile back.

⋆☆24☆⋆

A Once-in-a-Lifetime
Educational Experience

I walked home slowly that day. I guess because I didn't know exactly what to do with myself. The last week or so I'd sprinted for the farm, but now, what was there to sprint for? Like I'd told Bea, I'd messed everything up. I didn't have a solution for Miriam, unless I wanted to attempt whatever that exorcism thing was, which I didn't, even if I could figure out how. I didn't want to send Miriam to the Sitra Achra, if it existed. She was better off with me, even if we were both miserable. So I just trudged along, until out of nowhere, I was surrounded by girls. Swallowed up by the walking group. They were suddenly all around me on the sidewalk, talking and yammering. Minnah and Tess and Lane and Leah. And Bea, who didn't even make eye contact.

We ended up moving on like that, and I was trapped, forced to listen as Tess complained about homework and Minnah gossiped about some boy she liked, whose name I didn't catch. I tried to fade into the background until we made it to the intersection of Woodland and Ormewood, where the group usually turned for the coffee shop, and I knew I could escape. But when we stopped at the red light, I heard a familiar voice calling my name.

"Zippy! Zippy!" she sang.

I froze. It was Miriam. Miriam, in her long, stained dress, with her tangled hair and her huge dark eyes. Miriam, with her wings, even if nobody but me could see them. Miriam, sprinting toward us. "Zippy," she cried. "I was afraid I'd miss you. Come to the farm! We need to talk!"

The other girls all stopped and turned to stare. "Who's this?" asked Leah, pointing.

Bea narrowed her eyes curiously. "Why the farm?" she asked.

"She's . . . my friend," I said at last. "Her name's Miriam. She's new in the neighborhood. I've been showing her around." Which wasn't technically a lie.

"Hello," said Miriam, smiling. She looked much happier than the last time I'd seen her. "It's nice to meet you all. I haven't met any of Zippy's other friends." I cringed at the word *friends*.

Lane laughed. "Wild! You're like Zippy 2.0."

"Huh?" I asked. "What do you mean?"

"She kinda looks like you?" Lane said. "Only the reverse. Like, she's all long, light hair and a white dress, and you're all long, dark hair and a black dress. Or you were, anyway, until today. Maybe she's, like, your replacement, Bizarro-Zippy."

"Oh yeah," I said, examining Miriam, the ragged hem of her grass-stained dress. "I guess."

As the others turned away from us to continue their conversation, Miriam grabbed my hand, setting off prickles in my fingers that made me flinch. "I came to find you," she said. "I found another memory. I thought it might help us. That's good, isn't it?"

"Sure," I said, nodding as though I had any idea, really, what we were going to do with the memories. I hadn't turned out to be much of a detective. Plus, it was hard to give Miriam my full attention that day, with the walking group so close by. "What kind of memory?"

"Well," said Miriam, "there was water in this one too, only not a big ocean. I was sitting in a small pool, and above me, the sun suddenly changed into a black sun, with a bright rim all around it. The sky was orange, and my eyes hurt to look at it, but I did anyway. I floated in the pool and then everyone was singing, but I didn't know the song. What do you think it means?"

"I don't know, But that sounds like an eclipse, maybe?" Out of the corner of my eye I saw Bea pivot away from the group to stare at me, eyebrows raised, though I wasn't sure why. As the light changed and the walking group headed off, I turned back to Miriam.

"An eclipse?" asked Miriam. "What's an eclipse?"

"It's when the moon covers the sun," I said. "I've never seen one myself. They're pretty rare. . . . But hey, I guess if you can remember more, we might be able to figure out where you would have seen one and when. That might be helpful, sure. Or if you can remember the song . . ."

Suddenly Bea was standing with us. "What did you just say?"

"Zippy was explaining a memory I had," Miriam said with a friendly smile. "She said it sounded like an eclipse."

"Yeah," said Bea. "I heard that part. I also heard her say *she'd* never seen one, and I know that's a lie." She turned to me. "What's going on here, and who is she?"

"A lie?" I said. "What are you talking about? I'm not lying."

"Come on, Zippy," said Bea. "You know that's not true. We saw an eclipse together, just last year. Out near Athens. Remember?"

I blinked. "We did?"

"Seriously?" Bea said. "How could you possibly forget? My parents rented that Airbnb with the pool, and we both skipped? We decided to go swimming and watch the eclipse at the same time?"

"I . . . don't remember that," I said, shaking my head. "Not at all."

"That's just not possible," said Bea. "Unless you're like . . . seriously ill. You don't remember? Your mom said it was okay to miss school, because it was a 'once-in-a-lifetime educational experience.' We ate all that watermelon. . . ."

Just then I looked over at Miriam. She was nodding up and down. "Yes!" she said. "It was just like that for me too. There *was* melon. I remember spitting the seeds."

I glanced back at Bea. "Miriam said there was singing. Do you remember singing?"

Bea nodded slowly, and even before she began to sing, I knew what was coming. It wasn't a memory at all, only that I had known Bea too well for too long. We'd sung too many rounds of out-of-tune karaoke in her living room for me not to guess.

"'Nothing I can do . . . ,'" Bea sang under her breath.

"'A total eclipse of the heart . . .'" I finished the line.

"That's it!" Miriam said brightly, turning to me. "That's the very melody I heard. How did you guess? And how do you know it? Is this more of your magic?"

"No," I said to Miriam. "No. It's not my magic. And what you're remembering isn't yours at all, don't you see? It's mine. *My* memory with Bea. It's a moment from my life, that you . . . somehow borrowed from me."

"I don't understand," said Miriam. "It's my memory. I *was*

there. I know it. I saw it. I have a picture, in my mind."

What I felt then was dread like I'd never felt before, an ugly tangle of thoughts. The feeling when Miriam and I touched, that tingle of magic that soon became painful. What I'd thought was a pulse of energy, a way of sustaining her, was more than that. In a moment of terrible and sudden clarity, I knew what that pain was in me. It was loss, the pain of my own memories, slipping away.

"Don't you see?" I asked. "*That* must have been what was happening each time we touched. Everything you thought you remembered . . . Those are *my* memories. Or they used to be. Since I don't have them anymore myself."

"Oh," said Miriam, paler than I'd seen her in days. "Then, I've been stealing from you? All this time?"

"I don't know," I said. "Maybe." But I was lying. I did know, in that moment. I could feel the truth of it in my gut.

Bea had been silent all this time, watching Miriam and me. Now she spoke. "What exactly is happening here, Zippy? You said you only just met Miriam. But where did she come from? Who is she?"

"We don't know!" I said. "That's the whole problem. I don't know where I brought her from. Or how, exactly. Or *what* she is, even! I gave her the name Miriam myself. I told you, I made a big mess, Bea. It was an accident . . . just some words I said. I'm not sure how I did it or what the words meant.

But it's not a game. It's definitely real. *Too* real. And I can't seem to undo it."

I watched Bea process what I'd just said, take it all in. She glanced from me to Miriam, and then back to me. "I . . . I don't know what to say," she said. "You're suggesting that you, like, *summoned* her from some other world or whatever? That's . . . a lot. Wow."

"Yeah," I said. "I know."

"Magic?" asked Bea. "For-*real* magic? Seriously, Zip?"

I nodded miserably.

Then Miriam stepped toward me and spoke, in a calm, grave voice. "If that's true," she said, "this has to end, Zippy. Doesn't it?"

I only shrugged then. I didn't know what to say.

"It does," she said. "It *has* to be over. Wherever I came from, whatever I am, I don't belong here, do I?"

I shook my head. "*No*," I said, the word catching in my throat. "I *don't* think you belong here. But I don't know what to do about that, Miriam. I don't know how to help you, how to fix this mess I've made. I wish I did."

"And I'm hurting you . . . ," said Miriam. "I *am*, aren't I?"

She looked around then. I'll never forget it, how she stared around at Woodland Avenue, quiet on a weekday afternoon. She stared up at the sun and around at the lush trees and the late-summer flowers. She knelt down and pulled a fading pink zinnia from the garden beside where we were standing. "It's beautiful," she said. "This place, your world. I wonder if my world is beautiful too. Wherever it is that I belong." She looked down at the flower in her hand, and I saw that there were tears in her eyes. "Do you think I'll ever find it?"

"I hope so," I said, and discovered that there were tears in my eyes too. "I hate that I did this to you, Miriam. I'm so sorry."

Then, right there, in the middle of Woodland Avenue, Miriam unfolded her wings, shook them loose, and raised them above her head. She stood up on her tippy-toes, and suddenly she looked taller, straighter, as if she was reaching for something.

"What's she doing?" asked Bea.

"You can't see her wings?" I asked. "Really? Even now?"

Bea didn't have time to answer because a moment later, Miriam took off, lifted herself up into the air over our heads.

Whuff.

But that wasn't the only sound this time. Because as Miriam flew away, the blue sky filled with the sound of her screaming. An animal sound, of pain and rage and confusion. It was a sound I hadn't heard since that first afternoon at the farm.

I followed her with my eyes for as long as I could, and then I turned back to look at Bea. "Did you . . . ?" I started to ask.

She cut me off. "Yep," said Bea, still staring at the sky where Miriam had been. "Yep, I sure did. *That* I saw. Wow. I'm just . . . wow."

"I wonder why you couldn't see the wings then," I said.

"Maybe," said Bea, "because I didn't want to."

"Yeah," I said. "Maybe that's it."

We began to walk home then, just the two of us, like we'd done a million times before. Only it felt different that day. *We* felt different. Bea and I were both quiet, each of us lost in our thoughts. I didn't ask what she was thinking about, and she didn't ask me either.

But when we got to her house, Bea turned around and asked, "Hey, do you want to come in? It's taco night. You could stay for dinner. Mom was just saying she misses you."

I shook my head. "No," I said. "That would be so nice, so normal. But there's something I really need to do, if I can figure out how. I need to go home."

"Yeah," said Bea. "I figured. That makes sense. But then . . . do you want company? I could come with you and help—"

I cut her off. "No," I said. "Thanks for the offer, but I'm pretty sure I need to do this alone. Or fail to do this alone. Whatever *this* turns out to be."

"Okay," said Bea. "Well, just so you know, I'm here."

★☆ 25 ☆★

Face of Delusion

*H*ere's something I wonder: Did you understand about Miriam before you read that last chapter? Did you guess? Maybe you did, and you were thinking I was kind of an idiot all that time, because I didn't figure it out sooner. But the truth is that when things are happening to you, in the present, they're a lot harder to see clearly. Until Bea was there to remember *with* Miriam, to share her memory, I couldn't see that all the moments with Miriam were pieces to a big puzzle.

But now, I understood. It wasn't just that Miriam was stealing from me but that we were hurting each other. I understood how I could remember the flavor of smoked salmon, though I'd never tasted it in my life. I understood how I'd suddenly been able to play piano and read Hebrew. I understood how

Miriam had remembered a trip to someplace that looked remarkably like our family cruise to Alaska. And why I hadn't. I understood how she'd found her way right to the stone lion in Oakland. Though it was *me* who'd walked past it on a field trip, not her. How many memories had she taken that I would never even know about? How many pictures were gone forever?

Was this what a dybbuk actually was? Not a spirit who possessed people's bodies, but who possessed their lives, one memory at a time? If that was true, none of the old men in my book knew much about dybbuks. Was it possible the books were wrong? Miriam wasn't wicked. She wasn't just a thief. It was much more complicated than that. She was hungry, lonely, lost. And so was I. Maybe we can do wicked things without becoming wicked. I'll have to think about that.

In any case, I still didn't know how to do an exorcism. I didn't *want* to do an exorcism. But I felt cornered, confused. Miriam couldn't stay forever, stealing my memories, and she couldn't survive in this world any other way. As much as I hated to consider it, this might be our only answer, and so I had research to do. I didn't really even know what it was exactly that I was so scared to try. So I went home that day, took a deep breath, and typed the words "Dybbuk Exorcism" into my laptop.

What I found was really confusing, and kind of upsetting. Even if I wanted to *conduct a horrifying and sacred ritual to force the demon-spirit out of the host*, I wasn't sure where I was going to find a *tzaddik* (an extra-boss rabbi) or *ten men who had purified themselves* (I didn't know what that even meant), and *dressed in corpse-shrouds and holy parchment.*

But eventually, I stumbled onto another exorcism page, one that read *Jewish ritual for the expulsion of displaced spirits.* That sounded slightly less horrible. I read it carefully. And in the end, if we were going to have to do something to separate me and Miriam, I figured this was as good as I was going to find. Unfortunately, I couldn't find it in the original Hebrew, only the English, but that will probably make it easier for you, whoever you are, to follow it.

Who are you?
Depart from humanity and from the offspring of the holy ones!
For your face is a face of delusion, and your horns are horns of fantasy.

You are darkness, not light, wickedness, not righteousness.
The Commander of the Army, the LORD, *will bring you down into deepest Sheol,*
and he will close the two gates of bronze through which no light may enter,
and the sun will not appear for you that shines upon the righteous.

Holding the prayer or spell or whatever it was, I read silently, mouthing the words. Of course, the whole prayer felt really dark and weird to me, but still, I printed it out, folded the paper, and put it in my pocket. Then I went into the dining room for dinner.

Often, Jewish families will go to synagogue on erev Yom Kippur—but by this point, you probably won't be shocked to hear that we don't follow all the rules like that. We fast, and we go to services on the afternoon of Yom Kippur, and we break our fast with breakfast-for-dinner, which I love. But I don't think we've ever gone to the evening service the night before. That night, I was especially glad for that fact as I gobbled down a grilled cheese sandwich and drank three glasses of water (dehydration is the hardest part of fasting, trust me). After that, I asked Mom if I could go out for a walk before bed and headed straight for Red's Farm.

Walking there, I didn't even know what to hope for. But if I was being honest with myself, whether it was by exorcism or something else, I knew in my bones that if I could find Miriam where we'd always met, it was probably going to be the last time I would ever see her. I was scared of the spell or prayer or whatever it was in my pocket. I was sorry for Miriam. I was afraid I'd fail her, let her down. And I was frustrated, even angry, that this connection between us meant that I had to send her away. That felt so wrong. But that didn't make it untrue, did it?

When I got to the farm, I lingered on the gravel road that led into it, not quite ready for what came next. Unsure of what I was about to do. But I could smell honeysuckle everywhere, and that felt like an omen or something. I remember asking myself, *What would happen now if this were a book?* Now, of course, it *is* a book, since I'm writing all this down. But I didn't know the answer to that question then. I had no clue. I only knew that I was going to try. I took a deep breath as I swung open the gate to the farm.

"Miriam," I called as I walked down the hill, past the oak tree.

"Miriam!" I shouted as I neared the rock by the creek.

But she didn't come.

And she didn't come.

Until finally . . .

Whuff.

Then, she was beside me, on the bank of the creek. She folded her wings and walked over, sat down across from me on the rock. She was trying not to look hungry, but I could see it in her face and the way her hands trembled in her lap. She looked so pale and when I reached out a hand to her, she shook her head and looked away from me.

"Are you all right?" I asked.

Miriam shrugged.

"You're not," I said. "Please, let me help you."

"No," she said. "I won't take anything else from you, not

anymore. Your stories, your memories, everything that has happened to you, that's what you are. I can't do that to you. I've stolen so much already. . . . We'll never know what I've stolen. I'm a danger to you, Zippy. It was one thing when I didn't know it, but now I do."

"Well, then I've stolen from you too," I said. "It must be you who played piano, you who spoke Hebrew, knew the prayers. . . ."

Miriam shook her head. "Even if that's true," she said, "that doesn't make it better. It doesn't solve anything. I want this to be over, to go home . . . or to go somewhere other than here. To be done with this place. Whatever that means. I don't want to stay here and hurt you, or anyone else."

I looked at her for a long time. At least a minute. But I couldn't think of anything else to say, and so I pulled the folded paper from my pocket.

She glanced at the page in my hand. She already knew what it was; I didn't have to explain. She took a deep breath.

"You really want to try this?" I asked, staring down at the sheet of paper. "You sure?"

"If you *don't* do it," she said, "I'll just leave. I mean it. I'll fly away, to the loneliest cliff in the sea, and stay there forever. I won't hurt you anymore. It's worse than the hunger, even. Knowing that I'm hurting you. Please, help me end this."

"But what if I do this wrong and you—"

Miriam shook her head. "Then your fear is holding me hostage."

There we were, on the very same rock where I'd begun all of this. Not on Rosh Hashanah, but on erev Yom Kippur. It was cooler now than it had been then. The breeze tickled the hair on my bare neck.

So I stood up, took a deep breath, and began to read.

"Who are you?" I began. "Depart from humanity . . ."

Almost immediately, Miriam's eyes went wide. "Ahh . . ."

It wasn't easy to keep going then. Something was happening, only I didn't know just what. Still, I read. "Depart from humanity, and from the offspring of the holy ones! For your face is a face of delusion, and your horns are horns of fantasy. . . ."

Now her eyes were closed, and her wings had unfolded. She was trembling all over. Her back was arched, but I didn't know if she was in pain or if she was feeling something else. She was glowing now. Like a shell on the beach with the last bit of sunset shining on her.

"You are darkness, not light . . . ," I read. ". . . wickedness, not righteousness. . . ."

That was when she screamed. Bright and loud, she cried out. And when she crumpled to the ground, I stopped.

"No!" I shouted. "No, this can't be right. It can't be. You are *not* wickedness. You are good and this whole thing is a lie."

"Zippy!" cried Miriam from the ground. "Don't stop. You can't. . . ."

But I stood over her, and I shook my head. Because I was right. And that wasn't something I knew because I'd found it in a book or someone else had told me. It was something I could *feel*. Deep within me.

"I'm right," I said, putting the paper back in my pocket. "I am."

"Oh, Zippy," she said weakly, pushing herself up to sitting. "If only we could go back to the beginning, start over."

But when is that ever possible?

✦ 27 ✦

Thank God, I Guess

The next day was Yom Kippur, the Day of Atonement. So I feel like maybe I should tell you a little bit about that in case you don't know. Remember how I explained about tashlich, about how Jews like to start the holiday by making a list of regrets, and then tossing crumbs into the water? Well, that whole process ends ten days later, on Yom Kippur, when the Book of Life is sealed. I don't really know much about it, but apparently a lot of folks think that you have those ten days to apologize to people and straighten things out, to fix things and make peace, and then I guess God forgives you for all the bad stuff, and you start the new year off right. Something like that? Whatever you do or don't believe, it seems like a stretch to expect you can fix your life in ten days. But what do

I know? In any case, that whole process is called T'shuvah—which means "Return."

So yeah, on Yom Kippur, you fast and atone, and since you're super hungry and cranky and sorry and faint, you can't do much else that day. Everyone just sits in the synagogue, listening to other people praying, and watching the yellow sunlight stream through the big windows into the room. It's beautiful and peaceful and the music is nice, but eventually you sort of assume everyone is secretly thinking about exactly what they want to eat as soon as they can eat again, because that's how you're feeling.

Only this year was different. This year I had a lot to think about. So I sat there, listening to Rabbi Dan and a bunch of other folks lead us in prayers. I listened to the choir sing. I stood and sat when everyone else stood and sat. But I wasn't thinking about how hungry I was. Instead I was thinking about Miriam. I was thinking about what I should do next. What hadn't we tried? I thought back over the spells I knew, all the things I'd read over my years as a witch. But none of it got me anywhere. My magic just wasn't strong enough. And Rabbi Dan's book didn't seem to have the right answers either, from what I could understand of it. Anyway, they didn't offer any non-exorcism options when it came to dybbuks—if that was even what Miriam was. When you assume something is wicked, I guess one solution is enough.

Then, right there in the middle of the slow chanting of

the Ashamnu, something happened. I heard Miriam's voice in my head. Sharp and clear. As if she were sitting behind me, speaking in my ear. We were all standing and praying when it happened, when I heard her speak these words, just as she had the day before:

If only we could go back to the beginning, start over.

I flipped around, searching, but obviously, she wasn't really there. It was only a memory, an echo. And what would it help, anyway? We'd come as close to the beginning as we could come, hadn't we? Stood on the rock together, in that place where I'd summoned her.

Then I thought, was that right? Was that actually the beginning of the story? Was there something that came before?

A few minutes later, it happened again. *If only we could go back to the beginning, start over.*

This time, the voice gave me prickles. I gasped, and when I looked around me, it was the strangest thing—the light in the room changed. Something shifted, and the light through the window wasn't yellow anymore. It was clean and white, and it almost looked like there was glitter, swirling around the room. The dust motes, maybe. I couldn't have said. But I sat and watched the glitter fall and swirl and float all over the room, expecting to hear Miriam's voice again. Only I didn't, and when the prayer ended and everyone in the sanctuary sat down, I decided to take a walk.

Quietly, I excused myself and hurried from the room. I

went out into the yard, where I sat on a park bench to think.

Nothing came to me immediately. Nothing that could solve my problem. But it was nice in the yard, and I sat there awhile, until I felt like I might get in trouble for staying away too long. But just at that moment, someone tapped me on the shoulder, and I shot up and turned.

"I didn't know you were allowed to take breaks!" I said to Rabbi Dan.

He laughed. "Who's going to tell a rabbi when they're allowed to take breaks, Zippy? Gut yontif to you." (That means "Happy Holiday," pretty much.)

"Gut yontif," I said, hoping I was pronouncing it right. "Why are you out here?"

"I saw you leave," he said. "And you've been on my mind all week, since our lesson."

"I have?"

He nodded and took a seat on the bench, so I sat down again too. "Sure. You've asked a lot of hard questions, and I can see that you're working through something, so I wanted to let you know that this might be a good place to do that. We come here together as Jews, sure, but even more than that, we come here as people. We're a family, and this is a place for all the parts of you, Zippy. Not just the Jewish ones."

"Thanks," I said, blushing a little. I didn't know what else to say, and I was actually getting sort of misty, for some reason. Probably because I was hungry, I guessed. And there are allergies in Georgia in the fall. But also, it was really nice, what he'd said. It wasn't nothing.

"I was wondering, how did the story come out?"

"The story?"

"About the dybbuk," he said. "You were working on a piece of fiction, for school, I think? I lent you that book."

"Oh, that. It's . . . Well, it's not so great."

"No?" he asked. "What's the trouble?"

I tried to think of what to say. "I guess just that I don't know how to end it. The girl in the story, the one who discovered the dybbuk? She couldn't go through with it. The exorcism, I mean. She couldn't bring herself to say the words. She was afraid."

"An interesting choice!" said Rabbi Dan. "What was she afraid of?"

"They'd become friends," I explained. "And even if the dybbuk was doing bad things, it just didn't feel right to the girl, to send it away."

Rabbi Dan thought about that a second, then said, "Well, then it was the right choice for the story."

"Yeah," I said, searching my mind for a way to say what I needed to say. "But see, because of that, the story can't end. The characters are just stuck. The girl can't bring herself to hurt the dybbuk, because the dybbuk is so nice. But the dybbuk also can't stay, because it's hurting the girl."

"Hmmm," said Rabbi Dan. "I see your dilemma."

We sat a moment, just thinking on the bench, the rabbi and I.

"Maybe," he said after a bit, "if the dybbuk was so kind and friendly, she wasn't actually a dybbuk at all. Have you considered that?"

"What else could she be?" I asked. "In the story, I mean."

Rabbi Dan shifted on the park bench so that he could look me straight in the eyes. "In your reading, did you come across something called an ibbur?"

I shook my head.

Rabbi Dan smiled. "Ah, then you didn't finish the book."

"No," I said. "I tried, but I didn't understand so much of it. And honestly, I don't think they got a lot right about dybbuks. So those were the only parts I read."

Rabbi Dan laughed. "Fair enough. Maybe it was the wrong book. For you, for now. But you might want to read about ibburs. For your story, I mean."

"Okay," I said. "What's an ibbur?"

"Ibburs are less widely discussed today, and like with all folklore, there are many different and sometimes conflicting ideas about what they are. But the myth goes back just as far as that of the dybbuk. In the thirteenth century, it was believed that spirits could possess people in a fragmentary way, such that the possession was beneficial to both the host and the transmigrating soul."

"I'm not sure I understand," I said.

"It means that, while dybbuks make the host's life worse, ibburs improve things. They do mitzvot. Do you think that this creature in your book has made the world a better place?" He raised his eyebrows.

"I . . . don't know," I said. "Maybe. I'll have to think about it."

Rabbi Dan nodded. "Another difference is that ibburs don't just show up. They're summoned."

I froze. "What did you say?"

"I said that ibburs must be summoned. In much of the folklore, anyway. People call on ibburs to help correct things, to repair the world."

"But . . . what if the creature was stealing things? That can't be good, right?"

Rabbi Dan stood back up. "I guess that depends," he said. "On why the creature took the things they stole and also whether the things the creature stole were able to be spared. Sometimes, we don't need all we have. Does that make sense?"

"No!" I said. "It doesn't. It's like my *story* has all these missing pieces in it. Things I'm not sure of. Questions I can't figure out."

Rabbi Dan smiled, in that way grown-ups sometimes do when you're most confused, like they think they helped you and it's not their problem anymore. "Then we're back where we started a few weeks ago," he said. "Life *is* questions, Zippy. Life *is* uncertainty. But how lucky we are that we can come together here, in this place, to wrestle with the mystery. Just like this. In the sun. On a good sturdy bench. Such a blessing. That we never need to be alone with our struggles."

Then he left and I was by myself again, just sitting there.

"Back to the beginning," I said aloud.

A moment later, I said it again. "Back to the beginning."

Right before I jumped up from the bench, ran inside to get my parents.

"Miriam," I called as I ran the path into the farm, past the gate and to the old oak tree.

But for once, she didn't *whuff*. She wasn't up in the tree. Instead, she emerged from the garden, on foot, munching on a huge tomato, the juice dripping down her chin. She ate hungrily but sadly. As she neared, I could see she was fading again, growing thinner. In the dusk, she looked almost gray.

"There you are!" I shouted. "Come with me, to the rock."

"Why?" she asked.

"You said you wanted to go back to the beginning," I answered. "And that's where I was when this all began."

"But we've been there so many times, Zippy. What difference will it make now?"

"Because," I said. "It's not just a matter of where it began but how. Or I'm hoping that's true, anyway."

Once we were seated on the rock, Miriam still chewing her tomato, I pulled the little red book from my pocket. Why had

I kept it hidden all this time? Because it was empty. Or it had appeared so, anyway. I held it out in front of me, stared down at it. I was careful, gentle, since the spine was now cracked, the pages coming loose. I set it on the rock.

"What is it?" asked Miriam.

"It's where this all truly began," I said. "Or I think so, anyway. I found the words I spoke to summon you in this book. They're gone now, but the book is still here, and I thought maybe it could help us. I don't know where I called you from, and I don't know what you are. There's so much I don't know. But I do know that it all began here, with this." I patted the book.

"What does it say inside?" asked Miriam, looking down at the red-leather binding.

"Nothing," I replied. "It's entirely blank. There are no words. But there *were* words, just a few, and I think I remember them, now."

Miriam cocked her head at that; I don't think she quite understood what I'd figured out, not yet. But she would. And so, as the sun was setting above us, as Miriam's chin dripped tomato juice, I looked out over the farm, and I called the words of power. I called the words that felt true, even though they weren't mine. Without even knowing what they meant, I shouted, "PAOHLHA CHAI!"

And then it happened.

It happened!

There was no denying the magic this time. The air all

around us began to smell of cinnamon and woodsmoke. Overhead, we heard the *whuff* of wings, the barred owl, off for his evening hunt.

And on the rock before us, the little red book began to glow.

"Oh!" cried Miriam. "I remember this. I do!" She reached out and took the book. She opened it.

From within the small red book then, there was light. Something glowing faintly in its pages, shining up into Miriam's pale face. When I glanced down over her shoulder, I could see that there were letters scrawled on the pages now, perfect Hebrew lettering, dark markings in the blazing book. It looked like the pages were on fire, and I had to turn my face away.

But Miriam read the words.

"What does it say?" I asked.

Miriam didn't answer. She was too busy reading. It was like she was gulping the book, swallowing something delicious. She turned a page and gave a laugh, as all around her, the light from the book glittered and glowed, like a swarm of fireflies.

"What?" I asked. "What is it?"

Still, she didn't reply. She only sighed faintly. "Oh yes, that's right," she said somberly at one point.

"Miriam!" I cried. "Please. Tell me, what's in that book?"

At last she looked up, and her face was full of that odd light. Her eyes were still huge and dark, but they weren't bruised anymore, or lost. Now they were glinting, dancing with flecks of gold.

She smiled. "Why, everything!" she said. "*Everything* is in here. My whole story is in this little book, Zippy. This is my entire life. These are my memories, all the things that mattered to me, good or bad. I wrote them all down, many years ago."

"Oh," I said. "Okay. But . . . why?"

"Because it is good to write things down. A kind of mitzvah. I was training to be a scribe, you see," said Miriam. "I was not allowed to become a sofer, because I was a girl. I could not make a sefer Torah. But I learned just the same. I studied, and then, when I knew how and felt ready, I wrote my own story down, for practice and safekeeping. Everything I knew or remembered of my life, the world around me."

"Everything?" I asked.

She nodded happily. "Everything that mattered. Only after that, the book became lost, and somehow, so did I. *That* part of the story isn't in these pages. It came later, I suppose, and I don't know how it happened. But you see, now that I have my memories back, I'm not empty anymore, Zippy. I'm full again."

I didn't understand, but I nodded anyway. I was happy that Miriam finally knew who she was, but happy wasn't all I felt. Mostly, I was . . . uncertain. "Well," I said, "I'm glad it all worked out for you, Miriam. Thank God, I guess."

She smiled warmly. "Indeed," she said. "Baruch Hashem!

But I'm *not* Miriam, Zippy. Don't you see? My name isn't Miriam. It never was."

"Then what is it?" I asked.

"Well, of course you know!" she said. "You called me here with it, and returned me to myself the same way. My name is Paula. Paula Chaya."

"Paula Chaya?" I said slowly, as if testing the words, tasting them. "But that means all I ever did was say your name. It was never a spell at all. It was never even magic, was it?"

"Who's to say what's magic?" she replied. "Who is to say that a name can't summon? Isn't that precisely what names are for?"

"But then, are you a dybbuk after all?" I asked. "Or an ibbur?"

She shrugged. "I think we are all many things, Zippy," she said. "I can't say for sure *what* I am. But that doesn't concern me any longer. I remember my story, and so I know *who* I am, on the inside. Does it matter what others choose to call me?"

"I . . . guess not," I said. Though of course it was driving me bonkers, the not-knowing.

Miriam smiled. "All this time, Zippy, we were looking for answers, looking to understand things that we may never know for certain. And that was good, a journey we shared! But do you know what? Whether in magic or memory, even if we never understand, I will carry you with me forever now. You showed me things, cared for me, kept me as safe as you could,

and now, here we are, in this beautiful place, one last time."
She laughed out loud. "Isn't that enough for joy? I will always
be grateful."

"I . . . Me too," I said, feeling lost for words. It was true,
what she was saying. I knew it was. And yet. "I'll just miss
you," I said. "I'll never forget you."

Only that was a lie, and I knew it.

After that, she leaned over and hugged me, wrapped me
in her thin arms and held me tight for a quick moment, a hug
so brief I barely felt the prickles begin. Then she sat back and
handed me the little red book. "Here," she said softly. "*You
keep this. I have what I need from it now."

I ran a finger over the leather. "Really?"

She nodded. "I wrote my story down so I would remember
it. And now I do." Then she climbed to her feet, unfolded her
beautiful wings.

"But . . . ," I started to protest.

Miriam glanced down at me one last time. She closed her
eyes, smiled, and shook her head faintly, as if to say, *This part
of the story is over.*

Then she flew away.

Whuff.

"Miriam!" I called after her, jumping to my feet.

But by then she couldn't hear me, and all I could do was
watch her become smaller and smaller in the sky above my
city.

Then I looked down. I opened the tiny red book in my hands, and though the pages had stopped glowing, I saw that they were full of the most beautiful script imaginable. Like the Torah, with crowns and looping lines, thick and black.

Perfect Hebrew. Absolutely perfect.

Except for the fact that I could no longer read a word.

*☆*27*☆*

The Last Chapter Is Where You Wrap Things Up

So that was what happened to Miriam, in the end. Or any-way, it's the last bit of the story I know. What came after that is anyone's guess, and I am determined that this book be *The Truth*. Was she some sort of dybbuk? Was she another kind of Jewish creature I haven't even read about yet? Was she a ghost who just happened to have been Jewish in her lifetime? Was it *my* magic that altered her, or did the little red book have its own powers? And would I miss her forever? Or would my memories of her slip away?

I walked home that night and wondered about all those things. I went around and around in circles in my head. Though I think, in the end, there are just always going to be questions I can't answer about Miriam. I *hate* that.

But do you know what? That isn't the end of this book. Because even though Miriam was gone, I was still here, and *my* story was still going. I'd never thought about that before, the fact that when a story ends, everyone in it still has to go on living their lives. Even Cinderella, say, or Bilbo Baggins. They both woke up the morning after The End and had to brush their teeth. Isn't that funny? Nothing is ever really over, I suppose. Every story just leads to another story. Or maybe a million other stories. It's a little exhausting to think about.

What happened to *me* was that I walked home that evening after Miriam flew off. And even though what I'd just experienced had been pretty intense, I was ravenous from fasting all day, so then I sat down at the dining room table like usual. We lit the candles and said the blessings, and then we all gobbled up delicious waffles and veggie sausage and scrambled eggs with scallions, just like everything was normal. After that, Mom and Dad and I walked to Morelli's for ice cream, which is *our* Jewish tradition.

I guess I wasn't being very chatty, though, because at some point when we were walking home, Mom said, "Hey, Zippy, penny for your thoughts!"

And I sighed and said, "I was just thinking about Miriam."

Then Mom raised her eyebrows and said, "Oh? Is she doing okay?"

So I said, "Yeah, she's fine. But she's gone now. She moved away. For good."

And Mom said, "I'm sorry, honey, that's too bad." Though she looked sort of relieved when she said it.

That made me angry, so then I was like, "No you aren't! You never liked Miriam!" and sped up walking, left my parents in the dust.

"Always a pleasure, Zippy!" shouted Mom after me.

But you know what I realized later that night, when I was trying to fall asleep and couldn't? I think the reason I got mad at Mom was that *I* felt a little relieved too, about Miriam being gone. Relieved to not have to worry so much. Relieved to go back to being a normal kid for a little bit. (Even if I am a witch.) Of course, that made me feel terrible. Could I really let go of someone so easily? Could I really just move on without her? The way Bea had moved on from me? The more I lay there in the darkness, the more I thought maybe I could. But I didn't love that idea, and I found I still couldn't sleep. Until at last I climbed out of bed, pulled the little red book from my WitchKit, and slid it under my mattress. Somehow, after that, I drifted off.

The next morning, I walked over to Bea's house and knocked on the door.

"Hey," I said when she came out.

"Hey!" she said. "What happened with Miriam?"

"She's gone now," I said. "But I'm fine. I guess. Or I will be, anyway. I don't know. . . ."

"Well," said Bea, "I'm glad things worked out. But I'm dying to know—how did you do it? And how did she get here in the first place? There's so much I don't understand."

I thought for a second about what to say. "I'll tell you what I know . . . someday," I said at last. "I promise. But I don't think I'm ready yet. I'm not sure how to begin. Is that all right?"

Bea nodded. "Sure," she said. "Of course. But at least tell me—did you use magic? Like, *for-real* magic? A wand or a potion or something?" She grinned like she was waiting for juicy gossip.

I thought about the little red book and nodded. "Yes," I said. "I used magic. I think I did, anyway. But it feels . . . strange to me. Talking about it with anyone. The whole thing has been a secret for so long. I'm not sure I'm ready to share."

"I get it," said Bea. But I could tell she was a little annoyed. People don't like being left out of things. Still, I realized I wanted to keep the story for myself that day. I didn't want to try to explain how I felt, to pretend I knew exactly what had happened. It was hard enough, just sitting with all the confusing questions that lingered.

So Bea and I walked to school, and for the first time in weeks, I found I wasn't watching her closely, trying to guess what she was thinking and feeling about me. I wasn't worried anymore. I think maybe, compared to everything I'd just been through, it felt silly to stress about Bea. She'd been there forever in my life, and I could see now that she wasn't going away. So we walked along, just talking about schoolwork and other boring stuff.

Until at some point I said, "Hey, Bea, I'm not going to Fall Fling. I decided."

"Yeah, I kinda figured," said Bea.

I nodded my head. "I don't want it to be a big deal. It's just not my thing. You should go and have fun, and then come tell me all about it. Okay?"

"Okay," she said. "And does this mean we're good again? Bea and Zippy? Zippy and Bea?"

I glanced over at her. "It feels okay to me if it feels okay to you."

She nodded. "It feels okay to me."

"Look," I said. "The main thing is that I don't want you to feel like you have to include me in everything anymore. I don't care so much about some of the stuff you're into now, it's true, but I have my own stuff. So we can be friends, and it's still fine if you need to leave me out now and then, a little bit. Maybe that's not so bad."

Bea stopped walking. "No, Zippy . . . ," she said. "No, that's not it. And look, I really am *super* sorry, about ditching you, that whole thing with the walking group. It wasn't okay. I just wanted to see what it felt like."

"You don't have anything to be sorry for," I said. "Really. You're allowed to change, to like things I don't. Let's just be real with each other from now on, okay? Like sisters. And you can have *other* best friends too. I get it."

But Bea shook her head. "No," she said. "*You're* my best friend, Zippy. You always will be. I swear. And honestly, the walking group is kind of boring sometimes. *So* giggly."

"Oh my god, *so* giggly!" I said. We both laughed.

"The thing is," said Bea, "despite all that, it wasn't that I outgrew you. I just sort of . . . outgrew *me*."

"What do you mean?"

"Just . . ." She looked around, and for the first time I could remember, ever, Bea looked kind of lost. "The thing with Liv is that I . . . I *really* like her, Zippy."

"Sure," I said. "I know that. And even if she and I are never friends, that's okay."

"No," said Bea. "You don't understand. I think I *like* her like her. Do you see? She's *definitely* not my best friend. She makes me nervous. She makes me scared. But in a good way. You know what I mean? I get jittery when I see her. But I still just kind of want to be around her, all the time."

"Jittery?"

Bea nodded. "But I don't know how to tell her that. I don't know what to do. Do you get it? *Now* do you get it?"

I could feel my eyes go wide. "Oh! Yes!" I said as it dawned on me what she was telling me. "Of course I get it. And also . . . I don't."

"What do you mean?"

I stood there for a second, looking for the right words. "I

mean," I said, "I understand what you're saying, I just have absolutely no idea what that feels like. I'm just not . . . *there* yet, you know? I don't get jittery like that. I don't feel that way about anyone. But that doesn't mean I don't want you to tell me about it, dummy. And if you and Liv do, like, any *adult hugging* . . . I *really* hope you'll call me right away."

Bea burst out laughing then. "Are you kidding me, Zippy? Adult hugging?"

I shrugged.

Then Bea threw her arms around me and hugged me like she hadn't done since the start of middle school. "You are such a weird, wonderful witch, Zippy McConnell. There is nobody else like you in the world. And I'm glad we're best friends."

So *that* was okay.

After that, things got quieter. More predictable—though, anything after what had happened with Miriam would have been more predictable. I went to school like usual, but now Bea talked me into joining the walking group sometimes, and that was actually not the worst thing ever. I went to my bat mitzvah classes every two weeks, where I found I no longer knew all the prayers and tunes. I also couldn't read Hebrew. It was *hard* again. But I also wasn't scared of it the same way. I just knew I had to study, which I did. Sometimes I studied with Sophie, who turned out to be pretty nice. She wasn't a witch, exactly, but it turned out she read tarot cards and was into meditation. People will surprise you, if you let them.

But you know what I didn't do that whole time? I didn't do any magic. For months, I didn't even try. I went to bed every night with the little red book under my mattress, because it helped me sleep. But I never opened it, and I hid my WitchKit away in the back of my closet. The strange thing was that life was okay that way. Calmer. I think, after everything that had happened with Miriam, I just wasn't sure what I could handle anymore. I knew that my magic was absolutely real, but I also knew it could surprise me in ways I might not be ready for, in ways I couldn't control or understand. I didn't regret summoning Miriam now that she was gone. But I still wondered about her, every day. I still missed her. I still puzzled over what exactly had happened. And I knew I wasn't ready for anything else like that anytime soon. Regular life was confusing enough.

Then, months later, it was time for my bat mitzvah.

If you have never been to a bat mitzvah, here is what happens: Everyone you know comes to town. Family, friends, friends of family, family of friends. Then they all get dressed up and show up at the synagogue on a random Saturday morning. There, you stand at the front of the sanctuary, on the bimah, and everyone stares at you for hours, even though for a lot of the service, you're just doing nothing. Right away, the grown-ups start crying and dabbing their eyes with tissues while the choir sings and then everyone chants the morning service. You get to say some prayers, which is a little nerve-racking but not too bad, because there's a cheat card right there for you, with the English transliteration, just in case. (They should really tell everyone about that in advance. It would help a lot of kids to chill out, I bet.)

After that, it's time for the Torah service, so you get up to read your parsha. The rabbi makes a little speech about what's going to happen next, and then a line of grown-ups join you at the Torah. Some of them are basically strangers—I didn't even know I had a Great-Uncle Joe until that day—and they read the prayers before and after each chunk of your parsha. This is supposed to be a great honor, but I think that in our family, we just asked the people we thought could actually manage the Hebrew. In between those people, *you* read from the Torah, and this is the WHOLE POINT OF EVERYTHING. This is the reason everyone flew from Toledo or Los Angeles to see you point the sacred shish kebab at the scroll and read Hebrew. It's a little scary, and your voice shakes, but you chant and chant, and if you mess up, there's someone there—they're called a gabbai—to help you out.

Then, finally, you're done, and you say the final prayer yourself, and after that, you set down the yad and take a deep, cleansing breath, and when you look around, everyone says "AMEN" in a really final way, and then they all shout and cheer and yell, "MAZEL TOV!" The whole room starts clapping and singing and clapping and singing and singing and singing. They shout: "SIMAN TOV U'MAZEL TOV U'MAZEL TOV V'SIMAN TOV SIMAN TOV U'MAZEL TOV U'MAZEL TOV V'SIMAN TOV SIMAN TOV U'MAZEL TOV U'MAZEL TOV V'SIMAN TOV . . ." and the room is shaking with noise and relief and joy, and for some reason, people are throwing candies at your head.

Honestly? It feels *great*. It feels like you should be done then.

But you aren't.

Because after that, the rabbi says nice things about you, about how much he's learned from you, and about how meaningful it has been to watch you grow, and about how you will always have a place in the community. And then your parents say nice things about you—about how smart and unusual and loving you are—and they tell a story that is embarrassing but not *too* embarrassing. Your mom starts out reading that part, but then she begins weeping and can't talk anymore, so your dad takes over.

After all that, it's time for your d'var, which is the last big thing.

I think I sort of explained this already, but at a bat mitzvah, your d'var is a huge deal. It's your chance to say something *important*. You are supposed to talk about your parsha, about the lessons you took from it, and what you learned in the process of studying the Torah for all those months. But you know what? That wasn't what happened for me. I got up there, with this smart little essay I'd written, all about—you guessed it—Mekhashepha. I was going to draw connections between magic and miracles. I was going to discuss the women's narratives we don't hear much about in the Torah. I was going to connect the story back to my own life and the *world today*, tell everyone about how important I think it is to *tolerate the sorceress*, and everyone else too.

But I got up there, and I looked down at the pages I'd printed out, and somehow they felt all wrong to me. They seemed false, like I'd just written what I was supposed to instead of what I actually felt. Somehow I couldn't go through with it.

So I turned the pages over and looked at Rabbi Dan. "Is it okay if I last-minute change the plan and just wing it? This isn't what I want to say anymore."

He smiled. "You can do anything you want, Zippy. This is *your day*. And honestly, I'd expect nothing less."

So then I took a deep, brave breath, and I looked out at the sea of faces. At the people who loved me, and also a bunch of strangers who didn't, and this is what I said. (Dad recorded it—even though he wasn't technically supposed to have his phone out in the synagogue on Shabbat—so I can write it down here, word for word.)

"Hi! First, I want to thank you for coming today. I really mean that. I didn't think I wanted to do this, back in the fall, and a big part of that was not wanting to stand here in front of you all. Mom and Rabbi Dan said you were my community, but honestly, it didn't feel that way to me. It felt weird and phony. Still, I'm glad I did it and I'm glad you all came."

At that point, I took a breath and everyone started nodding and smiling quiet smiles, if you know what I mean.

I continued. "I also didn't want to do this because I wasn't sure what it really meant to be Jewish. I didn't feel like I totally belonged here, or believed in all of this." I gestured around the room. "I still don't believe in the stories, I don't think. I don't know how we could know what day the earth was created, and I definitely don't think God should be spending time stressing out about donkeys falling in holes when there's stuff like climate change to worry about. In my parsha, specifically, it made me crazy to read that Jews weren't supposed to *tolerate the sorceress to live*, because as most of you know, I happen to *be* a sorceress, and if anyone makes me choose between witchcraft and Judaism, they might not like my decision."

Everyone nodded more now, and someone in the back called out, "Preach!"

"But here is the thing," I said. "In a way, despite all of that, this whole day is a miracle. Because even if I don't believe that the stories are true or right, I've learned something really important this year. I've learned that *no* stories are entirely true or right. Because no stories are ever finished. Whatever we think we know or understand is incomplete and is going to change anyway, and so—even when we think we know something, we're really just asking a question, waiting for more information. We can read all the books in the world and drive ourselves crazy, but in the end, we are all going to grow and change our minds, so there's no correct answer. Isn't that right?"

I looked over at Rabbi Dan. He shrugged, which seemed appropriate.

"But that's not a reason to avoid the stories," I said. "Because if everything is incomplete, then nothing can ever be entirely false either. There's always room for the story to change, or for you to change the way you understand it, maybe? There's something to learn everywhere you look. I used to feel like I wanted to know everything. Because I thought that if I did, I'd be able to *handle* everything, control it all. But now I realize that most of the time, the moment I think I know something for certain, it turns out I'm wrong!

"So I don't really know what my parsha *means* any more than I know anything else. If you want to know the real truth, I don't know what most of the prayers mean either. I just memorized them, pretty much. And the big secret is that most people do that, I think, even though they never tell you about it.

"But that doesn't mean that I don't want to learn! I want to read and read and study and try new things and admit that I don't know anything, as much as I can, just like I'm doing right this minute, so that I can keep growing and reaching and asking questions and arguing and starting over. I want to just go ahead and admit *all* the things I don't know so that I don't waste time being scared I'm wrong all the time. And I feel really lucky that I did this, became bat mitzvah. Because you were totally right, Rabbi Dan: the world *is* full of mysteries. And they used to scare me, but they don't anymore. I'm okay—or I'm trying to be okay—with uncertainty. So thanks for that!"

I looked out into the crowd then, and from everyone's faces, I could tell I hadn't screwed it up, at least. Folks were looking thoughtful, mostly. Except my grandma, who was crying again and dabbing her eyes. Probably because I was being such a *mature young Jewish woman* or whatever.

"So I guess that's all I have to say. The stories in my parsha are weird. I don't really know if I believe in any of this stuff, and I'm not even exactly sure what it means to be Jewish. But I'm really happy I could come here today and say all of this to you. I'm happy we can ask these questions together, which, I know now, is way better than asking them alone. I'm grateful you came, and I'm really proud of myself. Also I'm glad it's over! Whew."

And after that, we went to Ziba's and had a party. Mom was so happy, it was annoying, and Dad made everyone drink Scotch and I ate too much cake, and Sophie and Bea got to meet. And all of that was pretty great.

* * *

But when I got home that night, after everyone had gone to bed, I found I couldn't sleep, not even with the little red book under my mattress. So I got out of bed and walked through the dark house, just thinking about everything that had happened to me. I stared at the piano I couldn't play any longer. The picture of the Alaska trip, which I had forgotten for so long. Then I opened the front door and peered out, trying to remember the last conversation Miriam and I had on the porch. But already, I realized, the pictures were blurring. Things were falling out of order in my memory. How would I ever hold on to her?

I went back to my room and slid the little red book out from under my mattress. Then I sat down at my desk, and opened it, being careful of the fragile pages, the cracked spine. I almost expected the book to be blank again, but it wasn't. Now, in the moonlight from my window, I saw that each yellowed page was covered in her Hebrew, her perfect hand. I ran my finger across one page and felt, gently, a prickle, a shimmer, the quiet pull of magic. I couldn't read the words, but maybe someday. Maybe, if I worked very hard, I would be able to know all the parts of the story Miriam had lived and recorded, forgotten, then found again. It was a wonder, what a book could do, I thought. Even if no story was ever exactly right or finished, a book was a kind of treasure chest. A vessel.

"A vessel!" I said out loud. "A book is a vessel."

And that was when it happened. That was when, in a wave so strong I could barely breathe, a new kind of magic crashed over me. Suddenly, the air in my room felt different. Rich and warm and full of possibility. I looked around, and I swear, there was glitter everywhere, floating in the moonlight, filling my room.

"Miriam?" I called. "I mean, Paula?"

But there was nobody else with me. I was alone with my thoughts. Just me, Zippy, in a night full of magic. I looked down at the little red book then, and I closed it. Someday I would read it, but I didn't need to rush. The book would hold everything. The book would wait.

So I reached into my desk drawer and pulled out a regular notebook instead. *This* notebook, that you are reading right now. I found a pencil, and when I put it on the page, something happened. Something hopeful and embarrassing and wonderful and terrible. Messy and full of questions.

But you know what? I can always revise it later.

Acknowledgments

*H*ow on earth do I acknowledge all the people who helped me with this, my pandemic novel? When I began sketching out Zippy's story in 2019, I thought it would be a relatively easy book to write. I was in the process of planning a spring bar mitzvah for my son Lewis, and it felt like the two projects—book and simcha—would fit nicely together. Then came March 2020, and the realization that nothing was going to be "relatively easy" or "fit nicely" for a very long time. As we pivoted to distance learning and began to mask, wipe down our mail, and socially distance, I found myself postponing first the bar mitzvah, and then the book. Daily living was just too difficult. Everything else would have to wait.

As time went by and the pandemic stretched on, *The Witch of Woodland* only became harder to finish. I blew past multiple deadlines, but the story I'd initially wanted to tell no longer felt true to me, and I wasn't yet sure what I *did* want to say. I came very close to giving up on Zippy, but Jordan Brown, my generous editor, had more faith than I did. And Tina Dubois, my brilliant agent, offered endless support. I started the book over again. And over again. And over again. Both Jordan and Tina read many drafts.

By the time we finally celebrated Lew's bar mitzvah (masked, proof of vax, party in the yard), I'd figured out what I needed to do. The day after our guests left town, I ran away to a quiet place in the woods with a cooler of party-food leftovers, turned off my phone, and tore the book apart yet again. Only this this time, it worked.

So here she is at last. Zippy, who, like me, isn't always sure how to tell her story. Zippy, who is messy, who questions and wrestles. Zippy, who believes in something.

The thing is that while I've lived with her for years now, she doesn't really belong to me, alone. She wouldn't be here if not for a huge community of people. But how, after the three blurriest years of my life, will I remember all the moments of support, all the helpful conversations?

I can only try . . .

With gratitude for keen eyes and thoughtful insight as readers: Natalie Blitt. Robbie Medwed. Sylvie Shaffer. Elizabeth Lenhard.

With thanks for the conversations that helped me puzzle this book out in one way or another: Rabbi Josh Lesser. Rabbi Malka Packer. E.R. Anderson. Susan Gray. Lisa Brown. Marc Fitten. Rachel Zucker. Brooke and John Marty. Rebekah Goode. Carly Kimmel. Kyle Lukoff. Sandy London. Phil Bildner. Dan Santat. LeUyen Pham. Joel Silverman. Minnah Dunlap. The entire (genius!) faculty of the Hamline MFAC. My writing quad—Jonathan Auxier, Grace Lin, Kate Milford. And the Ladies Sewing Guild—Anne Ursu, Laura Ruby, Tracey Baptiste, Kelly Barnhill, Olugbemisola Rhuday-Perkovich, Kate Messner, Linda Urban, Martha Brokenbrough.

Then there are all the people who kept me human. Who fed and hugged me, who called to check in at the just-right moment. I will never be able to mention them all here, but I'll try: Steve Snyder and Cheryl Hindes. Kate Hamill and Steve Gettinger. Henry Snyder and Maria Martin. Emma Snyder. Roy Snyder. Howard Sankofa. Abbie Gulson. Nancy Lamb. Sue Salvesen. Jenny Minkewicz. Darolyn McConnell. Stacy Platt. Kelly Yang. Jaime Ladet. Tamara Caldas. Liz Frayer. Melissa Manlove. Sonya Naumann. Annie Crawford. Kate Tuttle. Kate Rope. Pieta Brown. Virginia Prescott. Matt Arnett. Paula Willey.

I'd be terribly remiss if I didn't mention Zany Dunlap in particular. She watched this book take shape over my shoulder, listened to me rant, fed my kids while I worked. She's a rare friend and I will never be able to thank her enough for becoming family when I needed it most.

I also feel the need to send extra gratitude to Elana K.

Arnold, who has been on this journey with me for years, cheering Zippy on. As a reader, a friend, an occasional roommate, a puzzler of worlds and humans.

And then there is Debbie Kovacs, who is herself a (very good) witch. Who reached out years ago and has been there ever since. Who sent Shabbat dinner, when I was living inside a dollhouse. Who defies categorization and is always the right person to call.

I'm grateful to the South Fulton Institute for the time and space I needed at a crucial moment in my writing process. I'm so lucky to live in a community that supports the arts in this way.

And I could never have imagined Zippy's world without Brian "Farmer Red" Harrison, who created something unusual and perfect on five hilly acres in my South Atlanta neighborhood. I didn't know Farmer Red well, but he touched my life—my writing, parenting, and sense of home. Farmer Red passed away this year, and his absence will be felt by many of us, but he leaves a magical wilderness behind him, and I'm deeply grateful.

I'm endlessly impressed and bewildered by the team at Walden Pond Press and HarperCollins. I'm still not quite sure how you do it, but you do it all beautifully! To Patty Rosati. Amy Ryan. Barb Fitzsimmons. Jon Howard. Gwen Morton. Vicky Abate. Josh Weiss. Allison Brown. Robby Imfeld. Emma Meyer. Andrea Pappenheimer. Kathy Faber. Kerry Moynagh. Jen Wygand. Jenny Sheridan. Heather Doss. Jess

Abel. Jean McGinley. Suzanne Murphy.

And I don't know how I'd have managed these years without the faculty and staff of Maynard Holbrook Jackson High School and the Atlanta Neighborhood Charter School. Through these very difficult seasons, our schools have held the world together. To educators everywhere who may read this, I want to say thank you. You reinvented everything, and we all owe you a tremendous debt.

To Stacey Abrams, who doesn't know me, but whose tireless efforts have made Georgia a place I want to call home, and whose vision has given me faith in all sorts of ways. Every book is written within a certain moment. This book belongs to the Abrams moment. Onward!

And finally, of course, to Chris, Mose, and Lewis Poma. Who lived with me in a strange little bubble these last few years, and somehow made it a joy. No matter how many books I write, I will never find the right words to express how much I love you, or how wonderful I think you are.